CONDO

By

Kerry Costello

CONDO

This book is a work of fiction. Names, characters, places and incidents, are either the product of the writer's imagination or are being used fictitiously. Any resemblance to any actual persons, living or dead, and events or locations, is entirely coincidental.

DEDICATIONS

For; Joe Mainous, Capt. Dave Ramsey (Park Shore Marina), Pedro (part owner of Cibao - who passed far too early) and all our dear friends at The Orleans and Colony Gardens Naples Fl.

ACKNOWLEDGEMENTS

Lyn Costello

Edmund Pickett

Dr Gabi Rosetti

Jasia Painter

John Sansom

By the same author

No Way Back

The Long Game (Gibson series book 1)

Florida Shakedown (Gibson series, book 2)

Florida Clowns (Gibson series, book 3)

You Owe Me (Frankie Armstrong book 1

www.kerrycostellobooks.com

Chapter 1

2019

Day 1- Tuesday evening

Frankie

Frankie was sitting in his favorite chair on the lanai, talking to his business partner over Skype. The ceiling fans rotated with a gentle thropping noise, his little dog Charlie lay at his feet and yelped occasionally as he dreamed. Every now and then Frankie leaned down to stroke Charlie's head.

"So how hot is it there now Frankie, at what, seven in the evening?"

Frankie looked at the thermometer.

"Seventy-five," said Frankie

"So that's about twenty-four?"

"I guess so," said Frankie.

"Well lucky you. It's colder than a witch's tit here. We'll be lucky if the temperature gets above freezing this week."

"Hang on a minute Barnsie, got to open one of the sliders, let some cool air in."

"Yeah, rub it in why don't you? Anyway, don't you have air con?"

"I do," said Frankie getting up from his chair, "but I don't turn it on 'til I go to bed."

Frankie slid one of the floor to ceiling windows along, letting the evening breeze waft into the lanai. His condo was on the second floor, offering an uninterrupted view over Venetian Bay. He stopped briefly to watch the sunset, the sky now a mixture of blues, burnished copper and red swirls The sun was a red molten ball descending behind the high-rise buildings opposite, heralding another spectacular Naples sunset. He sighed, then lowered his gaze to look out over the condo gardens. About 150 yards away, he could just about make out a couple on the other side of the swimming pool, silhouetted in the fading light.

His view was partially obscured by the branches of the poolside bottle brush tree. The couple were standing on one of the boat docks having an animated discussion. *Odd for anyone to be out there this time of night?* He shrugged, went to sit down and resumed his conversation with Derek, *Barnsie* his business partner and friend. He took another sip of his cold Michelob.

"Okay Derek, I'm concentrating now."

"Okay, so, as I was saying… Do you think it's too soon to make Gareth a director? He's worked hard and really improved the IT department. We're getting loads of recommends from existing clients. Pen testing and cyber security in general is more in demand than ever. We're in a great position to make a killing. My suggestion is we make Gareth a director, move Jimmy up to office manager and employ a couple more techies. What do you think?"

"Yeah, sounds like a good move." Charlie suddenly woke up, went to the open window and started barking, "Just hold on Barnsie, give me a minute."

"What's up Frankie?"

"Not sure, something's going on outside," said Frankie putting his beer down. He stood and pushed the mosquito screen aside to get a clearer view, and straining to try to hear what was going on. The discussion between the two people had become more animated, but he was too far away to see properly and couldn't hear anything distinctly. They'd moved further along the boat dock. The woman appeared to be gesticulating, then seemed to stumble backwards. Frankie heard her scream, then a splash as she fell off the dock into the water. Frankie watched transfixed. A split second later another louder and more horrific scream rent the air. *Did the man push her, why isn't he helping her?* Frankie turned back to the laptop, then looked back briefly to where the couple had been. The man had gone. He turned back to the laptop.

"Sorry Derek, got to go, someone's just fallen in the bay," and with that Frankie rushed for the door, stopping only briefly to grab his cell.

He opened the condo door, ran along the walkway to the stair's door, opened it then dashed down the stairs two at a time and out through the ground floor door. He suddenly realized he didn't have any shoes on but didn't stop. Turning left and left again, he passed under the breezeway and along the path through the gardens, and on round the swimming pool towards the boat dock where he'd seen the woman go into the water.

He got to the dock and ran to the end. The docks were wooden pier-like structures, about thirty feet long. A boat was moored on the right-hand side of the dock, but no boat on the left-hand side where the woman had gone in. He couldn't see any sign of the woman. The sun had now disappeared beyond the horizon and illumination was limited to a small dim light on the dock, the security lights around the pool and some reflected light from the houses and condos alongside the bay.

Frankie ran back down the dock to the rear of the pool where there was an extending pole kept in a plastic tube holder. It had a large hook on the end. He took it out and quickly returned to the dock, nearly bumping into a man holding a flashlight. He recognized him as Hector Carmouche, one of the other residents.

"Frankie is that you?" the man asked, shining the torch in Frankie's face.

"Yes, it is," said Frankie holding up his hand to shield his eyes from the blinding glare.

"Oh, sorry," said Hector, "what's going on? I heard a scream," he said as he followed Frankie to the far end of the dock.

"Not sure Hector, but I saw a woman fall off the dock and into the water, or maybe she was pushed?"

"Pushed! Sweet Jesus, by who?"

"No idea." Frankie replied

Hector shone his light across the water

"Keep shining that light Hector."

Frankie got down on all fours, then flattened himself out on the wooden deck and leaned over trying to look underneath the dock. They were joined on the dock by another two of the residents who'd come to see what was going on.

"Anything?" asked Hector, waving his flashlight and trying to provide some light underneath the structure.

"Nothing," Frankie replied. "You know, when I got into the garden, Hector, I'd swear I could hear a sort of thrashing, not like somebody struggling in the water, something more, I don't know, a sort of heavy slapping sound, something violent."

"Oh, shit," said one of the others who had joined them.

"What?" asked Frankie.

"You heard about the gator?"

"What gator? no I didn't hear about any gator. I haven't been around the pool the last few days, been sorting out some business stuff. You're not saying...?"

"A few folks have seen an alligator near the docks in the last couple of days. Not every day but... Tom and Marge saw it and they reckoned it was a bull gator, well over twelve feet long, but then you know how people exaggerate?"

"Oh Christ," said Frankie, scanning the water as he took out his cell. "Did anyone call 911?" he asked the little group, now joined by one of the women residents.

They all looked at each other.

"No," said one of the men who Frankie recognized as Bill Ferenczi "I thought someone else would have."

"Jesus," said Frankie in frustration. He took out his cell and punched in the numbers 911.

"Yes, an emergency, someone fell, or was pushed into the bay, Venetian Bay that is. Anyway, we can't see her. Yes, Venetian Bay," he said again, then proceeded to give the operator the address and zip. "They'll be here shortly," he said to others. He looked around and saw some more people had come down to see what the fuss was. One shouted.

"Can we help?"

"I don't think so," Frankie shouted back. There were already enough people doing nothing useful he thought. "Someone fell in the water," he shouted back to them, "the emergency services are on the way." There was a collective gasp. Frankie turned his attention back to scanning the bay.

"Look, over there Hector, out there," Frankie said pointing "shine your flashlight. See that red thing?"

"Yeah, I see, can't see what it is though, clothing maybe?" said Hector,

"Might be the woman," one of the others said. Frankie went to the end of the dock and dove in.

Chapter 2

Day 1 - Tuesday - later that evening
Frankie & Detective Randazzo

"So, you're the guy who called it in?" asked the detective who'd arrived at his door ten minutes before. He'd introduced himself as Lieutenant Detective Sam Randazzo. He was a similar height and build to Frankie, but had shiny black hair, an almond complexion and intelligent searching eyes. He and Frankie were now sitting at the dining table in Frankie's condo. Frankie had showered and dressed after his unplanned swim in the bay earlier. He had a cup of piping hot tea in front of him, which he sipped at before asking.

"Have you heard anything more, have they found a body? Do you know who she was, was it one of the residents?"

"Hold up there buddy, one thing at a time. The divers are still out there, but it's obviously difficult searching in the dark, even using the arc lights. So, it's unlikely we'll find anything tonight," said the detective. "They'll probably keep at it for another hour max, then come back tomorrow morning at first light, see what they can find. As to the identity, well, that's what we're trying to establish. We're working to account for all the residents, but with people out for the evening, or away, or not in residence at this time, it's not easy."

"I've asked the Condo Association President," Randazzo consulted his notebook, "Err Rudy Sprouse?" Frankie nodded, "I've asked him to email all the residents telling them about the incident and asking them to notify him of anyone they can't account for. I also asked him for a full list of residents along with their cell numbers so we can contact them to make arrangements to speak to them all, probably tomorrow afternoon. I'll organize a couple of detectives to help me interview everyone who was here at the time. You're excluded on account of our present conversation."

"So, let's start at the beginning," said the Lieutenant, "mind if I record this? I'll make notes as well, but best to have a full record. Okay with you?" Frankie opened his hands in an expression of cooperation.

"No problem," he replied.

"You're a limey, right? Sorry, a Brit?" Frankie smiled, "so what are you doing in Naples, vacation or what?"

Frankie took a deep breath and blew it out. "You really need to know all that?"

"Yeah I do."

"Okay," said Frankie. "Well I first came out here, to Naples that is, in March 2017 to help a friend. An American soldier I met in the army in Iraq."

"Help him how?"

"His nephew had disappeared, and he asked for my help in finding him. Sort of returning a big favor he did me in Iraq."

"Favor?" said the detective, eyebrows raised.

"He saved my life."

"That's a big favor all right. But apart from the favor angle, why you? You have some sort of expertise in finding people?"

"No not as such, no, but I'm a partner in a security firm back in the UK, so I do have a bit of general experience in the area I suppose."

"And did you find his nephew for him?"

"Yes, I did, so it all worked out okay. And in the process, I got to know Naples and I like it here. I like it a lot, so I came back."

"For a vacation?"

"No, not really. I'm renting this place for six months, see how it goes long term. Then who knows? I might try to apply for a green card."

"What made you choose this place in particular?"

"The location mainly. It's on the bay, near the beaches, access to the gulf, if I ever get a boat. Great view out the back, and I also liked the name Acadiana."

"How long have you been here already?"

"Two months. I have a six-month visa."

"What about your business back in the UK?"

"Almost runs itself these days, and I have a great partner who manages it day to day. My role was always strategy and financial, so I was never really customer facing. These days it's as easy to work remotely as being in an office, so I work from here."

"I see, so no wife or kids?"

"No kids but I do have a wife, but things aren't going too smoothly at the moment, hence my extended trip here."

Randazzo made a note in his pad.

"Okay, so let's cut to the chase. Tonight, what happened?"

Frankie recounted the events from when he first noticed the couple at the pool. Randazzo listened intently, without interrupting, making a note now and then. Frankie finished his account and took a long swig of his now lukewarm tea. Randazzo checked his notes.

"So, two months, I guess you've had time to get to know some of the other condo residents?"

"Yes, they're a friendly lot. I think I know most of them by now."

"But you didn't recognize who the two people were, the ones you say were having a heated discussion?"

"No, they were too far away. The dock must be, what 150 to 200 yards away? And it was getting dark. Then there's the tree. It's not a big tree, but the branches were enough to obscure the view a bit."

"Show me," said Randazzo. They got up and Frankie led the way to his lanai where Charlie was lying on his bed. He got up and went up to the detective, wagging his tail. Randazzo bent down and stroked the dog's head briefly.

"Friendly little guy."

"Yes, Charlie loves everyone."

"So, you brought your pooch all the way from England?"

"No, he was already here. It's complicated. Charlie belonged to the missing man I was looking for, and for a while I looked after Charlie. He was good company. We took a shine to each other, so as part of the reward you might say, I got ownership of Charlie. I couldn't take him home at that time due to the rabies restrictions, but when I got here this time, I was able to get him, so here we are," said Frankie.

"Okay, so tell me where the couple were," said the detective. Frankie pointed out the boat dock where the two people had stood.

"See, the way the condos are built in a semi-circle, means everyone has a view of the rear garden, the pool and the bay, just from slightly different angles. So, it's possible someone else might have had a better view and recognized who the people were."

"We'll get to that when we start interviewing the other residents. Now, the other residents, the ones who came down to help, who were they, can you give me their names?"

"I think I can give you the names of the people who initially came to help, but then a bit of a crowd gathered, and I wouldn't be able to say who they all were."

"Okay, give me what you can."

"Let's see, there was Mr. Carmouche, Hector Carmouche, he was the first to come down and help. Fortunately, he had the good sense to bring a flashlight. Then there was Bill, that would be Bill Firenze, I think he was the one who said the noise I heard could have been an alligator. It was a bit of a shock when I heard that. I mean I had no idea there could be alligators in the bay."

"Yeah it's unusual alright. Not unheard of though. The guy who owns Park Shore Marina, Dave Ramsey, he told me about a six-foot gator that hung around his dock last summer for a couple of days. And I remember one turning up on a beach in Naples a few years ago. Made headlines in the Naples News. Anyway, we digress. So, who else was there?"

"Okay, let me see, Roger, Roger Tuckerman. There were definitely four in that first lot who came down, now who was it? Yes, the guy with the funny name, Bodo, that's it, Bodo Kellerman."

"Anyone else?"

"Yes, there was one woman, Nancy, Farr I think is her second name. Like I said more people came afterwards, but they stayed back by the pool. The ones I've told you about were the first ones to come to try and help."

"Okay," said Randazzo, "do you know if any of those people who came to help witnessed the argument?"

"I don't know for certain, but my impression was they didn't. I think they just responded to hearing the screams, but I can't say for sure."

"Okay, said the detective finishing his notes. "We'll interview them as soon as possible. So, going back to what you saw. You saw the guy push the woman off the dock and into the bay, then he ran off?"

"I couldn't swear I saw him push the woman, but it seemed that way. As I said, it was too far away to be certain, but why would he run away, if it was just an accident?"

"Yep, why indeed?" replied the detective. "So which way did he run?"

"He ran to the left and disappeared into the darkness, but I didn't stop to try and see where he went, I was already running out of here to get to the woman."

"There's another condo block next door, on the left, right?"

"Yes, it's called Blue Horizons I think."

"And that was the direction the guy ran in?"

"Yes, but he could have turned left again, around the side of Acadiana and out into the front parking lot area, then on to Bayline Drive."

"I see," said Randazzo making another note before he continued. "So, you didn't see any indication of any kind of weapon being used at all?"

"No, I couldn't say I did. But like I say, they were too far away, and in poor light. Why do you ask?"

"No particular reason. Just got to cover all the bases. The use of a weapon would suggest premeditation."

"Yes, I see."

"Having said that, it could have still been a premeditated attack regardless of not using any weapon, especially when it's a man who's the aggressor. On the other hand, it could simply have been an argument that got out of hand," said the detective. He tapped his pencil on his pad as he considered what Frankie had told him, then said, "the gator element, which seems a distinct possibility, especially in view of the thrashing noise you heard, and the reports of a large gator around here recently, that has to be a possibility. That and the fact that the body disappeared so quickly, it all points that way. You didn't actually see anything that might have been a gator?"

"No, I didn't, just heard a loud thrashing, or maybe better to describe it as a slapping noise as I ran towards the boat dock. It was those screams though. The first scream I heard sounded like a normal scream, if there is such a thing as a normal scream. The second scream was much more, I don't know, dramatic, or horrific, and louder, much louder."

"Yeah I get the picture," said the detective.

"What are the chances of finding the body, or the alligator, assuming there is one?" asked Frankie.

"Venetian Bay is what, three miles long and pretty wide in places and it's tidal so my guess is we'll be lucky to find either. Gators tend to take their prey down to the bottom Take their time to digest their meal." Randazzo stopped talking and looked at his notes. "Okay," he said turning around and walking back to the dining table to retrieve his recording machine.

"That about wraps it up for tonight. Just write down your cell number on my pad here and I'll leave you in peace, until tomorrow anyway. You around tomorrow?"

Frankie said he was and started to show the detective out.

"Have you accounted for an Ava Ledinski?"

Randazzo turned back to face Frankie.

"Why do you think it might be her?"

"Well I've just realized, I haven't heard her piano. Early evenings I can normally hear piano music. I think she gives lessons as well. It's never loud at all, but like I say, I can hear it, probably because her condo's next door to the one underneath me."

"Well," said the detective, "I think she's one of the people we can't locate at the moment. Her apartment's locked and no answer, so maybe it could be her? But she's not the only one we can't account for just now, there are quite a few. She could just be out for the evening, or out of town. So, until we get more definite information... But are you now saying it might have been her you saw arguing with the man?"

"No, no I couldn't say that. It was, just like I say, it popped into my mind that I hadn't heard the piano, that's all. Like you say, she could just be out with friends or whatever. And as I said, they were just too far away, the tree branches and so on…"

"Yeah, okay. Well as soon as we find out who it was, I'll let you know"

"Thanks Detective."

Frankie closed the door and suddenly felt exhausted. He couldn't face up to a telephone conversation with Derek, so he went back, picked up his laptop and placed it on his desk and fired off a quick email to him to explain what had happened, then went to his bedroom. He stripped off, got into bed and fell into a deep dreamless sleep.

Chapter 3

Day 1 - Tuesday Evening - the Breezeway
The Perp

The perp took a beer with him and joined the other Acadiana residents in the Breezeway. *Nothing folks love more than a gruesome tragedy to gossip about, especially in a place like this.* The residents were sitting around discussing the dramatic events earlier that evening and speculating as to what had happened. A few of them asked where his wife was. The perp explained she'd gone to Indianapolis to see her uncle, whose health was failing. Said she'd be back in a few days he told them. His wife was very popular.

A few of the residents had already been interviewed by the police and were discussing who the unidentified woman might be. Speculation was rife. There were a lot of expressions of horror that the woman had apparently been attacked by an unknown man, and then eaten by a huge alligator. Those who'd seen the gator swimming around the docks in the previous couple of weeks, drew the largest contingent of gossips. People speculated on whether the victim and the attacker were either residents, or maybe just the victim was, and the attacker was a stranger. Others theorized that it could have been the other way around.

There was lots of discussion on what could have been the cause of such an attack. One or two mentioned heated disagreements at the recent condo association meetings, but no one could imagine such arguments morphing into violence. Others weren't so sure. He learned from eavesdropping on various conversations that there were at least three, maybe four single lady Acadiana residents who weren't at home, but that didn't mean much.

A lot of the single residents often went to visit relatives and stayed away for a few days. They went on overnight trips organized by the various groups they'd joined, or organized events by the church they attended. His takeaway was that no one definitely knew who the woman was, and the police were no wiser. He began to make a plan.

***

After searching through Ava's bag, he'd taken out her keys and hidden the bag in his closet. He waited until 2:00 a.m. before venturing out *Hope there are no cops still around. I've got to get hold of her laptop. If I don't, and the cops get to it first, I'll be in big trouble, regardless of whether they could pin her death on me. My whole life could unravel.*

He'd prepared his cover story, ready in the unlikely event he bumped into anyone. *Couldn't sleep after what had happened. Such a terrible tragedy so I got up and went to make a coffee and found I'd run out. Then I realized, in the confusion, I'd left some shopping in my trunk…* and so on.

He took an old Publix plastic bag out of the drawer in the kitchen and put some miscellaneous items into it to support his story, a packet of coffee and a box of Grapenuts, *that should be enough* then he exited his condo. As he suspected, there was nobody around as he stole slowly down the walkway towards her condo. *The dumb cops haven't thought to post anyone to keep an eye on things.* As he approached the condo door, he donned some latex gloves.

He used Ava's keys to open the door and closed it quietly behind him, then walked around, cupping the flashlight in his hand to avoid it being seen from outside. He located her laptop, which was in a cupboard in the entertainment center in the living room. He found her iPad on the kitchen counter. He knew her iPhone had gone into the bay with her. The chances of the cops finding her phone would be extremely remote, *what, with the thick mud and the tides, no chance. The phone might even be in the gator?*

He left both items he'd found on the counter and went into the bedroom where he knew she must have a hidden camera. He'd done some basic research on Google just an hour before, and found an amazing array of spy camera products, some as cheap as $150. They came as air fresheners, picture frames, clocks, even one hidden in a coffee cup. He checked the bedside clock, then the back of a painting of flowers hung on the wall facing the bed. Then he lifted a framed picture of Ava receiving one of her many music awards, off the wall.

The camera was cleverly integrated into the frame assembly, which was patterned with decorative holes through which the lens could record whatever happened in the room. There was what looked like a motion sensor situated next to the small lens with tiny infra-red lights on either side to facilitate night vision. He pried the back of the frame off and it revealed a space with connections for the mic and USB port, plus a 32GB SD card. He knew from his research that the images were transmitted electronically via the wireless network to any nearby PC, laptop or smartphone. There was a small hole left in the wall where he'd extracted the picture hook, but hardly noticeable. He rubbed it with his finger to try to close it further, then stood back to examine his work. *Perfect.*

Checking that there were no other marks to indicate where the picture had been, he took the picture frame and placed it together with the laptop and the iPad, then looked around for any other method she might have used for keeping records or notes. He found a domestic filing cabinet in the other bedroom, but all it contained were the usual documents relating to the condo, her car, air conditioning, instructions and guarantees for various appliances she'd purchased. He checked all the wardrobes, kitchen cupboards, drawers and an ornate drinks cabinet in the lounge and found nothing to worry about.

Satisfied he had all he needed, he put the picture frame, laptop, iPad all in the Publix bag with his shopping and exited her condo, had a quick look around to check no one had seen him leaving, then made his way back to his own condo. He mused as he made his way along the corridor. *I wonder what the cops will make of not being able to find her laptop and iPad? Once they find out it was Ava, they'll search her condo and expect to find some sort of computer. They'll soon be able to establish that she owned a laptop and an iPad. Still, that's their problem not mine.* He smiled and hummed quietly to himself as he neared the door of his own condo.

As soon as he was back and safe inside his own place, he set the laptop on the kitchen counter, made some coffee, came back and sat on a stool, took a sip of coffee and opened the laptop lid. It asked for the password. *How likely am I to find out what the password is? Not very….* There was no password hint beneath the password box on the screen. *A lot of use this is if I can't find the password, On the other hand, I have deprived the cops of the opportunity to access all her data, a not insignificant result in the circumstances. Still, if I could crack the password and get into this thing, I could find what records she kept and who else the bitch kept records on. And, who knows what else I might find? She probably has a stash of cash hidden somewhere. She'd hardly declare earnings for the sort of services she provided - well apart from maybe reporting some of the money she earned giving piano lessons.*

He closed the laptop, examined it then turned it over and found a label stuck on the bottom with something written on it. The label was worn away with age, but he could still discern what was written on it *instrumentnos*. It took him a minute to figure out it was probably two words, an instrument and some numbers. *Fuck! How many kinds of instruments are there, and what might the numbers be?* He decided the likelihood would be that she chose a conventional instrument rather than some esoteric obscure type, piano being the obvious one in her case.

He knew that a date of birth was always a favorite number combination in passwords, so he googled Ava Ledinski. It turned out she'd won a piano contest in Memphis when she was twenty-five and went on to play in the state orchestra for two years after that, wining more acclaim and the odd prize. These events generated plenty of information about Ava Ledinski, including her place and date of birth. Pleased with himself, he combined the date of birth with the word piano. He tried various combinations - at the end of the word, at the beginning, in reverse order, and any number of other variations, nothing. He tried the same with a range of other instruments, guitar, trumpet, saxophone, and so on, but after two solid hours of trying, he gave up.

Cursing, he stood up, went over to the drinks cabinet and opened a bottle of bourbon, then went to sit in his lounge and switched on the TV. *Maybe I can find some computer whiz kid to break the code, or whatever it was that was required to gain access?* He went back to the laptop and tried a few more combinations. Nothing doing, then he looked at the battery "s*hit,*" the battery indicator showed red and a message came on the screen warning that unless the laptop was connected to a power source, it would automatically close down in sixty seconds. He stood up and hit himself on the forehead with the heel of his hand. *What a fucking moron I am, I forgot to look for the charger!*

He considered going back to the condo but decided it would be pushing his luck. *Far too risky. I can get a charger tomorrow at Office Depot. Maybe they would also know some likely nerdy candidate who could crack the password problem?* He looked at his watch 5:23. The adrenalin that had sustained him until now suddenly dissipated. He felt weak and exhausted to the point of near collapse. He closed the laptop lid, turned off the lights, staggered to his bedroom and fell on the bed fully clothed. He was asleep within seconds.

Chapter 4

Day 2 - Wednesday morning
The Perp

He woke up bleary eyed but strangely refreshed, made himself a coffee, then wandered to the lanai and looked out on a day dawned clear and bright. Hardly any wind disturbed the surface of the bay. The sky reflected on the shining water as if it was blue tinted glass, the calm serene surface, broken only by the odd morning fish rise. Then he cast his eyes left and saw something else disturbing the calm waters of Venetian Bay. Two divers had just fallen backwards from the side of a boat into the water. Nearer to shore, he saw a third diver, searching in the water around the dock. A man assisting him, stood on the dock talking into a mic. The perp took a sip of coffee and continued to watch.

Suddenly, the diver near to the dock surfaced, pulled his mask to the top of his head and gave thumbs up sign. *Shit,* thought the perp, and took another gulp of coffee. He'd been hoping they wouldn't find the body, *surely the gator would have chewed her into little pieces by now?* He looked on anxiously, hardly daring to breathe as he waited to see what they'd found. A few minutes later the diver appeared on the surface again, holding what appeared to be part of a severed arm. He handed it up to the man on the dock. *Phew,* thought the perp, breathing a sigh of relief, before going to make some breakfast.

After breakfast he tried firing up the laptop, but it was as dead as the proverbial doornail. He went to get the iPad, placed it on the counter, sat on a kitchen stool and pressed the bottom button. It woke up, and a number pad appeared as he'd expected. He checked Ava's date of birth again, wrote down the numbers on a piece of paper and began to try various combinations. He wasn't sure if the iPad required four numbers or six, or maybe more. It was hopeless. He wondered if he should simply destroy it. *I'll delay that decision for a while, then if I decide to get rid, I'll ditch it in the bay.*

Having heard that the media mob were likely to descend on Acadiana later that morning, he'd planned to get out to Office Depot before they arrived, but he was too late. They knocked on his door just after nine and asked for an interview. The woman had a cameraman standing immediately behind her, filming as he opened the door. He shielded his face and told the reporter he had nothing to say. They knocked again a few minutes later. He kept the door closed this time, but shouted through the door in no uncertain terms, that he would not be interviewed. His actual words were 'Fuck off and leave me alone!'

He decided to wait awhile. *Maybe they'd go away once they'd got all the interviews they needed?* And so he distracted himself by tidying up his living room, changing his bedsheets and getting all his dirty clothes ready to take to the laundry. Going to his computer, he checked his messages and caught up on paying some bills. As he was working, his computer dinged the arrival of a new email. He opened it. It was from the association president, Rudy Sprouse.

Dear residents (renters and owners)

You may know by now that divers have recovered part of a body from the bay, near the number 3 boat dock. The police are saying nothing more at this time and continue their search of the bay for the rest of the body of the unfortunate victim. They have advised that due to this development, it is inevitable that the news media will arrive in force over the next couple of days. It is obviously up to you if you agree to be interviewed, but the police request that you refrain from speculation about who the victim was and how the incident or accident occurred. Unfounded speculation at this stage may severely hinder their investigations and might serve to cast suspicion on innocent people.

Yours

Rudy

He waited another hour before venturing out, but still had to fend off some remaining persistent news people before he got to the relative safety of his car. Some of them were still gathered in clusters around other residents, who were apparently willing to be interviewed. *Some people will turn cartwheels naked to be on television,* he thought as he drove out of the parking lot. Driving to the mall, he parked outside Office Depot. As he got out of his car, he donned a plain blue cap with a large peak and pulled it down over his face. Entering the store, he kept his head down, and checked out the location of the security cameras. He wasn't going to risk leaving a trail of evidence.

Eventually he managed to get the attention of a sales guy and showed him a picture of the laptop he'd taken on his phone. The man took him to the appropriate section and handed him the charger.

"This should do it, but keep the receipt just in case, okay?"

"Yes, thanks. Oh, by the way, I wonder if you help me with a problem I have?"

"I will if I can sir, what is the problem?"

"Well, a relative of mine died recently and his wife doesn't have his password for his computer, and she asked me if there was any way it could be recovered?"

The man looked at him with more than a hint of suspicion and he suddenly realized how foolish he'd been to have asked such a stupid question and draw attention to himself.

"Tell you what buddy," said the salesman, "you get a letter from the lawyer handling the estate, or whatever, and we'll try to help, but without that my friend..."

"Yes, of course, and that's how it should be," he said, "I'll talk to his wife and pop back in tomorrow."

"You do that sir. Now, is there anything more I can help you with today?"

"No thanks," he said and went to join the line for payment. He paid in cash. Transaction completed, he walked out to his car and set off back to his condo.

As he drove into the condo parking lot, more press people were arriving. *Will this circus never stop?* Despite being accosted another couple of times by news reporters, he managed to get back to his condo without too much hassle. He unpacked the charger, plugged it in and connected it to the laptop, gave it a few minutes, then fired it up. The screen came to life, and after loading up a beautiful picture of the Rockies bathed in dawn sunlight, the password box appeared.

He began to try out a series of combinations of Ava's date of birth and the word piano, then the numbers backwards, then the letters backwards. He worked for over an hour trying every combination he could think of. He got angrier and angrier, pacing up and down the living room trying to think, and the more he tried, the more his mind refused to come up with anything constructive. He went to the lanai and looked out over the bay. He was tense, frustrated and upset. The boat and divers were still searching in the bay, but now much further out.

The weather had changed dramatically as the day had progressed. Dark clouds now appeared on the horizon. He needed some distraction, something to clear all the clutter from his mind. He closed the laptop, detached the power supply and hid the laptop in the oven. Opening the condo front door, he gauged the outside temperature. It was warm and humid.

Changing into his shorts and a short-sleeved cotton shirt, he left the condo and made for the beach on foot. Navigating his way through the news crews, he exited Acadiana, turned right, and walked over the bridge then walked the remaining several hundred yards distance to the beach entrance. There were a few other people walking along the shoreline along with the usual variety of feeding birds – gulls, herons, egrets along with busy groups of sandpipers running alongside the shore - seemingly in a constant panic as the waves washed up on the sand to send them scuttling further up the beach.

He walked further along to find a space where he was on his own and stopped as thunder rumbled. He looked out to sea. The sun was dimmed now, surrounded by black and gray clouds and a darkening sky. Lightning suddenly lit up the horizon, the sky now broody and threatening. The water became much rougher, egged on by the wind. White horses now topped the waves as the angry sea smashed on to the sandy shore, demonstrating its fearsome latent power. He waited, a loud thunderclap rent the air and made him jump. Then he saw rain, sweeping in across the Gulf. Looking around at the now empty beach he turned to run, then thought better of it and turned back to face the sea, arms open, waiting for the driving rain to come and drench him. *Cleanse my soul? A bit late for that.* He laughed a dry laugh. Then the wind and rain hit, nearly knocking him over.

He turned sideways, and head bowed, slowly made his way along the shoreline, and back to the beach exit. Heavy raindrops dripped off his hair, eyebrows and nose as he walked along. Once he was on Park Shore Drive the rain and wind eased a little. He became less tense, felt his shoulders relax and an almost serene calm came over him. The lightning flashed again, then another rumble of thunder. The warm rain and the storm seemed to have energized him.

The conundrum popped into his mind again, but this time it didn't make him angry *Instrument plus number? Has to be a piano, maybe another name for a piano? That could be it?* He quickened his pace and was soon back inside his condo. Stripping off his wet clothes, he toweled dry, pulled on a fresh pair of underpants, then some shorts and a shirt, and walked quickly over to his computer. He sat and Googled alternative names for piano. *Grand, baby grand, upright, square, concert grand, pianoforte, apartment grand, boudoir, cabinet...* he stopped and went back to pianoforte. *Pianoforte! Instrumentnos, could it be... piano40, I wonder?*

He felt a frisson of excitement, went back to the kitchen, took the laptop out of the oven, put it on the counter, sat down on a stool and opened the lid. He fired it up and gingerly typed in the word and numbers. He hesitated briefly before pressing the return key. He pressed, nothing. Then he typed in the same combination, but this time with a capital P for piano. The screen changed. *Welcome Ava Ledinski.* He leapt off the stool, did a lap of the kitchen and whooped, then realized he might be making enough noise to make his neighbors wonder what was going on.

He mentally scolded himself. *So, piano40, you clever bitch,* He looked quickly around the screen and clicked on the Excel icon and it loaded up. He went to open and saw a list of files, one of them titled Piano Lessons. He loaded it and it showed a list of fifteen names in total. *Jesus, she was a busy little bitch.* They contained all the contact details of each person, address, email, cell, plus marital status.

Finding his own details on the database made him feel exposed, and strangely vulnerable. He clenched his teeth and felt like smashing the laptop to smithereens. Taking a few deep breaths, he calmed down. There was a separate column containing an asterisk on the same line as some of the names. There was an asterisk by his name, so he guessed they were probably the other ones being blackmailed. The ones without an asterisk, he guessed, were probably genuine piano lesson clients.

Looking at the list in more detail, he recognized three of the surnames as potentially being residents of Acadiana. *Hmm, looks I wasn't the only resident being blackmailed by the lovely Ava. Could it be other men with the same surnames, nah, very unlikely...* They were all married men. *So, I'm not the only one with a motive for keeping her quiet?* There was another name he recognized, who was definitely not a resident, but a well-known TV news anchor who was owned a home in Naples.

That one also had an asterisk by it. *Jesus Christ, I wonder how much she was soaking him for? This is getting interesting.*

He decided to park the Excel program for the time being and go for the meat. He doubted she would keep the videos in a video library or any standard folders, so he looked for a large file, figuring that would be a tell-tale. He found it under the innocuous name of a file named Dates. *Yeah, very funny.* He opened the folder which revealed several more folders, each one with two letters, plus six numbers as the title.

He immediately saw his initials with a number tagged on. Thinking back, he realized the number was likely to be the date of his first visit to her condo. He hesitated then clicked on the folder, then clicked on the video. He watched the first few minutes. *God, she was one attractive woman…* Piano music played in the background, cover she said, should anyone wonder what was going on. He realized he was getting aroused and stopped the video. *The bitch is still manipulating me, even from the grave.* It was the same video she'd shown him on her telephone when they'd been on the boat dock.

*

She'd demanded they meet down at the docks that night, 'to discuss something important,' she'd said, which turned out to be an ultimatum for more money. She said he had to pay her $1,000 in the next two days, or she'd tell his wife everything. He told her he couldn't pay any more, the well was dry, but she wouldn't listen. She taunted him, told him she had more stored stuff on her laptop.

'I'm sure your dear wife would be very interested, don't you?' she'd said, as she'd taken her IPhone out of her expensive Louis Vuitton shoulder bag. *I probably paid for that* he thought at the time and became even more enraged. She pressed the screen a couple of times and breathless grunting noises began to emanate from her phone. She laughed and turned it round so he could see the writhing bodies on the screen, then she paused the video. 'And not only the sex stuff either, as you well know,' she continued, smiling. He tried to snatch the phone out of her hand, but she'd taken a step back to get out of his reach. That's when he'd looked over her shoulder and seen a large dark shape in the water, moving towards the dock.

He could only wonder at the evil opportunity fate had delivered. She took her bag off her shoulder intending to put her phone back in it. As she did so, he moved forward, the dark shape was now in the water immediately behind her. What little light there was reflected off the knobbly hide of the monster. He'd calculated the moment, then pushed Ava with all his strength. She'd dropped her bag as she'd stumbled backwards, screaming as she fell into the water, and almost on top of the huge creature. Her cell phone was still clutched in her hand. As she realized what was happening, she'd screamed - a loud, horrific, blood curdling howl.

The gator's reaction to her falling on top of it had been immediate and awesome. The huge creature turned, clamped her body in its powerful jaws, tossed her around like a rag doll then still clutching her shattered body in its mouth, quickly and silently disappeared under the silky surface of Venetian Bay. He'd grabbed her bag off the dock and fled.

*

He moved on to another folder, making sure it wasn't one with initials he recognized. He couldn't stomach watching one of his neighbors performing. The video showed a similar series of moves, some awkward cuddling, clothes being discarded, a move to the bed. This time he noticed Ava looking directly into the camera and smiling a secret smile while the guy wasn't looking. He wondered, *was this more than just about the money?* He shrugged. *Whatever any underlying motives she had, this stuff is pure dynamite, particularly explosive in one case, that's for sure.*

Despite all his other faults, he wasn't a voyeur, so he stopped the video and came out of the file. He looked at the video files again, sighed, grimaced and moved on. There were several video files. He had one more thing to take care of and clicked on her Outlook email icon *please don't let it be passworded.* It wasn't. It loaded up and began updating the folders. He gave it a couple of minutes then quickly speed read the received and sent emails. There were a few unopened ones, *no surprise there in view of recent events.*

From the selection he read, they seemed fairly innocuous, mostly gossipy emails to her sister, he assumed from the greeting *Dear Sis,* There were other emails to various friends it seemed. As far as he could tell, there were no emails regarding piano lessons, legit or otherwise. He wasn't surprised. She'd never communicated with him via email. *A blackmailer would hardly leave a paper trail of evidence, now would she?*

Feeling he'd achieved quite a lot for now, he turned the power off, closed the lid, then took the laptop to his bedroom, slid the wardrobe door open, kneeled down, removed six pairs of shoes and pried open the false floor he'd installed. He placed the laptop together with Ava's iPad, looked briefly at the other items his wife was unaware of, then replaced everything and went to make a coffee. He needed to think.

He went to the lanai and sat down and looked out on the bay. The storm had cleared, the sun now low in the sky as it began its downward arc to the horizon. Sipping his coffee, he tried to work out his next moves. *If only she hadn't remembered. Okay, the sex video was bad enough. My wife would divorce me for sure if she saw that. She isn't exactly a prude, but if she knew what I'd been up to with Ava, she'd kick me out in a heartbeat. But, then the other stuff on top of that. Ava, you really left me no choice.* He went back over everything again in his mind. He was confident he hadn't left any trail of evidence, check. He had all her devices, check. *But there are loose ends.*

There were no signs of any cloud back up application, or other back up service on her laptop. Her alternative option was copying data to some sort of external hard drive or memory stick. In which case, she would have hidden it. *What an idiot, I should have thought of that when I was in there…supposing there is a backup device, and the cops find it…? No point in speculating. I could search the place again, but that's risky.*

He decided to put that problem to one side for now and concentrate on tying up any other loose ends. He had her iPad, which he realized he had little hope of ever getting into. The device required the correct sequence of numbers to gain access, and he considered it unlikely in the extreme that he would ever crack the code. As remote as the prospect was, the cops might find it in his possession, together with the camera picture frame, so it nevertheless represented an unnecessary risk.

He concluded he had everything he needed on her laptop. He got up, went to the cupboard where he kept his tools and retrieved a hammer. Taking the iPad and the picture frame out of their hiding place, he went to the kitchen put a chopping board on the counter, wrapped the iPad in a towel and smashed it to pieces. He shook the shattered remnants into a plastic bag, and then repeated the process for the picture frame. He put the bag by the door, planning to take it with him on a late evening walk. Suddenly feeling tired, he realized he'd skipped lunch. He needed food and a drink. He badly needed a drink.

A while later he woke from his post dinner snooze still feeling tired and anxious. He looked at his watch, 8:42 p.m., time to go for that walk. Donning a light jacket he gathered up the plastic bag and set off. On his way to the bridge, he considered any remaining loose ends. First, Ava worked at the music shop, so was there a computer there that she might have kept data on? Maybe, but he doubted if she would leave anything sensitive, anything embarrassing or incriminating that might be accessed by her work colleagues. Still, he thought, *if possible, I need to check it out for my own peace of mind.*

Two, there had to be a backup of her data somewhere. And three, where did she stash her dirty blackmail takings? Arriving at the bridge, he looked out over the bay. It was a cloudless night, with a warm balmy breeze causing small ripples across the water below. He looked around, making sure he was alone and not being overlooked, then he brought up the plastic bag to rest on the top of the bridge in front of him and slowly trickled the shattered fragments into the bay. *The mud and the tides will make sure they're never found.*

Walking back, his mind once again turned to his financial situation. He didn't have that much left of his own money to speak of, and he was he was thoroughly pissed at having to ask the permission of his wife if wanted to buy this or that. Not that she ever refused, but that sigh when she agreed was enough to make him want to strangle her. *If I could just find Ava's stash? But first things first, I need to figure out where the bitch might have hidden a copy of her data, The more I think about it, the more certain I am she wouldn't be stupid enough not to have made a copy. But that's all for tomorrow, what I really need now is to get back home and try to get a good night's sleep.*

Chapter 5

Day 2 - Wednesday
Frankie

Wednesday morning dawned bright and sunny - another stunning Florida day. Frankie looked out from the lanai and saw that the police had cordoned off a large area around the pool area and boat docks. There was a police boat out in the bay. Two divers, equipped with scuba gear sat on the side of the boat briefly before falling backwards into the water, one after the other. Another man was standing on the boat dock wearing a radio mic. He was looking down into the water by the dock and talking. Frankie realized he was communicating with the divers under the water.

As Frankie continued watching, a diver's head and shoulders emerged from the water a few yards from the end of the boat dock. The diver took his mouthpiece out, moved his mask up to the top of his head and gave the thumbs up sign, then pulled his mask back down, put his mouthpiece back in and dove back down again.

"Oh Christ," said Frankie out loud, then continued to watch. A few minutes later, the diver re-emerged holding something as he swam the few yards back to the dock. The diver grabbed the lower ladder rail and Frankie saw him hand what looked like part of a human arm up to the man on the dock. The man on the dock immediately laid it down on the floor of the dock and covered it with some plastic material, then he turned and shouted something to one of the other men standing around the pool.

Frankie felt a mixture of revulsion and pity at what he'd just seen, *poor woman, what a horrible way to die.* He recognized Detective Randazzo as he began to walk towards the man on the dock. Frankie stood looking for a few minutes more, then Charlie barked and looked up at him, as if to say – *are we going for a walk or what?*

"You're right Charlie. Bugger all we can do here, come on let's go," and they headed out for their usual morning walk. Frankie jogged along the roads at a leisurely pace, occasionally having to halt briefly as Charlie strained at his leash to stop and bid other dogs good morning. This mainly involved a mutual sniffing of bottoms, much wagging of tails and the occasional growl. He watched absentmindedly, his mind returning to the image of the diver handing over the severed limb. He tried to extinguish the picture in his mind's eye. He resumed his jog and a few minutes later his run was interrupted by a young couple who jogged out of a side road with their Alsatian dog, then promptly stopped on the sidewalk, lay down and started doing push-ups on the spot. Frankie had to move out on to the road to jog around them, Charlie in tow. Frankie noticed as he passed, that the woman was heavily pregnant. *Only in Naples…*

As he continued jogging along be began thinking about the last time he saw Ava. *Was it only yesterday morning? No, the previous morning, he remembered now. She was dressed for work, a smart and attractive woman whose age was hard to determine. She looked happy enough, gave him a big smile as usual when they exchanged good mornings. He hoped it wasn't her, but if not Ava then who...?* Charlie pulled on the leash and brought Frankie back to the present. He'd unconsciously speeded up and Charlie's little legs were finding it difficult to keep up.

"Sorry Charlie," he said and slowed his pace.

An hour later he jogged back into the condo parking lot and was amazed to find it filling up with news people. Reporters were variously standing in front of cameras, talking into their mics and using the Acadiana Condo building as a backdrop. Vans and cars were parked on every available space on the roads around the condo building. The broadcasting vans were festooned with satellite dishes, antennas, aerials and other miscellaneous outside broadcast paraphernalia.

A couple of hapless condo residents were being assailed by reporters, mics shoved in their faces, questions shouted at them as they tried to make their way to their cars. Frankie managed to get through the media scrum by putting his hand up and repeating 'no comment' in answer to every attempt for an interview. Then one of them effectively blocked his path as he walked towards the stairs.

"Cute dog," said the attractive young reporter as she hunched down to pet Charlie. She was a stunner. Frankie had no choice but to stop while Charlie made friends, wagging his tail enthusiastically as she talked to him. She was obviously a 'doggie' person. She looked up. "Hey, aren't you the guy who dove in the bay to save the lady? They told me you had a cute little pooch. Frankie, right, Frankie Armstrong?" Frankie realized he'd been cleverly ambushed. The reporter stood up.

"Yes, I'm Frankie," he replied reluctantly.

"Nice to make your acquaintance Frankie," she held her hand out and they shook. "Daisy, Daisy Metcalf, Naples Daily News. From that accent, I'd guess you're a Brit, am I right?"

"I am yes," said Frankie.

"So, what's a Brit doing here in Naples Florida?"

"Do you know anything about the winter weather in the UK Daisy?"

"Yeah, fair point, although I heard the forecast this morning and we're due a cold snap tomorrow."

Frankie laughed. Daisy raised her eyebrows and cocked her head.

"Sorry," said Frankie, "just… well I saw a flyer on the notice board this morning saying, 'Falling temperatures, falling Iguanas'. I thought it was so funny, that's all."

"Yeah, well it's true Frankie. You just watch out, those critters can hurt if they fall on you. Cold weather they become unconscious and tumble out of trees."

"You couldn't make it up," said Frankie laughing.

"I guess it does sound a bit strange, but hey, back to the subject. So, don't tell me you brought your little doggie all the way here on vacation?"

"No, it's a bit of a long story, but I'm here for a while now..."

"Hmm, intriguing," she said, "well maybe you can tell me that story another day, but for the time being... look let's move over there away from the other newshounds." She pointed to the far end of the parking lot. As they walked along, she carried on speaking. "I can tell you're uncomfortable about this, but just give me a few words about what happened, and maybe a quick picture with my phone, then I'll leave you alone, okay?"

"Okay a few words, but no picture."

"Deal," she said and smiled and took a small notebook out of her pocket.

"No recording machine?" asked Frankie.

"One time I interviewed a guy who unwittingly incriminated himself on tape for his involvement in a murder. I got back to the office and couldn't wait to play it back to my editor, Scoop Metcalf in the making. Guess what? The tape was blank. So, in your own words Frankie, what happened? And don't talk too fast." Frankie recounted the events of the previous evening, without adding any comment or opinion, despite Daisy encouraging him to speculate.

"Okay, so did anyone else help in the attempted rescue?"

"I really don't think you could call it an attempted rescue."

"You dove into the bay, didn't you?"

"Yes, I did but…"

"In journalistic terms that's definitely an attempted rescue." She smiled.

"Okay, have it your way."

"Now, did anyone else come to help?"

"Yes, a few of the residents came down to help."

"Names?" she said

"I'm not sure I should be giving you this information."

"Why not? It's not confidential or anything is it? Have the cops told you not to tell anyone?"

"Well… no."

"Okay then. Come on Frankie, who came to help?"

He gave her the names and she wrote them down, asking how he thought certain ones were spelt.

"People hate having their names misspelt, get really pissed if we get it wrong," she said. "So, Bill Ferenczi, know how to spell that one, Hungarian mother see. Roger Tuckerman, easy, Nancy Farr, okay double r I assume, Bodo, love that one, Bodo Kellerman and Hector Caramouche."

"Carmouche, not Caramouche," said Frankie

"Okay, Carmouche," said Daisy correcting the spelling in her notebook.

"Carmouche, sounds French?"

"Yes, I thought so too, but when I asked the guy, he said his family were originally Brits, same as me, so…"

"Hmm, okay," she said. Then re-read what she'd written and continued. "So, you didn't recognize the woman, don't know who she is, or was?"

"That's right," Frankie replied. "I was too far away."

"Okay, so was the woman pushed or what, was she attacked? Someone said she was stabbed before she was pushed into the bay."

Frankie laughed.

"Well I didn't see any of that, so unless someone else had a better view… I'm not sure what the police have told you, but all I saw was two people who might have been arguing. I say might, because I couldn't hear anything and so it was just the body language. I didn't see any stabbing or pushing, but I'm not saying that couldn't have happened. I can only repeat what I saw. I won't speculate okay?"

"Okay Frankie, you made that clear," she said scribbling some more. "I was told the red fabric you thought might be something, wasn't anything to do with the woman who fell or into the water?"

"Apparently not, just some miscellaneous piece of flotsam."

"Well, at least you tried, and for that you get an A plus in my book."

*

Frankie quickly took the stairs before anyone else could grab him. He began to ponder. *What on earth could have been the motivation for such an act of violence? All the residents are of an age when violence isn't a natural response to any situation.* He knew there were disagreements between residents on some aspects of how Acadiana was run, but they were generally small matters. His experience so far had been that the residents were generally a happy lot, relaxed, polite and friendly. Around the pool there were lively conversations, a bit of ribbing now and then, but he never heard anything nasty said about anyone and no serious arguments. Maybe it was as the detective suggested, simply an argument between residents that got out of hand. *But, maybe the man wasn't a resident, or the man was, but the woman wasn't, or the other way round?*

Frankie shrugged. *None of my business really*, but he felt himself getting drawn in. He recognized the signs. *If I'm not careful, I'll be trying to investigate matters myself. Just back off,* he told himself, *you've got enough on your plate.*

As he opened the door to his condo, his cell phone rang. He closed the door, took his phone out of his pocket and looked at the screen, *no one I know.*

"Hello," said Frankie

"Hello Mr. Armstrong, Lieutenant Randazzo here. Is it convenient to speak, you sound out of breath?"

"No, its fine, I just ran up the stairs that's all. Been out for my early morning jog."

"Very commendable, wish I had the time. Anyway, I guess you already know we found a body part out there by the boat dock?"

"Yes, I was watching from my lanai when they found it," Frankie replied. "Did you find anything else? I mean, other parts of her…"

"Yeah, I know what you mean and the answer's no, not so far. But I just thought you should know that we're now certain the victim was Ava Ledinski."

Frankie was silent while he took in what he'd just been told.

"You still there Mr. Armstrong?"

"Yes, sorry I…. You're absolutely sure?" asked Frankie.

"Yes, we are, the body part was about three quarters of the left arm of a female. It still had a watch attached to it, a Rolex. It was inscribed, *to Ava from Ava* kind of a joke I guess, but it pretty well confirmed it was her. As the hand was intact, we were also able to get fingerprints, plus DNA. We got the condo chairman, Rudy Sprouse, to open her apartment up so we could check, and it didn't take the forensic guys long to confirm them as a match to fingerprints in the apartment, so that puts it pretty well beyond doubt. We'll check the DNA as a matter of routine. That may take until tomorrow to confirm, but we already have enough to go on."

"Well thanks for letting me know Detective. Do you have any clue yet as to who it might have been, the person who killed her, or pushed her in?"

"No, not so far. I suppose you'll find out on the jungle telegraph, so I might as well tell you, but it looks like someone managed to get into her condo, sometime after the killing. We were looking for clues in the condo and had one of her neighbors in to help us out, a Meg Tweenie. She lives next door and used to pop in for a coffee with Ava occasionally. She said Ava had a laptop for sure, and we did find what looks like a charger for a laptop, but no laptop. We'll check that out of course."

"Mrs. Tweenie said she was also sure Ava had an iPad too, but there isn't any sign of an iPad either, or for that matter, any sign of a cell phone. Course, if she had her cell on her yesterday evening, it would probably have gone into the bay with her. The divers have been looking, but again nothing. But the missing laptop and iPad, that doesn't add up. It could be that the killer has a set of keys to her place and was anxious to remove anything that might provide a clue as to who he is or the motive, assuming it's a he?"

"So, we'll arrange to get the locks changed as a matter of course. Anyway, now we have part of the body to work with we can formally establish that it was a gator that did the final fatal damage, not that you'd need to be an expert to conclude that's what happened."

"No, I guess not. Well thanks for letting me know lieutenant, and if there's anything more you need from me, please let me know."

"Sure thing," said the detective and ended the call.

Frankie showered then got dressed and fed Charlie on the lanai. While Charlie wolfed down his meal, Frankie prepared his own breakfast of fruit, yogurt, croissant and coffee, and laid it out on the dining table. Charlie had finished his breakfast by the time Frankie had started his and came to lie at Frankie's feet. Frankie stopped eating, he'd lost his appetite. He rubbed his forehead and thought about Ava, *poor woman, what a truly horrible death...*

Chapter 6

Day 2 - Wednesday mid-morning
Redwood Music Shop

Martin Redwood, owner and manager of Redwood Music, sat at his desk in the back of his music shop, his head in his hands. He sobbed. Detective Sergeant Dale Vogel had just imparted the news about Ava.

"I just can't believe it, Ava gone," he sobbed some more.

Detective Dale Vogel waited. Eventually the sobbing stopped. The detective took out his notepad and spoke. He asked if she was full time, what her duties were, what days did she work, her interactions with customers. Had she had any problems with customers, or staff, any disagreements or arguments?

"Ava never argued with anyone, she didn't need to. She could charm the pants off a snake. Sorry, maybe not an appropriate thing to say in the circumstances, I mean…"

"Yeah, I know what you mean Mr. Redwood. She was a charmer, got it. Let me ask the question in another way. Can you think of anyone who might want to cause harm to Ms. Ledinski, boyfriends, girlfriends, jilted lovers, anything like that?"

"No, like I say, Ava was lovely, and everyone loved her. I can't believe she's gone." He grabbed another tissue out of the box on the desk and blew his nose loudly, then began to sob again. The detective sat there saying nothing. Redwood recovered enough to speak again.

"My apologies, Detective, Vogel was it? I didn't mean to..."

"No, that's okay I understand Mr. Redwood, nothing wrong with a few tears when you've just gotten some bad news like that." The detective gave him a while more to recover his composure, then said. "Now, did Ms. Ledinski have her own computer in the office?"

"No, well not as such, I mean she used the office computer as we all do, but she didn't have her own computer. Although she did bring her own laptop in most days I think."

"Okay, and she wouldn't ever leave her laptop here by any chance?"

"No, definitely not, but you can ask Marcia, she knows better what happens day to day."

"Okay, so what would Ms. Ledinski use the office PC for?"

"The usual, recording sales, issuing invoices, that sort of thing. Oh, and I'm sure she kept a list of piano lesson clients on there as well."

"I'd like to see that please."

"Yes of course," said Redwood. He got up and led the way out of his small office and into the shop. He turned to the detective. "I'm going to have to tell Marcia of course, she's going to be very upset."

"I understand Mr. Redwood." As they walked into the shop, Marcia was leaning on the front counter pretending to read a music manual.

"Marcia, come over here please, I'm afraid I have some bad news. The detective here has just old me that…" Martin Redwood couldn't finish the sentence. Marcia looked perplexed.

"What bad news?" she said. The detective stepped in.

"It's about your work colleague, Ms. Ledinski, Ava Ledinski, I'm afraid she was involved in an incident and she's, well she's dead." Marcia put her hand to her mouth, tears sprang from her eyes and trickled down her face. She managed to speak.

"How, why, I don't understand… why a detective, was she…, was she murdered?"

"That's what we're looking into, but her death is certainly being treated as suspicious."

Marcia sat down on the chair in front of the desk where the computer screen was standing. Martin Redwood put his hand on her shoulder. The detective stood there waiting. Marcia was the first to speak.

"Sorry Detective, I just find it difficult to believe she's gone."

"Yeah, I understand, but can you help me with a few questions I need answers to?"

Marcia looked round and grabbed a tissue out of a box on the desk. She patted her eyes and blew her nose gently, then said.

"Yes sure, go ahead, how can I help?"

"I'd like you to tell me about anything that Ms. Ledinski used this PC for."

"Yeah, well she used it to record sales, print off invoices, or email them to the customers. Then she'd also use it for ordering stuff and that sort of thing. Ava and I both did those sort of tasks."

"Anything else? I mean Mr. Redwood here said she kept a list of piano lesson clients on here."

"Sorry, yes of course she did. I'll show you," and she pressed a couple of keys and brought up an Excel spreadsheet with a list of names on. The detective sat down and studied the list. Alongside the names were contact details, dates, invoice numbers and amounts.

"Did she use the computer for anything else?" asked the detective.

"No, just like I say, just for the things we all did, other than this list, which was only accessed and updated by Ava. I think she may have had other private clients, but she kept all that sort of stuff on her laptop."

"What about emails, you said Ms. Ledinski sent emails from this PC?"

"We both did, but just shop stuff, nothing personal. We're not allowed." She looked meaningfully at Mr. Redwood.

"That's correct Detective, no private stuff is allowed on the PC, all strictly business," said Redwood who had now recovered. The detective turned his attention back to Marcia.

"Could you show me the emails sent by Ms. Ledinski?"

"Yeah, sure," said Marcia clicking the mouse a couple of times, "these are all the emails sent and received by Ava in the last three months. I can show you further back if you want?" Marcia had organized the list to show only Ava's emails. Detective Vogel read through a number of them. They all appeared to be as claimed, just business matters.

"Okay, well we might want to come back and look at these again, in the meantime can you print off a list of the piano lesson clients, with all the contact details please?"

"I can do better than that, if Mr. Redwood doesn't mind me using one of the spare memory sticks."

"No, of course not," said Mr. Redwood. Marcia searched in the desk drawer pulled out a memory stick, plugged it in, checked it was empty, then copied over the Excel spreadsheet.

"Would you like a copy of those emails I showed you as well?"

"Yeah that would be real helpful," said Vogel. Marcia copied them over as well, then took out the stick and handed it to the detective.

"Thanks Marcia," said Vogel, then turning to Redwood said, "I think we're finished here." Fishing in his pocket he took out a card. "Here's my card. Just call me if you or Marcia remember anything you might think would be useful okay?"

"I will Detective, thanks," said Redwood and showed him to the door. Then thanking Marcia for her help, Martin Redwood went back to his office and closed the door. He was tempted to shut up shop for the day, but that would mean going back home to Mrs. Redwood, and he couldn't face that. He'd loved Ava, not that she'd known, or maybe she had. He sighed and stared at nothing in particular. There was a knock on his office door.

"Come in Marcia."

"You okay Mr. Redwood?"

"Yeah, I'll be okay," he dried his eyes once more with a tissue.

"You should go home Mr. Redwood, I can look after the shop."

"No Marcia, I'll stay, I'd only mope around the house if I went home, and I'd rather be occupied. Look we're going to have to contact anyone booked in for a piano lesson, tell them, I don't know, tell them she's had an accident or something for now."

"Okay Mr. Redwood, I'll get right on it," said Marcia as she closed his office door and went back to her desk.

Chapter 7

Day 2 - Wednesday mid-morning
Criminal Investigations Unit Riverside Circle Naples

"Okay guys, listen up," said Detective Lieutenant Sam Randazzo, as he walked to the front of the room and addressed the three male and two female officers. They stopped their chatter. "You all know about the apparent grisly death of one Ava Ledinski. I say apparent, because we've only been able to recover a part of her body, her left arm to be accurate. But in the circumstances, it seems pretty obvious that the unfortunate woman is dead, having fallen, or more likely, been pushed into Venetian Bay from a boat dock at the rear of the condo complex where she lived."

"Ava Ledinski was a fifty-eight year old Caucasian female who lived at the Acadiana Condo Complex on Bayline Drive, Moorings Naples. Originally from Michigan, she was single, having divorced soon after she was married at twenty-two years of age. The ultimate cause of death, as I'm sure you also know, is likely to prove to be due to a fatal attack by a large alligator."

"The gator is thought to have been coincidentally swimming near to the boat dock as she went into the water.

Now this is where it gets a bit tricky. She was allegedly arguing with an unknown male, who was in close proximity to her on the dock, and who, it seems likely, pushed her into the water. Did he know the gator was there? We don't know. He certainly couldn't have organized it that way, that's for sure."
Muted laughter.

"Did he intend to kill her? Was it an argument that got overheated? Again, we don't know. What we do know, is that he fled the scene immediately after she went into the water. So, our job is to find out who the guy is and interrogate the truth out of him. To that end, we will need to interview all the residents of Acadiana today. As you all know, the fresher the memories... Susie here will distribute a list of the residents, be they owners or renters. Split them up between you."

"There are twenty-eight apartments in total. According to the association president, a Mr. Rudy Sprouse, this list shows who was in residence at the time. I'm sure you all know that the condos at Acadiana are, as with similar condos in Naples, mostly second homes for snowbirds, or rented out to people on vacation. There are a few permanent year-round residents, and these are marked on the list as appropriate. There are three single male and four single female residents, all the rest are couples, married or otherwise. There may be some who had friends or relations visiting, so they need covering as well. If they've left, get their phone numbers and interview them over the phone. Yes, Harold," said the lieutenant in response to a raised hand.

"Stating the obvious I guess, but the perp doesn't necessarily have to be one of the residents. Could be any guy the vic was associated with."

"Yep, that's true. Could even be a resident from the Blue Horizons condo complex next door, or someone who doesn't live in the immediate vicinity at all. As we all know, you're more likely to be killed by a family member or a friend, than a stranger. And we can't interview the entire Naples community, so let's see what information we can gather from her fellow condo residents and go from there. It's also possible that one or more of the residents saw something, perhaps something they don't appreciate the relevance of, so there's that as well."

"Again, to state the obvious, we need to dig into Ms. Ledinski's past. Who her friends were and so on, but the task is complicated by the absence of any phone or personal computer. Her apartment was entered by a person or persons unknown, on the night of the incident, or maybe very early the next morning. In view of the lack of any evidence of a forced break in, it seems likely that whoever took the items from Ms. Ledinski's condo, had a set of keys. In any event, we can safely assume that whoever it was, took her laptop and iPad. Her cell phone probably went into the water with her when she fell or was pushed into the bay. This severely restricts our ability to find out the sort of useful information that is no doubt contained on those devices."

"Now, early this morning, Detective Sergeant Dale Vogel here, went to visit the music shop where Ava Ledinski worked, and had the onerous task of imparting the bad news to her boss and work colleague. Dale, take over please."

"Yeah, I went to Redwood Music in Waterside and informed the owner, a Mr. Martin Redwood, of Ms. Ledinski's demise. I was also obliged to inform her work colleague Marcia, as Mr. Redwood was too distressed to tell her himself. My feeling was that neither of these people were aware of the incident and I'd bet my pension on them not being involved."

"I was able to get copies of Ms. Ledinski's piano lesson clients, contact details etc. You all have a printed copy of that data. Again, we will need to interview each and every client to try to establish where they were on the evening in question, the sooner the better. I was also able to view a substantial number of Ms. Ledinski emails. These all appeared to be simply emails about piano lessons, fees and invoices as you might expect. Nothing untoward as far as I could see."

"Okay, Dale, thanks for that," said the Lieutenant. "Now one more thing, this morning, just as the diver found the victim's severed limb, Ava Ledinski's sister Lisa turned up. She was coming to visit and had no idea about her sister's death. She went to her sister's condo expecting to meet her sister and found a crime scene. The guys working in the apartment called me and you can imagine how difficult it was to explain the situation to her. Luckily I managed to keep her away from the actual scene of the crime and we sat in my car while I explained the situation."

"She was pretty broken up as you might guess. She wanted to know how it had happened, so I had to tell her, but I'm not sure how much she took in. She was plainly in shock and after I'd told her what had happened, or what we surmise had happened, she said she wanted to be by herself for a while and wanted to go for a walk. I've got her cell phone details and we agreed that I would call her later to arrange a further chat when she felt up to it."

"She has nowhere to stay now as her sister's condo is part of a crime investigation, for the moment anyway. I told her she could probably move in there in a day or two, so I think she's going to stick around and do that. In view of the apparent illicit entry and theft of the items previously mentioned, we've taken the precaution of having the locks changed. So, ladies and gentlemen, that brings you all up to date. So, let's get as many of those interviews done as we can, and we'll meet up back here tomorrow morning at 11:00 a.m. to discuss results."

Chapter 8

Day 2 - Wednesday

Frankie Meets Lisa

After breakfast Frankie read the UK papers online, then logged on to his business portal and read through the latest accounts and sales reports for his company, A& B Security. Then he called his business partner Barnsie on Skype to discuss these and other matters. It was early afternoon in the UK and Derek's secretary said he hadn't returned back from lunch. She said she'd get him, to call back. Half an hour later Frankie heard the Skype incoming call alarm.

"What's all this Barnsie? When did you start having lunches out?"

"Since Albert White from Barclays Bank suggested it. I thought all that business lunch thing was history, but not in the banking sector it seems."

"Barclays Bank, are you kidding me?"

"I kid you not, they're setting up a new division and they want it completely isolated from the main business. He heard good things about our IT security and invited me out for lunch and he's on the hook now, just got to slowly reel him in."

Frankie congratulated his partner. They continued talking and discussing ideas and proposals for taking the business forward, then they spent some time analyzing the results of the last quarter's trading figures.

For the next couple of hours, Frankie was totally absorbed and was unaware of the doorbell ringing until Charlie came over and barked at him. The little dog then ran across the open plan sitting room to bark and scratch at the door.

"Sorry Barnsie, someone at the door, won't be a tick," He opened the door and was slightly taken aback. Standing before him was a younger version of Ava.

"Sorry to bother you, but I'm Lisa Marie, Ava's sister. Mr. Armstrong isn't it?" Charlie stood at her feet wagging his tail and begging attention.

"Err, yes, please come in. Don't mind Charlie, he thinks everyone's his friend."

"Hello Charlie," she said bending and stroking his head. Charlie's tail wagged so much he created a draft. "Don't worry, she said, "I was brought up with dogs. He's such a cutie." She stood up, sniffed, pulled a tissue out of her pocket and dabbed at her eyes. "Sorry, I'm still trying to take it all in, I can't believe…" She stopped, unable to go on.

"Please," said Frankie, "take a seat," he said showing her to the sofa, "I'm just finishing a Skype call and then I'll be with you."

"Sorry, I can come back if I'm interrupting..."

"No no, I'd more or less finished anyway," he said, and went back over to his desk.

"I heard," said Derek. "Catch up tomorrow."

"I can see the likeness, Lisa Marie did you say?" Frankie said as he sat down opposite her.

"Yes, that's what my family calls me, but just call me Lisa, it's a lot easier."

"Okay Lisa. Oh, I'm sorry, would you like a drink, a coffee? Maybe something stronger in the circumstances?" he asked.

"No that's very kind of you. A glass of water would be nice."

"Coming up," he said and returned with the water. She sipped then put the glass down on the coffee table.

"The detective, Detective Randazzo, he told me how you dove in to try and save Ava, so I just thought I'd come and thank you. It was very brave of you."

"Thank you, Lisa, but I don't think I was being brave, instinctive maybe? I just happened to be the first on the scene, I'm only sorry I wasn't able to do anything more to help."

"Well, you tried and that's the important thing."

"You got here quickly. Do you live nearby?" he asked.

"No, I'd already planned to come and see Ava, we'd spoken a few days ago. I only found out what had happened when I arrived. I literally bumped into Detective Randazzo when I got to Ava's condo. I'm afraid I caught him by surprise."

"I'd arranged to come and stay with Ava for a few days and arrived just as they'd found…, well I'm sure you know what they found," she said, then bowed her head and wept softly. There was a box of tissues on the coffee table. Frankie moved them towards her and waited for the tears to subside. His instinct was to get up and sit next to her and hold her, but guessed that might not be acceptable, on such short acquaintance. As the tears subsided, she began to apologize.

"It's okay," he said, "please don't apologize."

She took a couple of deep breaths and spoke again.

"Ava told me about you."

"How do you mean? We only exchanged good mornings and the like and had the odd brief conversation. What did she say?"

"Not a lot, just that there was a new renter in Carl's condo. Well that's not quite accurate, she said a dishy new renter." Frankie felt himself coloring up. He still wasn't used to American women, who seemed to be much more direct and less inhibited than women back home in the UK, even in the new era of alleged equality.

"I'm flattered," he said, laughing.

"Sorry, I've embarrassed you."

"No, it's okay, my battered ego could do with a lift."

"You're very modest. On a more serious note, do you have any idea who might have had a grudge against Ava? Had she had any big fallouts with anyone?"

"Not that I know of, but maybe I'm not the best person to ask. As you know, I'm a relative newcomer, and although I chat with the others around the pool, it's mostly about the weather, restaurants, or fishing, nothing heavy. Anyway, from what I saw of your sister, she didn't seem the type to fall out with anyone, she always seemed quite jolly."

"She was as you say, jolly, and friendly, but she obviously had a serious problem with at least one person."

"Well, when you put it that way..."

Lisa hesitated and seemed to be considering something, then she spoke.

"Can I speak to you frankly? I don't want to burden you, but you seem a nice levelheaded sort of guy, and apart from the police, I don't have anyone here that I can speak to about Ava."

"Okay, but I don't know how I can help, but if I can, I will."

"Okay, here goes. See, Ava had a bit of a problem with men."

"Really, what sort of problem? She was a very attractive woman. I mean I can't imagine…" he left the sentence unfinished not knowing where the conversation was going, then said by way of diversion. "Are you sure you wouldn't like a coffee or anything?"

"No, I'm fine thanks. Look I'm sorry to burden you with my problems, but I'm determined to find out why my sister died in that horrible way."

"Yes, I can understand that. I'd feel the same if it were my sister. But the police, I mean they're investigating, so maybe they'll be able to answer your questions, given time."

"I'm afraid I don't have much faith in the police. Detective Randazzo seems to be a sincere guy, and quite competent, but they have so much call on their time. I hope they do discover who killed her and why, but in the meantime, I'm going to try. See one advantage I have is that I know my sister, well knew, and I know what she's capable of. Sorry I'm taking a lot of your time. I get carried away."

"Look, I'm sorry to have bothered you. Just let me know if you hear anything useful or find anything out. Here I'll leave you my number." She took out a small notebook from her purse and started to scribble on it. "Ava's neighbor, Meg Tweenie, has offered to let me stay with her until I can get access to Ava's condo. They don't want me in there until they've finished whatever it is they do, fingerprint dusting, whatever."

Frankie took the piece of paper, folded it and tucked it in his shorts back pocket. Lisa began to get up to leave. He felt he had to ask.

"What do you mean exactly by *capable of?*" Lisa sat back down, then looked him in the eye and seemed to make up her mind.

"You sure you want to know? I feel I'm unloading on a complete stranger and that's not fair."

Frankie laughed.

"I reckon I can handle anything you want to tell me. And if it'll help you in any way, then feel free to unload. Really, go ahead."

"Thanks, you sure? it's a bit of a long story."

"I'm not doing anything in particular. Got plenty of time to listen, so go ahead."

"Okay, well as my mom used to say, a trouble shared and all that. So, when Ava was nineteen years old, she fell in love with Matt Barr, a guy she met at a friend's party and when I say she fell in love, I really mean they fell in love with each other, hook line, sinker, the works. I know it's a cliché, but they just were so right for each other. There was little doubt in our close-knit community that they would get married and have lots of kids. Well they were going to get married alright, but then Ava had second thoughts, lost her nerve. Something happened, I never knew what, but she wasn't sure she could trust Matt."

"Ava told me she didn't want to risk being let down, so she got a job as an airline stewardess. In fact, she was based in your country for quite a while, a couple of years, I think. She loved England, or the UK, whatever it's called these days. Matt kept in touch and wrote her nearly every day. In the end, she succumbed. She chucked her job, came back and they were married within a couple of months of her returning. I've never seen anyone so pleased with life as Ava was then. She was happy as a clam, Matt too, but he must have been putting on a front. The fairy tale ended six months later when Matt ran off with Ava's best friend Jacky, a story as old as time I guess."

"That's tough," said Frankie.

"Sure was, particularly as he emptied their bank savings account in the process. They'd been saving for a deposit on a house and he took the lot, over $35,000. Anyway, as you might imagine Ava didn't take it well, she was inconsolable for weeks. But being Ava, she recovered, got angry and decided to go on a crusade, get her own back on men."

"She chased after married men and seduced them, then told their wives. I tried to reason with her after she'd broken up the first two marriages, but as far as Ava was concerned, she wasn't the one to blame. It was all the men's fault and they had to pay. Eventually, things got so bad that she had to leave the area. She moved around but never got into any long-term relationship that I knew about. When I asked her why, she said she wasn't interested. All men were the same as far as she was concerned."

"When she moved to Naples, she seemed to change. She certainly stayed here longer than she'd stayed anywhere previously. We always kept in touch, emails, phone calls and sometimes she'd visit me, and vice versa. On a recent visit, I remarked on her lifestyle. You probably know she had a top of the range Cadillac for instance, and when she took me out for a meal, it had to be the most expensive restaurant, with a wine cellar to match."

"She also wore expensive jewelry, Rolex watch, took vacations to health spas, trips to the Caribbean staying in top class hotels, the works. You get the picture? I asked how she could afford such things, teaching the piano. I mean I know that apart from giving piano lessons, she also sold pianos at the music shop she worked at. But that couldn't explain where the money came from. She got quite annoyed with me for asking about how she could afford expensive things, so I let it slide."

"Then one night on my last visit here, the night before I left, I asked her if she had a secret sugar daddy, a rich married guy or something?" She laughed and said, 'Why rely on one guy for money when you can play the numbers game?' I'm no prude, but that comment shocked me. I said, 'you're not telling me you're a call girl?' She laughed and said no she wasn't, at least not in the way I meant. She also said she would never be subservient to any man again, ever."

"On the way home, I kept thinking about what she'd said in that last conversation, and I wondered if she was still playing the same game she played back home, but instead of telling their wives…?" She looked at Frankie and raised her eyebrows.

"You mean blackmail? She used sex to blackmail men for money?"

Chapter 9

Day 2 - Wednesday

Frankie

After Lisa Ledinski left, Frankie made himself another coffee and sat on the lanai, pondering the conversation he'd just had with her. As he looked over the bay, an osprey flew from one of the nearby buildings. Frankie never tired of seeing these magnificent birds in action. He stood and watched the bird as it flew over the bay, then swooped down. It was near enough for Frankie to clearly see the colors of its gray, blue and white plumage.

It neared the water's surface closing in on its unsuspecting prey. Leaning back in the air with talons extended, it hit the surface of the bay and grabbed the fish, causing a huge explosion of water, then flapped its powerful wings and simultaneously fighting the resistance of struggling fish, gravity and the clinging water, leaned forward and rose majestically into the air, its prize firmly clasped in its talons.

Frankie shook his head in wonderment and remained standing as he watched the bird fly to a nearby rooftop where it began to methodically tear the fish to pieces and devour its catch. His UK mobile phone rang and roused him out of his reverie. He looked at the screen, *Penny*. They hadn't spoken since he told her he was going to Naples. He hesitated.

"Hi," he said.

"Hi yourself," she replied. "Am I talking to the local British hero?"

"Oh", said Frankie, "you know?"

"Well it would be difficult not to know, you're all over the UK news. Brit Dives Into Crocodile Infested Waters to Save Drowning Woman."

"That's just not true, and they're alligators in Florida, not crocodiles."

"So, you didn't dive in to save someone?"

"Sort of, but it wasn't that dramatic. I actually saved a piece of red material floating on the surface of the bay. I think the woman was long gone. Anyway, to what do I owe the pleasure?" Frankie could have bitten his tongue as soon as he'd said the words. "Sorry Penny that sounded a bit trite."

"No problem," she said, "I, well, I don't know why I'm calling you really. We both said a lot of things before you went away and I suppose I didn't want to leave things as they were left."

"Look Penny, I thought we'd agreed to give it six months and then talk again, maybe."

"Oh, well that doesn't sound too hopeful."

"That's because I'm not hopeful. Have you forgotten last year, when you left me for your friend Jill? Made a big mistake you said, asked me to forgive you and then we got back together, and I thought we were getting along fine, better than fine. Then for some unfathomable reason, which I still don't understand, you went cold on me again. When I asked why, said you thought getting back together had been a mistake, you needed to be on your own for a while. Well you got your wish, and being honest, I'm getting used to being on my own now, and it isn't that bad."

"No nasty surprises waiting around the corner, so …" There was silence at the other end of the line. "Penny? Look I'm sorry but…"

"I'm still here Frankie. Listen, sorry I called, it was a mistake." And with that the phone went dead.

"Great, just call me anytime you want to and try to fuck my day up why don't you?" Frankie said to the empty room. Charlie trotted up to him alerted by his raised voice "It's okay Charlie, nothing to do with you. Come on, I think a walk would be in order, clear my head." As he walked along, he replayed the last encounter he'd had with Penny, the one where the camel's back got broken.

*

"So, what's the problem Penny?

"No problem."

"Bollocks, you've been moody for nearly a week now, I didn't say anything hoping it would pass, but there's something, so out with it."

"Well I have been feeling…I don't know a bit unfulfilled."

"Unfulfilled? You know what your trouble is?" *as soon as the words were out of Frankie's mouth, he knew this conversation was going to end very badly.*

"No, I don't Frankie, care to tell me?"

"Naval gazing. Thinking about how you feel all the time, how unfulfilled you are. Last time it was worrying about your sexuality, were you straight or were you gay? So, you had to go and break up a perfectly happy marriage, at least that's what I thought we had, but you, you had to go and find out."

"Yes, I did have to find out!" Penny replied, her voice rising in anger.

"And how did that work out? And no, you didn't have '*to find out*', he said "I could have told you if you'd simply asked me. You were no more a lesbian than I am, was" (*oops that came out wrong*). He was shouting now, "I meant gay," he added limply.

"Oh, go fuck yourself," replied Penny, slamming the door as she stormed out of the room. He stood there and listened as she ran up the stairs and slammed the bedroom door hard enough to make the house shake. He slept in the spare bedroom and the next morning when Penny went to work, he sat down and wrote her a long letter. He called his business partner and told him he was taking a long vacation to Florida, and then made reservations for the first flight he could get on, packed and left.

*

Frankie came back from his walk and went straight to the coffee table where Lisa had left a scribbled note with her name and number on it. He took his cell out of his pocket, and then hesitated. Charlie had jumped up and now lay on the sofa looking at him.

"What?" he said to Charlie, "well, I'm single now, certainly feels like I'm single." He looked at the number and dialed.

*

Frankie arranged for an Uber to collect them at 7:00 p.m., took a long shower then got dressed and went downstairs and knocked on Meg Tweenie's condo door. Meg answered the door.

"Hi Frankie, come in, Lisa won't be a moment." He and Meg briefly exchanged small talk until Lisa was ready.

They arrived at Cibao.

"Nice place, very busy. How did you get a table at such short notice?" she asked when they walked in. He winked and pulled up two bar stools for them.

"Eating at the bar okay for you?"

"Perfect," she replied. "So, you come here a lot?"

"Yes, I eat here at least once a week, great food, and wonderful staff. What'll you have?"

"What are you having?"

"Martini, straight up, or neat gin if you like."

"I'll have one of those please."

"He shouted over to the barman, "Hey, can a guy get a drink around here?" he asked in a mock bad-tempered tone.

"Yeah, when you pay your last bar bill," said the large barman who came to serve them, the smile on his face belied his words as he offered his hand. They shook.

"Rommel, meet Lisa, Lisa, Rommel."

"Hey," said the barman, "you know who you're drinking with Lisa? Florida's answer to Crocodile Dundee."

"I know," she said, smiling.

"Heard what you did Frankie, pretty awesome," continued the barman, "first drinks on the house for a hero," he added, "now let me take your order."

They both ordered walleye pike and after the initial chit chat, the conversation inevitably turned back to Ava and the investigation.

"The cops say I can move into Lisa's condo tomorrow if I want to."

"You're planning on staying then?" asked Frankie.

"Yep, I'm staying. I'm gonna stick around and try to find out what happened to my sister, keep the pressure on that

Randazzo guy, the detective. I might not have approved of some of her lifestyle choices, but family is family when all is said and done." Frankie noted the steely look on her face as she said it. He couldn't help feeling pleased she was staying.

"You don't have a problem getting the time off, I mean, come to think of it, I don't know what you do for a living."

"Time off isn't a problem, Got a house cleaning franchise, great manager. The business can do without me for a couple of weeks, more if necessary."

"Okay, so you don't have much faith in Detective Randazzo?"

"No, not on present performance. Anyway, I think me being here will put more pressure on him and I'm going to have a poke around myself, see if I can turn anything up. I have the advantage of knowing the victim intimately, so maybe I can find something out, poke around, I don't know, but I can't just do nothing"

"Fair enough," said Frankie, "so where are you going to start, I mean how are you going to approach this? Seems to me, if she was doing what you think she was, there are just so many potential suspects. I mean how would you find out who her clients were for a start, and I don't mean those that were having genuine piano lessons?"

"Haven't got a clue at the moment, but I'll work something out. Every journey starts with one small step and all that."

"It does," said Frankie, thinking the idea of Lisa her finding the killer seemed a bit fanciful, but he understood her need to try. He decided to change the subject. "Enjoying the food?" he asked *subtlety*…

"This fish is delicious," Lisa said, taking another sip of her martini, "as is this," she continued, raising her glass.

"And the company?" asked Frankie.

"Hmm… so so," she replied wiggling her hand to emphasize the point, while trying to keep a straight face. Frankie laughed. "So, are you in?" she continued.

"In?" said Frankie.

"Yes, in, as in cahoots with me? Finding the vicious bastard who killed my sister."

"Oh, well... err, yes. Yes, sure, absolutely, love to be in cahoots with you." Lisa looked over the rim of her martini glass as she took another sip of her drink. She paused.

"Okay partner, it's a deal," she said.

"It's a deal," replied Frankie, wondering what he was getting into and what the parameters of being in a *cahoots* relationship were. He could only hope…

The Uber driver didn't speak much English and didn't seem to understand his GPS either, so the journey back to Acadiana took a little longer than Frankie expected.

"Do you think the guy was an illegal, or had a driving license even?" Lisa asked as they strolled through the parking lot towards Meg Tweenie's condo.

"Probably yes and probably no," Frankie replied. "Here we are, delivered back home safe and sound," he said as they reached Meg's door. Lisa turned to him.

"Thanks for a really lovely evening Frankie." There was a brief awkward moment, and then Lisa leaned forward and planted a kiss on his lips. He savored the taste of her moist lips.

"Maybe we can do this again?" said Frankie in response.

"I look forward to it Frankie. I move into Ava's condo tomorrow but give me a couple of days to get stuff done. I need time to get some family things sorted out. I have to talk to the bank, the insurance company and all that kind of stuff. I also need to establish if Ava had a mortgage or owned her condo outright. Depending, I then need to discuss with the other members of my family about keeping it or selling up. Then there's a funeral to arrange, or at least make some preparations for when they release Ava's...well remains I suppose. How the hell do you bury an arm Frankie? Sure as hell it won't be an open casket affair." Lisa struggled as she spoke the last few words, making a noise somewhere between laughing and crying. Frankie took a step forward and held her.

"And I still have to talk to my brother about how we break this to mom," she said with her head resting on Frankie's shoulder. "She's in a nursing home, dementia. Depending on the day, she might not even remember who Ava is," her voice faltered again. Frankie hugged her tight, but she broke away and managed a smile,

"I'm okay Frankie, got to be strong, can't afford to grieve properly, not yet anyway, too much to do."

"What about your father?"

"Passed a few years ago, which was when mom started to disintegrate."

"Oh, I'm sorry," said Frankie.

"Happens to us all in the end. Come on, let's stop talking about morbid subjects. I'll call you the day after tomorrow, or you call me if you like."

"Okay" said Frankie, "so Detective Randazzo had no issues with you moving in?"

"No, they've finished with it for now. They think someone must have had a key because some of Ava's things were missing. They couldn't find her laptop or her iPad, so as a precaution, they had the locks changed. They gave me a set of new keys, so I'll move in tomorrow. Listen Frankie, I've really enjoyed tonight so thanks again."

"The pleasure was all mine Lisa." She put her key in the lock and Frankie turned to walk away.

"Hey Frankie, maybe you get invited in for coffee next time?" He turned around. She winked and smiled before disappearing into Meg's condo. Frankie grinned, then made for the stairs which he took two at a time.

Chapter 10

Day 3 - Thursday

The Perp

He'd had a bad night, couldn't sleep thinking about all the loose ends. *I hate that woman and I'm glad she's dead, but maybe I should have just found the money she demanded, taken my time to plan things better…. still too late now.* He made himself some breakfast then thought about his next move. *I need to check out the music shop she worked at. Maybe she kept records there, maybe a backup? I need to know.*

He wasn't sure which music shop it was, but the online Naples Daily News helped out with that, providing the information in its lead story of the day. 'Gobbled up by a Gator?' was the headline. He skimmed the article then stopped when it mentioned Redwood music.

There was a photograph of the shop, located in the upscale Waterside Shopping Centre in North Naples. A plan formed in his mind.

He drove along the 41, entered the shopping center complex and parked. Redwood Music was located in a small retail unit towards the rear of the mall. Before he entered the shop, he peered through the windows to try and establish the location of any security cameras. There didn't appear to be any surveillance cameras in the shop, so he entered and approached the young lady on the counter.

"May I help you?"

"Yes, my name's… he coughed as he realized he was about to blurt out his real name. *Shit, I'm so busy bothering about cameras I nearly blew it.* "Sorry, bit of a tickly cough," he said quickly. "My name's Kenneth Parkinson. I booked some piano lessons with, erm, Ava is it?"

"Oh dear," she said, "haven't you heard the news?"

"Sorry, what news?"

"I'm afraid there's been an accident, well sort of, and Ava has," she drew a deep breath before speaking the next words. "Well she passed, yesterday," she hesitated, then added., "Well, technically I suppose it was the day before that." Her eyes filled up.

He feigned shock.

"Oh dear, that's terrible, and such a lovely looking young woman." There was an uncomfortable silence, then he spoke again. "Look, I don't want to appear insensitive, but will there be alternative arrangements for the lessons? You see I was going to treat myself to a piano. I used to play quite well when I was younger, but Ava suggested I have some lessons to brush up before going ahead and buying one. I'd set my heart on that one over there." He pointed at what looked like a very expensive white Baby Grand.

The young lady appeared to get over her grief and went into full sales mode.

"An excellent choice Mr. err...?"

"Parkinson, Kenneth Parkinson, but please call me Ken."

She smiled.

"Of course, Ken, well, it's a Yamaha and quite a good price at $10,000."

Inwardly he blanched at the ten-thousand-dollar price tag.

"Is that all?" he said smiling. "About the lessons?"

"Oh yes," she said, "well Mr. Redwood is looking for a replacement, but he's very choosy and piano teachers don't grow on trees, he says. Not good ones anyway. I presume Ava took all your details?"

"Yes she did, but I've changed my email since I gave them to her. Getting so much spam, I decided it was the only way. Maybe you could check she took all my details and update my record?"

"Yes of course, won't be a moment." She left the counter and went to the rear of the shop where a computer screen sat on a desk. She sat and clicked her mouse a couple of times. He could see a chart appear on the screen. Swiveling round on her chair, she asked.

"Parkinson, spelt as it sounds?"

"Yes it is, why?"

"I can't find a Parkinson, nor anyone called Ken or Kenneth.

This is it, he thought

"Really," he said, "may I have a look, I mean I'm certain I saw her type my details in."

"Well I shouldn't really." He feigned disappointment, she relented, "but okay, yeah sure, come and look. Just mind the drum kit, people are always banging into it. I keep meaning to move it." He navigated his way around the drums and through the gap in the counter.

"See, the names, they're in alphabetical order," she said as he looked over her shoulder. "And there's no one here with the name Kenneth or Parkinson." She scrolled own the list of names. His relief at noting there was no record of his name was so great, that he lost concentration and felt a little faint. *Hadn't realized I was so anxious.*

"Mr. Parkinson? Oh, sorry, I mean Ken. You okay?"

"Yes, sorry, just having a senior moment," he laughed briefly. What he'd seen was a much shorter list and one without asterisks. This was obviously the list of genuine piano lesson clients. He decided to push his luck. "Might she have another list?"

"No definitely not, not on here anyway. I think she may have had another list on her personal laptop. I think she had some other private clients. Ones that she'd got before she worked here or didn't come through the music shop. Recommends and such, I imagine. She only worked here four days a week."

"Oh, I see, well thanks for all your help," he said and started to walk away. All he wanted to do now was get out of the shop as soon as possible.

"Don't you want me to put your details in now, Ken? I mean we will be getting another teacher soon, and that baby Grand, it is such a beautiful instrument." He stopped and turned around.

"Yes, yes of course," he said. "So, Kenneth Parkinson," she typed as he spoke. He continued making up a fictitious Naples address, which she dutifully typed into the database. He then provided a bogus email address.

"Okay Mr... sorry, Ken, I'll email you as soon as I have some news. Would you like to leave a holding deposit on the piano maybe?" she said hopefully.

"I would love to, but I'm afraid I'll have to run it by the boss for a final decision, but I'm sure she'll agree. Got to be diplomatic with such matters." he winked. "You understand?"

She laughed.

"Of course, we don't want to get you into trouble do we?"

"We certainly don't," he said.

She stuck out her hand.

"Very nice to meet you Ken,"

"Likewise," he said. They shook and he left.

Chapter 11

Day 3 - Thursday

Police HQ Naples

Detective Randazzo stood up.

"Okay folks, here's what we have so far on the lady and the alligator case," he hesitated, "well, not much is the short answer. No real progress on any front. No more than you know already, other than we have more suspects than an Agatha Christie whodunit. Yes Pedro," he said to the man who had just raised his hand, then muttered loudly, "why do I have the feeling you're going to ask me who Agatha Christie is?"

"You're ahead of me boss," said the man unabashed.

"Okay, substitute Colombo for Agatha Christie, okay?" The others laughed.

"Sure boss," said Pedro sheepishly.

"So, as I was saying, I don't want to sound defeatist, but we have very little new to go on, and a shitpile of other homicides to deal with. No murders for weeks then…well you know how it goes. We got the body washed up under Naples Pier, a shooting come mini massacre out in Golden Gate, three dead, four injured and no perp arrested so far.

We got a suspicious looking 'suicide," he said using air quotes
– "out at the trailer park on Airport."

"Don't forget the road rage killing on 41," shouted one
of the female detectives.

"Yeah, that one too. So…, we carry on gathering
evidence on the condo gator death, as and when we can, but
I got to be realistic with resources. The vic's condo has been
dusted and crawled over by the CSI guys, with nothing to
show. We're 99% certain that either the perp who shoved her
into the bay, or some other interested party, gained access to
the victim's condo the night of her death, and removed her
laptop and iPad. There were no signs of any break in, so safe
to assume whoever it was, had a set of keys, or maybe picked
the lock."

"Also, fair to assume that this same somebody, didn't
want us to find whatever was on either of those devices. Yes
Pedro?"

"Could that indicate some sort of blackmail boss? Could
be the reason she was killed, and also the reason someone
stole the devices?"

"That's a fair deduction Pedro, we'll make a first class
detective out of you yet." *laughter* "And I agree, but, if she was
involved in blackmail, then the person who attacked her and
killed her, doesn't have to be the same person who entered
her condo and stole the stuff. Could be more than one
blackmail victim, if that's what was going on here. But we'll
keep an open mind. However, her condo is no longer

considered a part of the crime scene. The vic's sister stated her intent to move into the condo and we've given her permission to do that. We've also of course had the locks changed."

"So, all witness statements and interviews have been collated and examined and alibis checked, zip, nada, nothing. So, we're by no means abandoning the investigation, and I encourage you to follow up any leads or theories. Use your own time if you want to, but no overtime unless sanctioned, okay? But like I say, we have some other urgent incidents to deal with, so go check with your immediate superiors for allocations of crimes to teams. Meeting over, get to it folks."

Chapter 12

Day 3 - Thursday

Prattling by the Pool

"Hey Nancy, lovely morning, haven't seen you for a few days, not since the incident. Roger was in the pool, using a water noodle to float around. "That was something else wasn't it," he continued, "who would've believed something like that could happen here in sleepy Acadiana?"

"Oh, hi Roger, Yeah, I'm still in shock," said Nancy Farr as she spread her towel on the sunbed, "Can't even face drinking Gatorade at the moment."

Roger laughed.

"You're joking right?"

"I'm serious Roger. Every time I get hold of a bottle I think of poor Ava." She stopped talking and looked down to hide her face, then took a deep breath. "You've been interviewed by the police I guess?" she asked.

"Sure have, everyone has. That right Mick?" he said to Mick Sharkey who was sitting at one of the poolside tables reading his book. Mick looked up when he realized the question had been directed at him.

"Interviewed? Yeah, thumb screws an all," he replied then laughed. "They even insisted on talking to my wife."

"Yeah, that happened to all of us," replied Nancy, "well spouse, not wife in my case, though these days…"

They all laughed in agreement.

Tony Yassaman who was floating on his back at the deep end, wafted his arms to propel himself into the shallow end and stood.

"What on earth is an alligator doing so near to a place like this?" he said to no one in particular, "I thought they only lived in fresh water?"

Nancy Farr replied,

"Don't know about that, but those varmints are all over the place round here. You know my cousin Michael? You must've met him, the stockbroker guy, appears on TV giving tips, all that?"

"Yeah, I remember meeting him, I think?" replied Tony,

"Well, a few weeks ago, he and his buddies were playing a four ball at the country club, just around the corner on Crayton, which is what, a mile and a half away at most? Well they were just teeing off on the 9th when a gator appeared from the left and sauntered, yeah that was the word he used, sauntered across the fairway and slipped into the lake.

He said they all stood there and watched. He said it must have been eight to nine feet long and no more than fifteen yards away. They called it in then carried on with their game."

"Yup," said Roger, "they regularly show up in swimming pools in Naples. Well regularly might be a slight exaggeration, but I read somewhere, there are well over a million gators in Florida, and a lot of those are in the everglades, just around the corner."

"And snakes now, foreign ones that don't belong," said Nancy, "big mothers too by all accounts, some so big they can eat a gator whole. They should let me open a big handbag factory. The Everglades Handbag Company, genuine snake and alligator handbags, that would do it."

"Did anyone actually see the gator attack Ava?" asked Tony Yassaman changing the subject.

"Ask Hector, he was there with Frankie at the dock… Where is Hector?"

"He was here a minute ago," said Mick Ramsey putting his book down, "I think he went to the bathroom. Here he is now."

"Hey Hector, said Mick, "Tony here was asking if you actually saw the gator attack Ava?"

"Me, no, I didn't see it happen, but I heard the scream and ran down to the dock. But Frankie was already there, and she'd gone. Frankie was the only one who actually saw it happen."

"Maybe not the only one," said Roger.

"What do you mean Roger?" said Nancy.

"Well, there was the guy who pushed her in, right?"

"Now you're just being silly, said Nancy. "So, who was at the dock when you arrived Roger? I remember Bodo being there and you Hector. The police asked me who got there first and I could only remember you two, and Frankie of course."

"The cops asked me that too." Then using his fingers to count, he said. "There was me, Frankie, Hector, you, Bodo and Bill, Bill Ferenczi."

"You don't think the cops assume it was one of us, just because we were the first there?" asked Hector Carmouche.

"No, course not" said Nancy, "look, here comes Bodo. Hey Bodo, we were just discussing the gator attack. Wasn't you who pushed her in was it?" Bodo walked over to one of the spare loungers and put his towel and book down.

"Yup, it was me. I confess, been having an affair with Ava for years. Just don't tell the cops… or my wife, okay?" They all chuckled. Bodo walked to the steps and down into the pool. "Ahh, that's lovely. Tell you what though, I wouldn't have minded having an affair with Ava, it'd probably have killed me, but what a way to go."

"Bodo!" Nancy said loudly, "you can't say that about the poor woman, she's only been dead a couple of days!"

"Sorry, bad taste, but she was a looker."

"Amen to that," said Roger.

"So, who killed her and why?" asked Mick to no one in particular. Nancy rolled her eyes. It wasn't lost on Roger.

"What?" said Roger addressing Nancy, "come on, give with the gossip."

"Well, all those men, going for piano lessons. You know she really wasn't allowed to operate any kind of business under the rules, but the committee never objected, did they?"

"What are you suggesting Nancy?" Asked Hector. "A few of us had lessons. I certainly did and she was a great teacher. I wasn't a bad player as a kid, but now, well just don't have the same dexterity these days."

"I'm not suggesting anything Hector, just saying is all."

"There were women too," said Roger.

"One woman," replied Nancy, "your wife Myrtle, but she gave up, didn't she?"

"True, but still. Anyway, are you saying she wasn't just giving piano lessons, what've you heard? I had a few lessons, but I was all fingers and thumbs - and no, there was nothing else on offer, sadly. So come on Nancy, what've you heard?"

They were all looking at Nancy now.

"Oh nothing, it was like you say, some idle gossip I overheard. Speculation at best. I withdraw any suggestion that there was anything… funny going on."

"It's how rumors start Nancy," said Mick.

"I know, forget I said anything. Have any of you met her sister Lisa? She was staying at Meg's condo, but I believe she's moved into Ava's condo now. Meg Tweenie told me the cops have changed the locks, said they think someone got into Ava's condo and stole stuff."

"You mean someone else had a set of keys?" asked Bill Ferenczi

"I asked Meg the same question and she said the cops said there was no sign of a break-in as such, just that stuff was missing, a laptop and things. They'd asked Meg if she could go and help them identify what might have been taken."

"I saw her the other night," said Bodo.

"'Saw who?" asked Nancy.

"You know, the sister, Lisa Ledinski, at Cibao... with Frankie!"

"She's another looker. Lucky Frankie I say," said Roger.

"Meg told me that Lisa Ledinski is really smitten with Frankie, and vice versa," said Nancy

"Smitten? You don't hear that word much these days," said Mick, "showing your age Nancy?"

"I'll show you the back of my hand Mick my lad. Don't forget I raised three strapping boys and they're still afraid of getting on my bad side, so you just be careful Mick Ramsey." *Laughter all round* "Anyway," Nancy continued, "Apparently Frankie couldn't wait to take her on another date. He's taking her out again on Saturday I believe."

"My God Nancy, you know everything about everyone round here. You make the CIA look like amateurs," said Mick to laughter from the rest. Nancy gave him the finger.

"So, I've missed my chance with Lisa?" asked Bill Ferenczi

"You never stood a chance Bill," Nancy replied. "Why would a gorgeous young woman like Lisa fancy a dirty old man like you?"

"Ouch! Said Bill laughing,

"Experience," said Roger, "younger women appreciate a bit of experience."

"You wish, Roger Tuckerman, you're just another dirty old man," said Nancy.

"I certainly am Nancy, whenever I can get away with it. You free later on by any chance?" They all dissolved into laughter.

***

The Perp

On his way back from the pool, he ruminated on what he'd just gleaned from the pool gossip. *Maybe Saturday evening would be a good time to search the place and look for a backup then? Is it worth the risk though? Maybe there isn't a backup? Nah, no one relies on just one copy of valuable data, particularly a blackmailer. Seems like the cops didn't find anything, but that doesn't mean diddly.*

It didn't look as if she had any kind of cloud back up, so if she copied it to a disk or whatever, it's either still in her condo or stashed somewhere safe. Still I need to have a crack at seeing if I can find anything. Her condo has to be the obvious place to look first.

He'd become increasingly worried and obsessed about the possibility of a backup of the stuff he'd seen on Ava's laptop. *If she made a backup copy and anyone else finds it, my life will be blown apart. Not only will I become a murder suspect, bad enough, but worse would follow, much worse.*

Although he wouldn't normally drink this early in the day, he needed a drink badly now to help him relax and calm down. He couldn't think properly in his present agitated state. Going to the drink's cabinet, he poured himself a generous two fingers of Jack, then went to sit on the lanai. *Now concentrate! So, the cops have changed the locks. They obviously knew someone had been in her condo and removed stuff.* He continued his train of thought, *I need to get in, have a good look around, if I find nothing, okay. But then, her sister might come across something in the meantime? If she does find anything potentially incriminating, I need to know before she tells anyone. How the hell do I do that? I have to think this through very carefully.*

He had another gulp of his bourbon and set his brain to analytical. *Maybe I could I bug the place…* Going over to his PC, he googled *remote listening devices*. He was surprised to find that for less than $50 you could buy a listening bug disguised as any number of household objects, including plug sockets, which he thought particularly clever. You could access and listen to them, using a cell phone, voice activated if required.

He went to check the plug sockets in his living room, and concluded that part of his plan was feasible, but it was of no use if he couldn't gain entry into Ava's condo.

He thought his plan through *I need to break in to plant the bugs, then break in again if I hear she finds anything. I obviously can't leave any trace of having got in there.* His next stop was YouTube to see if there were any vids on picking locks. He was amazed to find step by step instructions. It just didn't seem that difficult. They said you could even buy lock picking tools on Amazon for a few dollars. *Unbelievable… okay, so I can get the tools, but can I get them in time?* He went on to Amazon and purchased the listening devices and the lock picks, paying a premium for next day delivery. *If they don't arrive on time, I'll just have to move my plan to another day, but if I could do it tomorrow…* He ordered two single plug socket versions and two double versions.

Going back to the instructions on the listening devices, he read that he'd need to buy a throwaway cell phone, two bugs, one for the living room and one for the bedroom, plus three sim cards. He read on…

So, Saturday it is. *Gives me plenty of time to get organized.* He then went back to the YouTube vid on lock picking and studied it again. *Shouldn't be a problem.* He closed the browser down and went back to the lanai, picked up his drink, sat down and smiled.

Chapter 13

Day 4 - Friday

The Perp

The next day he felt anxious. Waiting to find out if the items he'd ordered would be delivered on time was getting to him. He busied himself with household chores and going to Publix to buy groceries. First thing that morning, he'd checked online with Amazon, but all it said was that his orders had been dispatched. He checked again an hour later and infuriatingly, their system wouldn't move on from telling him that his goods had been received at a local delivery depot.

He decided to go for a walk along the beach, which always helped him deal with stress and tension, but as he opened the door to leave, his cell phone pinged. It was a text message from Amazon telling him his orders would be delivered by 8:00 p.m. *So, could be earlier maybe?* He put his cell back in his pocket and was walking down the steps and out to the parking lot when his phone pinged again *call me when you can Mable xxx* He decided to wait until he was on the beach before calling her back.

*

He walked along the beach towards Doctor's Pass. A few people were fishing off the rocks so he stood and watched for a while, then found a smooth looking rock where he could sit and call Mable.

When he'd dropped her off at Fort Myers Airport for her flight to Dallas a few days previously, she'd pecked him on the cheek and said she'd be away for maybe a week, possibly longer. Although she wasn't a regular at the pool, claimed the sun was aging, she still kept in touch with all the other ladies. Lunches and long phone calls. She, like everyone else, had been consumed by the killings and in subsequent phone calls, kept warning him to be careful 'don't forget, there's a killer on the loose,' she'd said more than once.

She'd been unable to say how long she'd be away for. Her uncle's doctors were unable to predict if he would recover or not. They thought likely not this time. 'Depends on how long he holds out, so can't say when I'll be back honey,' she'd said. He knew she'd stay as long as it took, Uncle Akocha was rich, very rich. After they'd married, Mable had told him the story of where all the money came from.

'It was all down to serendipity,' she'd said, "As you know, my ancestors are Muskogee Indians and back in the early nineteen hundreds, one of them a lady called Sarah Rector, was said to be the richest native Indian girl ever.

It's claimed that the US Government of the time swindled our tribe out of their land, sold the arable pieces off to white settlers, and then handed back the remaining useless rocky parcels of land to the tribe.

The joke on the government was, that under those rocky parcels of land was liquid gold. Uncle Akocha's family invested the rewards wisely, managing to keep their fortune intact even during the bad times, and it just grew and grew.

He thought back about their 'accidental' meeting some years previously.

Chapter 14

Five years before
The Perp & Mrs. Waldroop

"Can I help you sir?" said the assistant getting up from her chair and walking round her desk to where he was browsing a cruise brochure taken from the wall rack.

"Yes possibly. I've never been on a cruise, but I really think I'd like to. My wife, bless her, she couldn't tolerate being on a ship, got seasick in a rowing boat." He laughed waiting for the penny to drop with the travel agent.

"So, the booking would be for erm... how many…?"

"Just me, a single cabin. Are there any cruises suitable for single people?"

"Oh yes sir, many cruises are very suitable for single folks, ideal. We book lots of cruises for people travelling on their own. Cruises can be very sociable, if you choose the right one. See the lady over there," the assistant said in a lowered voice, nodding her head slightly in the direction of a woman at another assistant's desk, "that's Mrs. Waldroop, she's a regular. Been going on cruises on her own ever since her husband passed a few years ago."

"Waldroop?"

"I know," said the assistant, "unusual name isn't it?"

"It is, but I knew some Waldroops many years ago. It isn't Cynthia Waldroop by any chance?" He smiled, then looked over at the woman, *late fifties, early sixties, well preserved, nice clothes. just the type.*

"No, afraid not, her name's Mable," said the assistant.

"Yes of course. That would have been too much of a coincidence," he replied, making a mental note of her name.

His finances were getting a little low. He'd made some unwise investment decisions and realizing he was no financial genius he'd been wondering for a while what alternative ways there might be to improve his long-term financial situation. Getting a job was not something he relished, *but if I can't think of something pretty quick, it might come to that.*

He'd often fantasized about marrying a rich widow, *after all, I might not be in my first flush of youth, but I know women find me attractive.* His other aspiration was for a vacation. Searching online for a suitable, but affordable break, he became drawn to the idea of a cruise. During his research, he came across an article about older widowed women, and some men, who took cruises with the specific purpose of meeting a replacement partner, although it was couched in more subtle terms.

The same article, while recommending a cruise as an excellent venue for meeting a suitable older partner, also warned against being taken in by predatory gold diggers.

Bingo, he thought, *two birds with one stone.* Then he laughed at himself using the word bingo – *how very appropriate!* Deciding further research was needed, he visited a number of travel agents over a period of weeks, seeking advice and trying to establish which cruise and dates might present the best opportunity for his requirements.

There were escorted cruises for singles, but he decided that might be a bit too obvious. There were historical trips, cruises for all manner of special interests. But he decided to confine his selection to those recommended for the 'more mature and discerning traveler' as the brochure termed it. He was quite spoilt for choice. Miami or Fort Lauderdale seemed to be the convenient ports, being just a couple of hours away – and… *maybe I could get a late booking deal?*

The assistant was now trying to get him to come and sit at her desk where she could take his details and look for a suitable cruise, but he had other ideas. Serendipity might have provided him with a possible target, and he wanted to incorporate that into his plan. He looked at his watch and tutted.

"Oh dear," he said to the assistant, "I'm late for my dental appointment. It's not far away, so I'll pop back in about an hour or so if that's okay?"

"Of course, Mr… sorry I didn't get your name. He gave her a false name. He had no intention of returning to the agency.

"Before I go, are there particular boats you'd recommend for people of my age, I mean, for instance, what would Mrs. Waldroop over there, what sort of cruise would she book?"

"Oh, she always goes on a Silversea Cruise out of Fort Lauderdale, twice a year."

"I see, and what sort of time would be a good time to go? I mean when would Mrs. Waldroop over there book for?"

"Oh, I really couldn't say. That sort of information is confidential, I'm sure you understand?"

"Oh, I didn't mean specifically, but just as a general guide."

"Yes of course, but there's no best time as such. More a case of what's best for you. The lady you were asking about, well she goes twice a year, once on her birthday and once on the anniversary of her late husband's passing. She says that's how he would have wanted it."

"I see, sort of celebration. Nice idea."

"Yes, isn't it?"

He walked out of the travel agency humming to himself.

*

After a light lunch, he sat in front of his PC and began his research. Her unusual surname helped. He just hoped she wasn't one of those women who kept her maiden name when she got married. She wasn't.

Chapter 15

All Aboard - Cruising and Schmoozing

O nce on board and settled in his cabin, the perp made his way to the reception area. The purser was a great help in answering his questions about cruise etiquette and other aspects of cruising protocol.

"It's all pretty relaxed these days, although most people do observe the request to dress appropriately for special evenings. Ladies in nice dresses and men in jackets, that sort of thing, but generally it's 'wear what you're comfortable with'. Smart casual at dinner most nights," he said. "During the day, pretty well anything goes," he added.

He delayed any implementation of his plan for the first couple of days and relaxed on deck building up his tan. He'd spotted Mrs. Waldroop the first afternoon at sea and was pleased to note she was on her own. His research had confirmed what the travel agent had told him. Mr. Waldroop, a very successful investment broker, had died some three years previously, on April 22nd.

Mrs. Waldroop's date of birth was also easy enough to find from the public records, as she'd been a minor political figure in the Republican Party in the past and all her details were duly recorded online. The anniversary of her husband's passing was the date for her next cruise. He'd booked accordingly, the first part of his mission accomplished.

Being an optimist by nature, he reckoned that even if his charm didn't work on Mrs. Waldroop, there were likely to be other suitable prospects on board. Albeit, Mrs. Waldroop already living in the vicinity of Naples had some considerable advantages for him. By means of observation, and some not so subtle bribery of the head steward, he was able to ensure a seat next to Mrs. Waldroop at dinner on the third evening. The steward showed him to the table and walked away.

"Is this anyone's place?" he asked the man sitting to the left of the vacant chair. The man looked around the table to see if anyone had any prior claim for a guest. There were no protests, so the man stood,

"No, I don't think so, please..." he gestured for the new guest to sit. "Do please join us."

He sat and introductions were made around the table. The waiter came over and took his drinks order, then the small talk ensued. He managed the conversation to ensure that he ended up speaking mostly to Mrs. Waldroop but resisted the temptation to become too friendly. *Plenty of time for that*, he thought. The evening went well.

He had a smooth tongue when it suited him and a store of interesting stories about his life, some of them true. When asked if he had a 'significant other', as the lady across the table put it, he feigned sadness and keeping it brief said that he'd been married but sadly his wife had passed some three years previously. The truth was quite different, he'd courted many women but avoided any long-term relationship, including marriage. Now though, he found the idea of marriage to a wealthy woman extremely attractive and wondered why he hadn't considered this much earlier in life

He soon had the table laughing at his tales and finished the night feeling he'd accomplished phase one satisfactorily. The next few days required delicate handling in order to avoid the impression of being a gold digger. He'd already concluded during their conversation at dinner, that Mrs. Waldroop, was no fool. Nevertheless, bumping into her by accident wasn't difficult on a cruise ship.

By the tenth day of the cruise he was sharing her sunbathing space on deck during the day, then lunch together at the sumptuous buffet, followed by sitting side by side at dinner in the evening. By the twelfth day he was sharing her bed in her Ocean View Suite. Within four months of the cruise ship arriving back in Fort Lauderdale, he'd managed to convince her to sell her condo in Pelican Bay (he needed to pry her away from her friends who he knew didn't approve of him) get married and move into his condo in Acadiana.

It was maybe a step down in size from her huge penthouse apartment in Pelican Bay, but she loved the location of Acadiana. She also loved its art deco construction, the manicured lawns, the magnificent entrance, and the pristine block paved parking lot flanked by shrubs and pretty, well-tended, flower beds filled with exotic plants.

As he knew she would, she offered to pay him half of the value of his condo before agreeing to the proposal. He graciously (initially) declined to accept, but eventually *and reluctantly* agreed, saying that although her money mattered little to him, he would accept if it made her feel more comfortable. A top up of his coffers was just what was needed, particularly welcome as he hadn't paid for the condo in the first place.

Chapter 16

Day 5 - Saturday

Frankie

Frankie followed his daily routine and went for his usual morning jog, which doubled as a fast walk for Charlie. Once again, his mind turned to Lisa. He'd thought about little else the last couple of days.

"I think I made a good impression the other night Charlie. Good looking woman… intelligent and obviously appreciates a man with charm and eloquence." Charlie briefly looked up at Frankie as he ran alongside him. "What? said Frankie. They jogged along a while longer. "Have to be careful though Charlie boy, don't want to seem too interested, do I? That can put women off. I know this Charlie, as I have a vast knowledge of the workings of the female mind." Charlie stopped to defecate. "Okay Charlie, I can take a hint," said Frankie as he bagged up the dog poo and tied a knot in the bag.

Half an hour later he was back in his condo. He showered, then fed Charlie, then prepared his own breakfast. As he ate, he listened to the BBC UK news on his iPad. After breakfast he checked the fridge for essentials and made a shopping list. He looked at the clock and called his business partner in the UK. An hour and a half later he left the condo for a trip to Publix to stock up on basics and to collect his dry cleaning. Getting back to his car, he laid the dry cleaning on the back seat then put his hand in his pocket to get his normal cell to check for any for any messages. *Not there. When did I have it last? Did I check it when I was in Publix, no, I left it in the condo, dumbass!*

Frankie drove back hoping he was right about having left it behind in the condo. *Amazing how anxious the potential loss of a phone could make you feel,* he thought as he tried to keep his foot off the accelerator. As he approached his condo door, he could hear his distinctive *Third Man theme* ringtone. By the time he'd put his shopping down, opened the door and found his cell, the call had expired. Looking at the screen, he saw three missed calls from Lisa.

"Damn."

Frankie was about to call back, but he was hot, sweaty and uncomfortable and felt the urgent need for a shower. It was in the high eighties today. Ten minutes later, showered and feeling much cooler and comfortable, he picked up his phone, sat on his comfy chair on the lanai and dialed.

She answered, he spoke.

"Armstrong male escort service, I believe you called earlier. How can I be of help to you today?"

"Oh... yes, well, do you have a sexy hunk available for a dinner date this evening?"

"Sorry, all hunks booked out already, but could we interest you in our special of the day. A witty Brit, fully trained with excellent table manners? The bonus: he also works for nothing." Lisa tried a serious reply but started to giggle.

"I'll take the Brit," she eventually managed to say.

"Excellent choice, what time would you like to have him pick you up?"

"Six thirty would be good."

"Your escort will be there at six thirty prompt."

"Look forward to it."

"Me too Lisa," said Frankie reverting back to his normal voice.

"See you later Frankie."

*

He pressed the doorbell on Ava's condo. Lisa appeared. She looked excited.

"The Uber's in the parking lot. I thought we might go to Pepe's Pizza if that's okay with you. Hopefully we can get a table outside."

"Perfect," said Lisa.

*

The Perp

He'd been sitting in his car for a while, near the exit for Lisa's condo, and watched as an Uber car arrived at 6:00 p.m. but was disappointed to see it was David and Jane Blaga who came out of the complex and get into the Uber. He ducked down to ensure he wasn't spotted. Then twenty-five minutes later another Uber arrived. Lisa came out of the corridor exit followed by Frankie Armstrong. He watched them leave but waited a while before getting out of his car. He knew from experience it wasn't unusual for a woman to suddenly realize she'd left a valuable item of clothing or make up behind and insist on returning to collect it.

He looked at his watch and let the finger reach the ten-minute time he'd set himself before moving. His own condo door had served for practice at lock picking and considered himself now quite proficient, but he was still nervous.

He needn't have worried, all that practice paid off and he was inside Ava's condo in less than a minute and a half. Once inside, he took his time looking around. He was reasonably confident they wouldn't be back for at least an hour, probably much longer. He checked the plug sockets near the sofa and found a double socket where the side table lamp was plugged into and replaced it with the bugged version, then re-plugged the light.

He went to inspect the bedrooms. It was obvious which one was being used. Memories flooded back, but he banished them and concentrated on replacing the single plug socket by the bed which the bedside lamp was plugged into. Switching the television on in the bedroom, he lowered the volume, then closed the bedroom door and went to stand near the front door. He took the throwaway phone out of his pocket and pressed the redial on a number in *Favorites*, then held the phone to his ear. He could hear the television okay. Satisfied, he repeated the exercise with the other bug, then went back to ensure there was no trace left of his presence. He peeked out of the windows to make sure the coast was clear, then listened at the condo door and quickly exited into the main corridor, pocketing his gloves as he walked back to his own condo ruminating on just how long he would need to bug her condo for.

She may of course never find anything, probably because there's nothing to find. If there was, then the cops would surely have found it? Those scene of crime guys are trained to find stuff, that I know. Not many people are ingenious enough to hide stuff where they can't find it. Always a chance Ava did though? He decided he'd listen in for a week then re-assess the situation. In any event, he knew the batteries in the bugs would only last about a week before they needed replacing. In the meantime, he'd try to find out how long she intended to stay. Gossip around the pool should reveal that information, or he could casually drop the subject into a conversation. Somebody was bound to know, they always did.

*

Frankie

When Frankie and Lisa arrived at Pepe's, they had to wait a few minutes for a table, then sat down. They both ordered beers while they perused the menu. Frankie stole a glance at Lisa and got the feeling there was something going on, *she looks distracted or excited, or both*? They ordered calamari between them for a starter. Mains were spaghetti vongole for Lisa, and lasagna for Frankie. Frankie suggested a bottle of Chianti, Lisa agreed but wanted another beer first. When the waitress had gone, Frankie spoke.

"All settled in now?" he asked.

"I am thanks," she replied.

"Is there something going on?" asked Frankie.

"You could say that," Lisa said in a lowered voice, "but the people on the next table are about to leave, so let's wait until they've gone, then I'll tell you." Frankie was more than a little intrigued.

"Cheers," he said and raised his beer glass. Lisa clinked her glass against his. The people at the next table finally got up and left.

"Okay," said Frankie, "come on Lisa, let's have it."

"Well, as you know, I moved into my sister's condo this morning and started getting all her stuff together. Stuff I wanted to keep, things I thought other members of our family might want as keepsakes, and stuff for the charity people. It wasn't easy, and I broke down a few times. Seeing her belongings in that way… Ava's clothes smelt of her favorite perfume." Lisa stopped talking to wipe a tear from her eye, then she buried her face in her hands and sobbed quietly. Frankie felt useless and waited.

"Sorry Frankie…, it just brought it all home to me."

"Nothing to apologize for Lisa, take your time." Just then the waitress brought their starter, two more beers and the bottle of Chianti. She laid them all on the table. Sensing there was something private going on the waitress left quickly. Lisa sniffed, blew her nose then laughed. She took a swig of beer.

"She thinks we've just had a fight," she said, "now, where was I? Oh yes, so after getting all the stuff organized, I began to have a good poke around." She stopped and looked at the food. "That calamari looks wonderful. I'm starving, come on, I can talk while we eat."

"Sounds good to me," said Frankie and began to share the calamari out on to the two plates the waitress had provided. In between mouthfuls of calamari and beer, then wine, Lisa continued her account of what had happened during the day.

"After a while I felt a bit tired, sorting out all that stuff, and the emotional bit, so I went to lie on the bed, grab a few minutes shuteye. It felt very warm and I realized I hadn't switched the air con on. I found the thermostat and switched it down to 72. I lay back down on the bed and I started to doze off. I was looking at the shafts of sunlight streaming through the windows, and you know how the dust motes dance around in the sunlight?"

"I do," said Frankie, in between dipping his calamari then stuffing it in his mouth. "Mmm," he said, "this is good. And yes, I've always been amazed at just how much stuff there is in the air that we can't normally see. And how much you must breathe in every day, so...?"

Lisa ate some calamari, then said,

"Well, as the dust motes were passing the two air con vents above the window, I noticed that when they passed the air vent on the left, the motes sort of swirled around in the airflow, but not when they passed the other one." Lisa stopped talking to take a drink of wine and eat some more calamari.

"So?" said Frankie.

"So, I just thought, strange, then I closed my eyes and I was drifting off again when I recalled what Detective Randazzo had said when he gave me Ava's keys back that morning. He said they'd been unable to find anything useful and handed the keys over. When I asked him what they'd been looking for, he said, anything really, but in particular, something that Ava might have kept a copy of her laptop data. Maybe on a memory stick, that sort of thing, but they found nothing." Frankie put his knife and fork down.

"You mean you found something in the air vent?"

Lisa smiled.

"I had to search around for a screwdriver. Ava had some basic tools in a drawer in the kitchen, I unscrewed the air vent cover and there was quite a large hole behind it. Ava maybe got someone to make it specially. There was this oblong metal thing, which I'm sure is a hard disk, or drive whatever you call them, anyway some sort of back up device I'm guessing, something bigger than a memory stick for sure."

"You clever girl," said Frankie.

"I am, aren't I? But that's not all."

"Go on…"

"Along with this hard drive or whatever, was a bundle of cash. I counted it and there's over $33,000, mostly in hundreds."

Frankie stopped eating and sat up straight.

"My God, what did Randazzo say when you told him. Bet he felt a bit stupid?"

"Wouldn't know, haven't told him."

"Not told him. Why on earth not?"

"Not sure, well I am really. I want to know what's on that disc first. I'm not having the cops rooting round in my sister's underwear drawer, metaphorically speaking."

"Hmm okay, I understand. Least I think I do" said Frankie, "but they might be pissed if you wait too long, withholding evidence, that sort of thing, and the money I mean…"

"They won't know, will they? I'm not going to tell them when I found it, not yet anyway, and I presume you won't either."

"So, you haven't had a look to see what's on it?"

"No, I'm no good at that sort of thing, and I'm not sure I could anyway. All I have is an iPad and I don't think I could see it on one of those. Anyway, there were no cables with it."

"Okay, so what's your next move?" Frankie asked.

"Well I can see our waitress coming out with our main dish, so I'm going to have a big glug of wine and enjoy my vongole."

Frankie laughed.

"Good call," he said and poured some more wine for both of them. They were both silent for a while as they tucked into their main courses, Frankie took another swig of wine and looked at Lisa.

"What?" she said, "I can almost hear your brain analyzing something."

"Not analyzing, speculating," said Frankie forking another portion of lasagna into his mouth.

"Come on, don't make me drag it out of you."

"Well, seems reasonable to assume, if you're right about Ava having sex with guys so she could blackmail them, that the disc backup you found has some videos on it." Lisa stopped eating and took a sip of her wine.

"I'd say that's a reasonable assumption Dr Watson."

"Dr Watson? Sherlock surely?"

"Sorry pal, that post has been taken by someone of superior intellect. So, Watson… carry on with your theorizing."

"Well if there are videos of Ava having sex with men, then were they taken with or without their consent or knowledge? My guess would be without. I mean I know some people enjoy recording themselves having sex, but that wouldn't fit with the blackmail angle." Lisa was about to reply, when Frankie held a hand up. "And…" he continued, "and, if that is the case, then again, assuming there are different men involved, one of them, by definition, would be the likely killer. Correct?"

"I agree," replied Lisa," so?"

"Well, that being the case, you'd have to hand the back-up disc over to Randazzo. So, why not hand it over now, with the cash, and leave it to the cops? I mean I know you said you don't want the cops, what was it you said? Rooting around in Ava's underwear drawer, but even so…"

"Yeah you're right, but still."

"What?"

"I've been thinking just how much damage that would cause to the men's lives, if that is what's on the disc."

"Sorry, I don't understand. If the disc contains what we think it probably contains, one of those men is likely to be the guy who pushed your sister into the bay and got her killed."

"Possibly. No, make that probably," replied Lisa.

"So, you'd keep it to yourself, I don't follow. Surely you're not willing to let the potential killer off the hook?"

"No, but I was wondering if there's a way of limiting the damage, the collateral damage anyway. Look, Ava found it was easy to take advantage of men. Where sex is concerned, most men are easy meat for someone like Ava. She gives them the come on and they lose their critical judgement, least most of them would. Way back then, she learnt how to do it to get some sort of twisted revenge on her husband. So, if she was doing what I think she was doing here, then she simply changed revenge for money."

"So, what exactly are you proposing to do, if things are as we assume?"

"I don't know, but if Ava was either charging for sex, or more likely, extorting money by threatening to expose her 'clients' said Lisa, using air quotes, "then she's not entirely innocent, is she?"

"No, but I have to say Lisa, most people wouldn't care a fig about these men. They'd say they probably deserved whatever was coming to them."

"Well I'm not most people. And don't get me wrong, I still want them to nail the bastard who killed my sister. On the other hand, there's such potential to damage some people's otherwise innocent lives."

"I understand Lisa, but I don't think you should concern yourself with such matters. At the end of the day, these men, her clients, they bear quite a bit of responsibility for getting involved don't you think?"

"Yeah, I guess you're right Dr Watson," she said suddenly smiling. "Now what about desert?"

Frankie was grateful the conversation had moved away from the subject of Ava and possible sex videos, and the evening progressed more than satisfactorily from Frankie's point of view. They were easy in each other's company and he began to think that this relationship could very well develop into something more meaningful than a few casual dates.

*

This time the Uber driver spoke English and understood his GPS. They arrived back at Ava's condo within ten minutes. Frankie was invited in for coffee.

*

"Make yourself comfortable Frankie," Lisa said, gesturing to the sofa. "You want coffee or another glass of wine, or maybe something stronger? Ava has a nice collection of booze, vodka, gin, and a very expensive looking bottle of cognac."

*

As Lisa spoke her first words, the perp received an alert. He dialed in and listened to the transmission.

*

"Cognac and coffee sounds very good to me, can I help?" Frankie replied.

"Maybe you can find some music on the radio? It's on the display unit."

Frankie found the radio and fiddled round with it, eventually finding some acceptable music.

"That okay?" he shouted.

"Sounds ideal Frankie, very romantic. Here we are, two coffees and two cognacs," said Lisa as she laid the tray down on the coffee table. Frankie took a sip of cognac,

"Hmm, very smooth, so where's this backup disc you found?"

"I'll go get it." She came back, sat down next to Frankie and handed the disc to him. Frankie looked at it, turned it over to read the details.

"One terabyte, so, plenty of capacity for all sorts of data, videos being particularly hungry in that respect. And it was in a false air vent?"

"Yes, in the bedroom, I'll show you after, but let's have our drinks first."

"Okay," said Frankie and took another sip of his cognac, "here's to us?"

"Here's to us Frankie," and she sipped her drink. So, how do we find out what's on it, the disc?" she said, "like I said, I only have an iPad, so…?"

"Okay, well why not bring it round to my place tomorrow, late morning, about elevenish?"

"Yeah, that suits me… Frankie..."

"What?"

"Are you going to make a move or are we playing hard to get? A girl might think she's not as attractive as she thought she was…."

*

He could hear their voices quite clearly despite the background music. *How the hell did she find the backup?* He listened in as their initial lovemaking began, then annoyingly, had to close down the connection and redial into the other bug as they moved to the bedroom. It was an improvement in terms of the lack of background music, but he felt strangely embarrassed listening in to their intimate grunting and moaning.

Trying to mentally detach himself he went to recharge his glass. At last they stopped the sexual activity. He listened intently.

*

"So, which vent was it you found the disc and money in?" asked Frankie as they snuggled up in bed after their strenuous, enthusiastic and noisy lovemaking.

"That one on the left," said Lisa pointing to the right-hand bedroom wall, "You want to take a look?"

"Not now, I'm too comfortable lying here," said Frankie closing his eyes, "show me tomorrow maybe?"

"Are you going to stay the night?" asked Lisa,

"I'd love to, but Charlie needs to have his walk around the parking lot before I turn in, and then I have to take him out in the morning. Maybe next time you can stay at mine, and we won't have that problem?" She sat up and punched him on the arm.

"Next time? We're a bit presumptuous, aren't we?"

"What?" said Frankie.

"I want to be wooed, not taken for granted."

"Oh, I'll woo you all right. In fact, I'll cook you my specialty, ply you with wine and charm the pants off you." Lisa laughed, then in a serious voice said.

"You know what Frankie? I'm a bit nervous about what we might find on this disc tomorrow. That's if I'm right about what she was up to."

"But you were just guessing, right? Might be just normal stuff." Frankie replied.

"Yeah, as if? I know my sister and it's more than a guess. Listen is there any way we can have a peek at what's on it now?" She said, walking two fingers up his arm as she spoke.

"What..., now?" asked Frankie.

"I'm just never going to go to sleep wondering. I mean I could be completely wrong about all this. My mom always said I had a wild imagination. I need to know."

"I suppose I could go get my laptop and we could have an initial look, but we'd probably need a lot more time to look at the whole thing, depending on what's on it. And I'd rather do it after a night's sleep and with a clear head.

"Yeah, I get that, but if you had a quick look, then…" Frankie knew when he was beaten.

"Okay, I'll just go and get my laptop and a cable, but just a quick look okay? But I need my beauty sleep so regardless of what we find, we leave a proper look until tomorrow, deal?" Lisa smiled.

"Deal partner," she said.

*

He got up from the bed where he'd been sitting while he listened in on their conversation and walked round the bedroom to try and shake off the tension. He realized his next move would be extremely risky. He'd got away with getting into Ava's condo without detection twice now but knew his luck couldn't last indefinitely. He took some deep breaths and tried to calm down. Keeping the cell phone next to his ear, he soon heard Frankie return to Lisa's bedroom.

*

"If anyone saw me coming into your condo at this time in the morning, the tongues would be wagging from now till

Christmas. Here pass me the disc." Lisa took the small oblong metal object off the top of her bedside cabinet and gave it to Frankie.

"What did you do with the cash?" Asked Frankie.

"In my bedside drawer," she answered.

"Okay, well I suppose it's safe enough for now, but you'll have to take care of that tomorrow, as soon as you've seen what you want to see."

"I know and I will Frankie."

Frankie turned his attention back to the disc and inserted a cable to connect the disc to his laptop.

"Here we go. Now I just click on the icon here and here we are. No passwords required so far. Let's look at the files." Frankie looked at the size of each file. "Can you see the screen okay?" he asked Lisa.

"Yes, fine thanks."

Frankie opened the largest file called Dates, then opened the main folder and some sub folders appeared, each sub folder was titled as a combination of two capital letters and six numbers in sequence s of two, the last two digits ranging from 17 to 19.

"Do those numbers seem like dates to you Frankie?"

"They do, don't know what the letters signify though." Frankie clicked on the first folder and revealed a video icon.

"How do you want to do this Lisa? If this video is what we think it might be…"

"I'm no prude Frankie. Porno doesn't, well you know, bother me, but the idea of seeing my own sister fucking people is going to be a bit icky. I really don't know."

"You want me to leave you on your own Lisa? I can go and sit in the living room, just click on the video icon and..."

"Yeah, I know how to do it, but it seems almost weirder to watch on my own while you're in another room. I… Oh fuck it, we're both grown-ups, just click and let see what's on the damn thing." He clicked and they watched as the video loaded up.

Ava walked into the bedroom, the very same bedroom they were now in themselves. Frankie was sure the irony wasn't lost on Lisa. Ava was followed by a man. She turned and looked directly into the camera over the shoulder of the man facing her. There wasn't much talking. What little there was, was hard to hear over the piano music in the background.

Ava patted the bed indicating the man should sit, then while still standing in front of him, started to shed her clothes. When she got down to her bra and panties, she walked out of camera shot. The man had turned his back to the camera by then, his face partially exposed for a fleeting second. He was now bent over the end of the bed.

"What's he doing that for? Do I recognize him?" Lisa said, "Have I seen him around in the last few days? Could he be one of the residents?"

"I don't think so, he maybe looks a bit like Roger Tuckerman, same build anyway."

"You know him then?"

"Know him? No, I don't know the guy on the vid. All I'm saying is he has a similar build to Roger. Roger's a friend, a good friend. He and his wife Myrtle were very kind to me when I first arrived here. They invited me to dinner at their condo and I've been out fishing with him on his friend's boat a couple of times. Great guy, army vet like me. I think. He's on the condo committee, and a regular at the local Episcopalian church. So no, I can assure you it isn't him."

"Well I hope it isn't. See that's what Ava was capable of, an otherwise respectable married guy, I don't mean this guy, but Ava could flash those eyes, and…"

"Uh oh, she's coming back." Ava came back into shot with a cane in her hand. Lisa gasped.

"Well I'll be a monkey's uncle, so that's what that was?"

"What?" asked Frankie.

"I found a cane in that wardrobe over there." Lisa pointed.

"Oh," was all Frankie could think of to say. The man turned his head slightly, but they still couldn't see his face.

"Jesus Christ," said Frankie.

"Oh no, she's taking his pants down. I don't know how much more of this I can watch," said Lisa, then Ava bent him over and she started to cane the man's bare backside, putting some heft into the job. Lisa started laughing uncontrollably, and Frankie joined in. They eventually stopped. Tears still running down their faces, they watched as the man's body flinch as Ava administered the punishment.

"Stop it Frankie please, I really can't watch any more, this is excruciating." Frankie stopped the video. "Why do people do that, I mean why would you like being caned on the ass like that?"

"I really don't know Lisa. If he'd been brought up a Catholic like me, he could've enjoyed a lot of ass caning for free, he could've had my share as well."

"Did they really do that to you when you were a kid?"

"They sure did. Not so much the priests in my case, but the teachers. A cane, or a galoshe as they were called then, like a trainer, sorry sneaker. Take your pants down in front of the class, sometimes the whole school, and give you six of the best, they called it, not sure what was so best about it. They enjoyed it too, you could tell."

"Perverts," said Lisa.

"With a capital P, they'd be locked up today, but hey, water under the bridge now." Frankie looked at the rest of the files on the disc.

"This is interesting," said Frankie, "an Excel file titled piano lessons, with some of the same initials and dates as the videos files, but with more information, names and addresses and more. This is potential dynamite Lisa, Detective Randazzo is going to have a field day when he sees this.

"Yeah, but like I said, how much damage is going to cause if this were to come out. Most of these men are probably decent guys who just wanted sex. Maybe their wives had lost interest, I don't know, but part of me feels sorry for them. I loved my sister, but…" Lisa looked away unable to finish the sentence.

"Yeah, but these guys, assuming there are more of them, they really should have known better. Anyway, not for us to judge, that's for the authorities to deal with. We have to tell Detective Randazzo as soon possible tomorrow Lisa."

"I guess you're right, I got carried away. Look I'm really tired now, so let's leave the rest until tomorrow as planned. At least now I know I was right about what I thought Ava was up to. We'll tell the detective tomorrow I promise, but not until we've had a chance to look at the rest of my sister's sordid private life, then we tell the cops. Hopefully Detective Randazzo can then nail the guy who killed Ava."

Frankie detached the cable closed his laptop and handed the disc back to Lisa. She took it and put it in her bedside cabinet drawer. Frankie stood up, leaned over and planted a kiss on Lisa's lips, then made to take his leave.

"Do you want me to take the disc with me now? Asked Frankie

"No, it's okay, I'll bring it with me in the morning."

"Okay Lisa, see you tomorrow, about eleven. Sweet dreams." he said as he walked toward the condo door.

"You too Frankie, and thanks for everything," said Lisa as she got up and followed him to the door. I'd better lock up behind you."

*

The perp listened as Frankie finally left her condo, then checked his watch. 3:15 a.m. *still time…*

Chapter 17

Day 6 - Sunday

Frankie

More often than not, Frankie would have a lie in on Sundays, but not today. Despite the previous late-night activities, he felt energized and fizzing with enthusiasm to get the day started. He looked at the clock, 07:15. *Plenty of time for an early morning jog with Charlie before breakfast.*

By 10.00 a.m. he was exercised, showered and fed. Frankie then emailed his business partner on a couple of matters that he'd left in abeyance over the last couple of days. Making himself some more coffee, he read the online newspapers to catch up on the latest developments in the UK, then distracted himself by watching the US cable news channels, switching from one to the other to get a balanced view on all matters American.

He checked his watch again, 11:16 a.m.

"Hmm, what do you think Charlie, should we be worried?

He busied himself tidying up in the kitchen then checked the time again, 11:25. *Strange?* He went to find his cell and punched in Lisa's number. It rang out then went to voicemail

"Hi, this is Lisa, leave your name and number and I'll call you back."

He went to stand on the lanai and looked out over the bay. *Where the hell is she, surely she'd have called if she was going to be this late?*

"Better take a look Charlie," he said, and left his condo.

Her door was closed and locked. He pressed the bell again and again and knocked on the door. No answer. He waited, then hit the door with the flat of his hand several times, still nothing. He called her cell again, no answer. He tried to look through the window, but the blinds were down. Just then Virginia McCrea walked down the corridor. He'd seen her before and knew she was a resident. They'd exchanged greetings before, but no more than that.

"Having trouble... Frankie isn't it?"

"I am yes. Lisa, Ava's sister, she's moved into Ava's condo."

"So I heard, so, what's the problem?"

"Well she was supposed to come to my condo at eleven this morning and didn't show up, and now I can't get any response. She doesn't answer her cell nor does she answer the door."

"Maybe she's just gone out and left her phone in the apartment?"

"It's possible but I doubt it. Do you know if anyone would have a spare key?" Virginia raised her eyebrows.

"You and she are…?"

"Yes, we've been out on a couple of dates, so…?"

"I see. Well my guess is Rudy Sprouse, the condo president, he would probably have a spare key. I have his number on my cell if you'd like it?"

Rudy Sprouse arrived some ten minutes later.

"Hi Virginia, Frankie. What's the problem?" Frankie repeated the explanation he'd given Virginia. "Okay, well let's try the doorbell one more time and maybe call her cell as well?"

Rudy pressed the bell push and Frankie called her cell phone. No answer to either. Rudy inserted the key in the door, opened it and entered Ava's apartment, followed by Frankie. Rudy shouted a loud *hello?*

"I'll wait out here boys, this is none of my business," said Virginia. Rudy wandered through the living room and on to the lanai. Frankie made straight for the bedroom. What he found there made his legs buckle as he felt his heart explode into a million pieces.

"No, no. Dear sweet Jesus, please no," he whispered, managing with effort, to stay upright. Time seemed to stop as he took in the scene. Lisa's body was lying on the bed face up, partially covered by the tangled sheet. Her blond hair splayed across the pillow, her face, normally a healthy light tan, now showed the unmistakable gray pallor of death. Frankie noticed faint bruise marks on her neck.

His face contorted in grief and tears began to roll down his cheeks. He realized he would never see that stunning smile again. Never hear that laugh, never kiss her or hold her in his arms as he'd done just a few short hours ago. She'd gone.

Frankie had witnessed many deaths during his time in the army. He could tell the difference between a recent death and the various stages that followed. Sometimes a recently dead person could look as if they were merely asleep, but he knew it didn't take long for that false look to fade as the heart, starved of oxygen, stopped pumping blood around the body and the inevitable process of decomposition kicked in.

As he began to recover from the initial shock, he walked the short distance to her inert body and stroked Lisa's face with the back of his fingers. There was no point in looking for a pulse. He could tell she'd been gone for some time now. He managed to speak. A small croaky voice was all he could muster. He stroked her hair and spoke.

"Lisa, I'm so sorry I left you." He felt the need to gather her up in his arms, but managed to resist, knowing that he might well further compromise what was now obviously a crime scene. He played their lovemaking back in his mind, *was it possible to have fallen in love so deeply in such a short time*? He'd hoped that their relationship would develop into something much more than a fling, something much more meaningful. He was sure Lisa had had similar feelings, *but now?*

He'd experienced before the void that opens up when someone close dies, the feeling of utter devastation, of impotence, helplessness.

Rudy shouted from the living room.

"Frankie, where are you?" Frankie took a deep breath

"Rudy, come here, now!"

Rudy walked into the bedroom.

"No, sweet Jesus no, this can't be happening, not here Frankie," said Rudy, his face drained of color, standing there stupefied. Frankie had his cell phone out and was dialing 911.

A few minutes later the emergency services showed up, sirens blaring. Paramedics rushed into the condo. Rudy showed them to the bedroom. They examined Lisa and went through the pointless routine process of checking her vital signs. A short time later, one of them came out of the bedroom, looked at Frankie and Rudy, and Virginia who was now standing with them in the living room.

"Sorry she's gone, but I guess you knew that. You need to all leave and stand outside the condo. This is now a crime scene. Who called it in?"

Frankie held his hand up.

"You need to stay. The cops are on their way."

The words were no sooner out of his mouth when Detective Randazzo walked swiftly through the door.

"Where?" he said to the paramedic. The paramedic pointed to the open bedroom door. Randazzo went in and exited a few minutes later, speaking into his cell phone. He finished his conversation. "Anyone touched anything?" he asked Frankie who was now standing by the door.

"Yes, I did. I found her," Frankie replied, "there was just me and Rudy Sprouse, the condo president. I called him because I was told he had a spare key to Ava's condo, and I wanted…" Randazzo cut him off.

"We'll get to the how what and why later, just tell me what you did when you entered the apartment, condo, whatever."

Frankie told him. By now two uniforms were standing by the door.

"Come with me," said the detective to Frankie, and as they exited the condo, Randazzo gave instructions to the uniforms about sealing off the crime scene. A small crowd of residents had gathered in the corridor. "And get these people out of here," he added. "Okay, Mr. Armstrong, you and Mr. Sprouse, follow me to my car." They followed him to the parking lot.

The detective leaned against his car, and making sure there was no one in listening distance, he took out his notebook.

"We've met before Mr. Sprouse, so I know where to find you if and when I need more information. But can you tell me briefly, what your involvement was in this... this incident?"

"No involvement as such, other than getting a call from Virginia McCrea. Apparently, she'd bumped into Frankie here, outside Ava Ledinski's condo. He was trying to get her, her being Lisa Ledinski of course, to answer the door." Randazzo held up his hand.

"Please don't tell me what Mr. Armstrong was trying to do, just tell me what your involvement was."

"Oh, Okay, well I got a call from Virginia, one of our other residents, she asked me if I had a spare key to Ava's condo and could I come and open the door for Frankie, who was trying to... Erm, sorry. Anyway, I came down with the key, but before I opened the door, I rang the bell and asked Frankie here to try her cell again."

"Time?" asked the detective.

"Around 11:45 this morning I guess."

"So, you went into the apartment, and then?"

"Nothing, I wandered over to the lanai, then I heard Frankie shout for me to go to the bedroom and I saw Lisa lying there, dead. Frankie was standing by the bed. I just stood there in shock. Frankie called the emergency services. That's it."

"Okay, thanks for your help Mr. Sprouse, you can go." Rudy Sprouse walked away head bowed.

Whilst the detective was asking Rudy about his involvement in the grim discovery, Frankie's mind was racing. *The most obvious motive for the murder was to get the back-up disc, but how would anyone else know about the existence of the disk, or more to the point, that Lisa had found it? What was he going to tell Randazzo? How much trouble was he in for not telling him about the disc already? Would he be charged for withholding evidence?* Two more police cars drove into the parking lot, blue and red lights flashing. They parked and disgorged two uniforms each.

All four policemen walked over to Randazzo.

"Detective?" said the senior officer holding his finger up to his hat in a vague salute.

"Hi Al," replied Randazzo, "send your guys to help the others secure the scene until the CSI's get here will you and take any statements from anyone who saw anything. Knock on neighbor's doors. You know the drill. When did anyone last see the victim etc.? I'll need you to stay with me Al." Al sent his men off and stayed with Randazzo, who was getting his notebook out.

"Okay Mr. Armstrong," said the detective, "let's get in the car," Frankie noted the formal name. No Frankie on this occasion, "I'm going to need you to make a formal statement down at headquarters, but in the meantime, tell me what you know about what happened here." The detective sat in the driver's seat, Frankie in the passenger seat and the cop sat in the rear.

Frankie began by telling Randazzo about his first date with Lisa and how it had led to the second date, when she'd told him she'd found what looked like a backup disc and a wad of cash.

"How much cash?" asked the detective.

"In excess of $33, 000,' Lisa said." The detective made a note.

"Carry on Mr. Armstrong."

Frankie left out the more intimate details of the previous night. Randazzo showed no reaction during Frankie's telling of the rest of his story, other than to grunt occasionally, raise his eyebrows at various points and ask for clarification on certain points as he made his notes. Frankie finished his story at the point where the detective had shown up.

The detective made a few extra notes, then looked over his shoulder at the cop sitting in the rear seat, then back to Frankie.

"You said she found this back up disc in a false air vent, and the cash, that right?" Frankie answered "Yes. It was quite a large capacity disc."

"Did you see what was on this disc?"

"Some of what was on it, not much but yes. Lisa only had an iPad, so she was going to bring the disc round to my place this morning at eleven. I have a PC and we planned to look at what was on it then."

"But?" said Randazzo.

"But Lisa said she wanted to know what was on it last night, well early this morning would be more accurate I suppose. She wanted to have some indication of what was on it. She said she wouldn't be able to rest until she knew. It was a funny situation. On the one hand she was convinced she knew what was on it, but on the other, she thought she might be wrongly accusing her sister of something she might not be guilty of. Does that make sense Detective?"

"In a convoluted way I guess it does. So, what was on this back up disc?"

"There were various files. We only looked at one because it was the largest one and seemed likely to be the one containing videos. Lisa thought that's what Ava might have been doing, making secret videos of her having sex and then charging, or more likely, blackmailing the men in them. Seems she might have been right as it turned out."

"Go on," said Randazzo.

"We only looked at one video, from the largest file which was called Dates. It showed Ava in a state of undress caning a man. We stopped looking at that point. Lisa said she didn't want to see any more. She'd seen what she needed to, to know that what she'd thought was going on, had been true. She was upset."

"And did you recognize this man?"

Frankie hesitated

"No," he said. *I can hardly say he looked a bit like Roger Tuckerman, that just wouldn't be fair.*

"Are you sure, you seemed to hesitate?"

"Hand on heart, I can honestly say I didn't recognize him."

"Could you describe him?"

"I could give you a general description, yes," said Frankie.

"Okay, you can do that later in your formal statement, but you definitely didn't recognize him as one of the residents?"

"I couldn't say one way or another, I mean if he was or wasn't one of the residents, just that I didn't see enough of his face to be able to recognize him," said Frankie.

"But the woman in the video was definitely Ava Ledinski?" Frankie told him there was no doubt about that.

"And you didn't see any other people on that video or on another video?"

"No, like I said, we only watched that one, and only the first few minutes."

"You didn't keep a copy on your laptop?"

"No, I didn't. I'd have told you if I had Detective."

"Okay, so, as I obviously can't ask Ms. Ledinski, why do you think she didn't immediately let me know when she found this potentially vital evidence, why would she not do that?"

"She said something along the lines of, she didn't want the cops rooting around in her sister's underwear drawer. She was obviously speaking metaphorically."

"Yeah, I think I could have worked that out," replied Randazzo sarcastically.

"Sorry," said Frankie, "didn't mean to sound... patronizing."

"So, you admit you were in possession of the knowledge of this vital evidence being found, for what, nearly twenty-four hours?"

"Well yes, I suppose so, but it was only last evening Lisa first told me about it, so not really that long."

"Far too long in my book Mr. Armstrong. Do you know how much trouble you're in - and do you realize, if you'd told us as soon as you found out about this backup disc, that young lady would probably still be alive?"

Frankie looked the detective straight in the eyes.

"That's a cheap shot Detective Randazzo. If I'd have thought for one split second that not telling you would put Lisa in danger.... I mean we couldn't have known what would happen in between..."

Randazzo's raised he voice to shouting volume,

"It's not up to you to make that sort of judgment. You could've easily called me. I gave you my cell number. If you had then…?"

"Okay, I was wrong, tragically wrong. But Lisa insisted we wait and well…"

"Well nothing Mr. Armstrong. On the face of it, you were colluding to deprive the authorities of evidence with the potential to catch a killer. Withholding such vital evidence is an extremely serious matter Mr. Armstrong, you do realize that, don't you?"

"Yes, and like I said, we'd agreed she'd tell you when she came round this morning, I…" Randazzo cut him off.

"But not before you took a look at what was on the disc. Even if I believe your story about this disc, or you persuading Ms. Ledinski to hand it over to us, you can add interfering with vital evidence to the charge of withholding." Randazzo turned to address the cop sitting in the rear, "You getting all this Al?"

"I am, yes sir. Withholding evidence and interfering with evidence." Randazzo turned back to look at Frankie, then consulted his notes. Frankie had a sinking feeling. This was getting much worse than he had imagined it could.

"When she first told you about finding the disc, you say Ms. Ledinski speculated on what might be on it?"

"As I said, she believed it might contain videos of her sister and her clients..."

"I'm wondering why she would think this. I can see the cash is something that could point to blackmail money, but people keep cash hidden for all sorts of reasons. Could have been cash paid for piano lessons over the years, money she didn't want to pay tax on?"

Frankie took a deep breath and blew it out before speaking.

"Yes, it could be but there's some history. It's a bit of a long story."

"Do we look as if we're in a hurry to leave?" replied Randazzo, "and you're certainly not going anywhere in a hurry that's for sure."

Frankie sighed, and told him Lisa's story of Ava's husband leaving her and the revenge affairs she had with married men to get her own back. Then Lisa's suspicions about where the money came from to fund her jet set lifestyle. He continued.

"Lisa initially thought Ava might have become a high-end hooker, an escort or something, but Ava scorned that idea. So, Lisa finally figured out that maybe she was up to her old tricks, but instead of actually telling her lover's wives, she was making money by threatening to expose them unless they paid her."

"So, she suspected even back then that her sister was a blackmailer?"

"Yes, that's what Lisa suspected."

"And neither she, nor you, thought to immediately come to us with that information?" Randazzo's voice had risen in volume and anger as he spoke, simultaneously striking the top of the dashboard with such force that Frankie was surprised it remained intact. Randazzo got out of the car and stood for a minute, before getting back in. The officer in the rear remained silent. Randazzo composed himself, then spoke again.

"You say you came back from the pizza place at around 9:30 p.m. and Ms. Ledinski invited you in for coffee, that correct? Frankie nodded. "And did you have coffee, or something stronger?"

"We had coffee and cognac."

"Coffee and cognac," repeated the detective as he made a note. "And how long did you stay in Ms. Ledinski's condo?"

"Till about 3:00 a.m. I guess."

"Did you and Ms. Ledinski have sex?" Frankie hesitated. 'There's going to be an autopsy Mr. Armstrong, so let's not mess about here, did you and…" Frankie cut him off.

"Yes, we did."

"Before or after you watched the video?"

"Why is that important, you think we got off watching a man being caned?"

"Just answer the question Mr. Armstrong, before or after?"

"Before."

"Did it get rough?"

"What?" said Frankie suddenly realizing where this was going. "No, it didn't get rough." *Well it did a bit, but not from my side.*

"So, we won't find any marks on the body consistent with rough sex?"

"No," replied Frankie, trying to sound convincing. "Just what are you trying to say, that I strangled Lisa during rough sex?"

"It wouldn't be the first time that's happened." Frankie was about to protest again, but Randazzo kept talking. "See, we have a situation here. You are the last person to see Ms. Ledinski alive."

Frankie protested.

"No, I'm not. Clearly, the person who killed her, who strangled her, whatever, is the last person to see her alive… and dead for that matter. When I left Lisa, she was perfectly well, healthy and very much alive. It's obvious the killer somehow got into her condo to get hold of the disc."

"So that's your theory, interesting. Any idea where Ms. Ledinski put the disc after showing it to you?"

"No… hang on a minute, yes, she put it into her bedside cabinet drawer." The detective made a note.

"Bedside cabinet drawer." He said as he wrote it down. He looked up at Frankie, then turned to the officer in the rear. "Okay Al, go search the bedside drawers for a disc or anything that looks like a backup storage device. And don't forget the plastic gloves and shoe covers before you go in."

"No sir, and yes sir, will do," said the officer as he got out of the car. Frankie began to speak.

"Look, I didn't harm Lisa. I'm not a violent person Detective, and I liked Lisa, I liked her a lot, more than liked."

"Problem is Mr. Armstrong, we only have your word for all this. Plus, there are no obvious signs of a break in. How did the killer get into the condo? And even if the killer did manage to gain access without any obvious signs of a break in, how exactly did he do that, and...how do you explain this killer knowing about the back-up disc you say Ms. Ledinski found, and that the killer obviously took?" He said the last two words using air quotes.

"I can't explain," said Frankie realizing just how weak his story now sounded. A couple of minutes later officer Al returned and got back into the rear of the car.

"Nothing in the drawers, other than some make up, underwear and stuff like that."

"Okay Al, arrest Mr. Armstrong here on a charge of withholding evidence and take him downtown. That should be enough to hold him until the crime scene guys have conducted their initial assessments and the results of the autopsy come in."

"Yes sir," said the officer. He exited the car and stood by the passenger door waiting to arrest Frankie as he got out. The detective turned to Frankie.

"Mr. Armstrong, may I have the keys to your condo, I assume you have no objection to us conducting a search of your apartment?" Frankie reached into his pocket and handed his keys over.

"Here, no objection, but you're wasting your time," said Frankie, "you're making a big mistake Detective, you've got the wrong man, and the killer is still out there." Then as he began to get out of the car, Frankie suddenly realized, in all the drama of Lisa's murder, he'd forgotten all about Charlie. Frankie sat back down.

"I have a problem Detective Randazzo. My dog Charlie, he needs to be looked after while I'm being detained, or whatever it is that's happening to me."

"I'll get the dog pound people to look after that problem, okay?"

"No, not okay, not okay at all. If you'll allow me to call my friend Joe Nelson in Naples, the guy I told you about, the guy whose nephew I found. He was the original owner of Charlie and he'll come and get him I'm sure." The detective hesitated.

"Okay but make it quick. And if he can't come right away, it's the dog pound. Tell your friend to come to your apartment and ask for me"

Frankie took his cell out and called Joe Nelson. He explained the situation as quickly as he could.

"He's on his way," Frankie said to Randazzo and got out of the car.

"Please put both of your hands forward sir," said the officer as he placed the handcuffs on Franke's wrists and read him his rights. Frankie turned to the detective and spoke again to him through the open window.

"I didn't do it Detective Randazzo."

"Maybe, maybe not? Look, I'm cutting you a bit of slack here Mr. Armstrong. Just be thankful I'm not arresting you on a charge of homicide, at least not yet."

Chapter 18

Day 6 - Sunday
The Perp

Acadiana, like most condo complexes, had a very efficient, if at times, wildly inaccurate rumor mill. This time there was no need for exaggeration. One murder was certainly unusual, but two in the space of a matter of days, was nothing short of shocking and sensational. Word got around the residents in record time and he hadn't long to wait until the 'news' reached him when one of his fellow residents stopped him in the corridor.

"You heard about what happened last night?" asked Imke Bogdasarian.

Acting surprised, he articulated the expected expressions of shock and horror as she relayed what she'd heard.

"What!? The British guy Frankie Armstrong arrested?" He exclaimed as Imke rattled through the details of what she'd been told with obvious gruesome glee. He had to turn away to hide the wry smile that he simply couldn't resist. Smile, he almost laughed out loud. It wasn't clear precisely what Frankie had been arrested for, but he could take an educated guess. He guessed eventually they'd realize they had the wrong guy and let him go, but the more confusion the better as far as he was concerned. *Hopefully the cops won't find any evidence of the condo being burglarized. I was so very careful not to leave any evidence behind...*

Getting into Ava's condo had been a breeze, both times. The second time he'd removed the bugs and replaced them with the original plug sockets. That was after the stupid woman had been strangled. *If only she hadn't ripped the mask off. Well it's done now, so can't turn the clock back. All we have to do is sit tight and hold our nerve.* He absent mindedly scratched at the small sticking plaster on his neck as he re-ran the burglarizing of the condo through his mind, mentally checking off the precautions he'd taken to avoid any detection of a break in. He couldn't think of any glitches and decided to go for a walk to shake off the tension.

Chapter 19

Day 6 - Sunday

Frankie

Frankie was taken to the Naples Jail Centre on Tamiami Trail, where he was formally arraigned, read his rights again, fingerprinted and swabbed for a DNA sample. He was allowed a phone call which he used to call Joe Nelson. One to check on Charlie, and two, to fill him in on what had happened and three, to ask his advice. Joe confirmed he'd collected Charlie and told Frankie not to worry on that score.

"Hmm," said Joe, "I'm no legal expert, so I guess I'd advise you to get an attorney. I know a guy you can trust, but he don't come cheap. And so far, you haven't been charged with the woman's murder, so I don't know. I spoke briefly with the detective guy, Randazzo when I went to collect Charlie. He wasn't really giving anything away, but I got the impression he was still very much looking for the killer. So, if he really thought you'd done it… Listen Frankie, the one thing I do know is, the less you say the better. So, just take the fifth and answer no comment to everything until things become a bit clearer, or you get an attorney."

"I've already answered a lot of questions."

"Was that before or after you were arrested?"

"Before."

"Okay then I don't think that can be used, so just keep your mouth shut from now on. I'll get hold of Michael Riley, that's the attorney. See if he can come down to sort things out." Frankie thanked him and the officer led him to the cells where his possessions were taken from him and he was incarcerated.

*

Randazzo called the meeting to order. He brought the assembled detectives and researchers up to date on events. Hands went up.

"Yes," said Randazzo pointing to a squat Mexican looking man who had got to his feet. "Miguel?"

"So, the guy you've arrested, is the same guy who dove into the bay to rescue the first vic?"

"Yeah he is."

"And you think this guy killed both women?" Detective Randazzo blew air out of his mouth before answering.

"Honest answer? No, I don't. In fact, I don't think he committed either crime. Truth is, I was so angry with this Frankie Armstrong character, I arrested him on a charge of withholding evidence to teach him a lesson. The evidence in the possession of the second victim could have got us the jump on the original perp, but now it's gone."

"But the guy had the opportunity and no alibi, that right sir?" asked one of the female detectives.

"He did, but no motive, no obvious motive anyway. He's just not a good fit and I don't want us wasting our time sitting on our fannies, thinking we've got the perp in custody when the real perp is running around free. I've asked the autopsy to be expedited and I'm hoping the results will be in this evening. If there's nothing to indicate Armstrong's involvement in her death, I might think about letting the guy go."

"The uniforms conducted the initial enquiries, interviewing neighbors and so on, so these are being collated and copied as we speak. So, Francesco, get copies and organize a couple of teams to follow up tomorrow morning. I'll let you all know the results of the autopsy as soon as I get them. That's all for now."

*

Frankie wasn't intimidated at being locked up in jail. He could handle himself if it came to it but cautious about getting on the wrong side of any potential violent cellmates. *No need to go looking for trouble* was his motto.

"Hey, now what have we got us here? Gangster, burglar, murderer?" said a scrawny looking individual as he went to sit down on a hard-wooden bench. "Come on buddy," the man continued, "fess up."

Frankie laughed.

"Sorry to disappoint, but I'm not any of those things." He replied.

"Don't tell me," continued the joker, to the amusement of the other cell mates, "you're innocent, it was all a mistake, you didn't do it." Then he laughed again.

"Spot on," said Frankie as he sensed this was more a question of amusement rather than anything with sinister intent. "As you say, it's all a mistake and I really am innocent."

This last comment caused even more mirth, Frankie laughed along with the others and relaxed a little.

"Well you've convinced me," continued the joker, "I'll just call the captain and tell him to let you out."

Frankie had been assessing the characters of each of his fellow jailbirds and decided he wasn't in any imminent danger, although as the conversations between the others continued, he began to wonder. Each of the inmates told stories about some of the violent psychopaths they'd each been locked up with from time to time. Frankie concluded they were exaggerating for effect, trying to outdo each other.

His big concern, out of the many he now had, was being moved to a real prison, rather than this local holding facility. He just hoped Joe's attorney could work his magic and get him released before that could happen. There was a lull in the conversations between the other men.

"So, come on then buddy, what did they bring you in for?'

Frankie wasn't sure he should tell them, *but what the hell* he thought.

"Okay, if you really want to know, I'm a suspect in a murder. The death of a friend, more than a friend. Someone I cared for very much, which makes it all the more ironic that I'm in the frame for the killing. Just because they think I was the last one to see her alive. But that's all they have, so, like you said, it's a mistake and I'm innocent."

"Hmm," said the joker, "you actually do sound as if you are innocent, that'd be a first in here." *More laughter*

Having satisfied the curiosity of his fellow inmates, he asked what each of them was in for. More for something to do and to take his mind off Lisa's death, for a while at least. There was Larry who was drying out, having been arrested trying to rob a bank with a plastic water pistol. Then there was Greg, who was in for beating up a man he caught with his wife. *He had everyone's sympathy.* Said he was still going to beat the guy to a pulp when he got out, but he was going to plan it properly, and *next time, wear a mask.*

The most interesting, as far as Frankie was concerned, was a serial burglar by the name of Denis. He reckoned he'd been really unlucky to get caught. Said he'd burglarized hundreds, if not thousands of homes in his thirty-year career and only been caught twice.

"This time was a real pisser," he said, "you wouldn't believe." Of course once he'd said that, they all wanted to know.

"Okay but promise you won't laugh. See, I'm in this ground floor condo, easy peasy lock a kid of five could have opened. I found some nice jewelry, nothing fantastic, but sellable, plus a genuine Rolex watch and a couple a hundred bucks in cash. I'm just leaving through the front door, acting casual, when two cop cars come screaming up and stop just in front of me. They got out of the car and were only a couple of yards from me. I can't run these days, gammy leg, so I drop the briefcase. Briefcase is better, looks like you been there to sell something.

"Anyways, I drop the briefcase, stand there and put my hands on my head. The cops didn't move at first, then one of them pulls his gun and tells me to get down on the floor. They stand around me and one of them puts his foot on my back so I can't move, then he says."

"What do we do now?"

"I don't know," said one of the others, "call the cops I guess," then they all started laughing fit to burst. Just then a van rolls up and a guy and a girl get out with like movie cameras. Turns out they were shooting an ad and they'd chosen this condo complex as the location. The fuckin cops were pissant actors and I was up the wazzoo big time!"

When they'd all stopped laughing, Frankie had an idea.

"Can I have a word with you Denis? He said.

"Sure, step into my private office," said Denis, gesturing to the corner of the cell where there was a separate metal bench, bolted to the floor. They sat.

"I told you why I'm in here," said Frankie, "so you know the general circumstances, but I didn't murder the woman as they're suggesting. She was very special to me…. Anyway, put that to one side. Although I'm in the security business back in the UK, I don't have any particular experience in, what would you call it, household burglary? Anyway, I've had a few hours in here to think about how the killer managed to do what he did and why. And I'd like to try my theory out on you, you being, with all due respect, an accomplished professional in this area, you might say."

"With all due respect," Denis laughed uproariously, "You limeys are really somthin' else."

"I didn't mean to offend."

"No offence taken, Frankie my new buddy, no offence taken, you're one of us now," said Denis and winked mockingly as he nudged Frankie in the side with his elbow. Frankie smiled back. "So, shoot, try me out with your theory. Let's see how it stands up to 'professional scrutiny' he said making quotes with his fingers. Then he laughed again.

"Okay, here goes," said Frankie and told him his theory about the burglar, come killer, planting a bug in the condo, then breaking in to retrieve the backup disc.

"Thing is," said Frankie, "this person had to have got in and out of her apartment, without leaving any obvious traces of a break in. And he had to have done it twice in a matter of a day or two at the most. So how easy is it to break into a condo without leaving any trace? Before you answer, there were two new locks on the door, and I'm fairly certain both were locked."

Denis smiled.

"If you're talking about a standard set of locks. By the way, how old are these condos?"

"Not sure, not modern, a bit art deco really, so I guess built in the sixties maybe?"

"Yeah, so unless here was a serious recent upgrade to the locks, and if they just replaced like with like, but with new keys, it would take any competent person with a set of picks, probably less than a minute for each lock. Man, I could probably do both of them in less than thirty seconds. You can even buy lock picks on Amazon these days, would you believe? Wear some plastic gloves and bingo bongo, you wouldn't leave a trace."

"Okay well that fits with what I thought, although I didn't know such things as lock picks were that readily available, but there you go. So, what about my theory on him planting bugs, how feasible is that?"

"Very, and if it was me, I'd plant two or three bugs in the main areas, maybe four if the place was big. I mean we're speculating here, but like I say, the level of sophistication of the listening devices these days is impressive. Your question about constant monitoring, I'm pretty sure you can get voice activated devices, even the cheap ones, so they only record when someone talks, saves battery life."

"And they can alert your cell when someone speaks, so you can listen in to a conversation. There's plenty of info online about these things. I've never used them myself, but it's a real pisser, all this online stuff available to amateur villains. Makes it hard for a regular professional burglar like me to make a decent living these days," then he burst into laughter again.

*

As Frankie bedded down in the holding cell for his first night in captivity, he lay on the bunk bed, his head on a thin pillow. He thought about his theory and wondered if Detective Randazzo would buy into it. Being convinced he wouldn't sleep a wink, if for nothing else because of the loud snoring of his cellmates, he was surprised to be woken the next morning by a guard shouting his name. Frankie was surprised to realize, he'd slept like the proverbial log.

"Wakey wakey rise and shine. And Armstrong the limey guy, you just made bail, which means you miss our wonderful gourmet breakfast."

The other prisoners laughed. Frankie got down from his bunk as the guard opened the door of the cell. He said goodbye to his newfound jail buddies, all three of whom had added to Frankie's knowledge of the human race, in ways he could not have imagined.

"Good luck Frankie boy," shouted Denis as he was led away. Frankie turned back and waved goodbye. He was taken down a corridor into a small room with a steel table bolted to the floor and two chairs on either side of the table, similarly anchored to the floor. He was told to sit and wait. The guard left and then a few minutes later, the door opened again, and a smartly suited man came into the room. He was tall and wiry, and wore a big smile on his face, showing whiter than white teeth. Frankie stood and they shook hands.

"Riley, Michael Riley. Joe asked me to come see what I could do." Riley sat and gestured for Frankie to do the same.

"How much trouble am I in?" asked Frankie.

"You want the good news or the good news?" replied Riley. "Silly question. The fact is they're letting you go, so I'm here under false pretenses as it were." Frankie couldn't hide his surprise.

"How so?" he asked.

"They have the initial autopsy reports in and there's a development. The victim, Ms. Lisa Ledinski?" Frankie nodded. "She must have put up a bit of a fight. The pathologist found minute traces of skin under one of her fingernails. The killer must have realized the potential for this to be a problem, so he, or she, had scraped the nails clean, but there were some tiny traces left, just about enough for a reliable DNA sample. As the sample didn't match your DNA, you're off the hook for the time being at least."

Frankie's shoulders slumped. He hadn't realized how tense he'd been.

"Christ, that's a relief. You said for the time being?"

"Yeah. Unless they find some compelling evidence to link you directly to the death of that poor woman, they've concluded you're not a great suspect. However, you were the last known person to see the victim alive, plus as I understand it, you don't have a great alibi. So, they're letting you go, but you're still a person of interest shall we say."

"What about the charge for withholding evidence?"

"Dropped. From what I saw of the arrest details, it was never going to fly anyway. But in any event, they'll be wanting your cooperation to help find the person who did it. So, like I say, you'll soon be good to go, a free man again. And, as you're a friend of Joe's, and I haven't really done that much, my services on this occasion are on the house. You want a lift anywhere? Shouldn't take long for them to process you out of here."

Chapter 20

Day 6 - Sunday

More prattling round the pool

"I got mobbed by the news guys this morning when I came back from Publix, Had to fight my way through. Those guys just don't give up," said Barbara Tyskewicz as she floated on her pool mattress in the shallow end of the pool.

"Yeah, same here," said Bodo Kellerman, "mind you this is probably the biggest story since Ted Bundy. Naples's very own serial killer."

"Be serious Bodo," said Deanne Boswell, "two women murdered in the space of a week, It's not funny. I mean, apart from anything else, what's this going to do to the price of our condos? We'll be living with this for years."

"Trust Deanne to focus on the practical," said her husband Pete, as he sat up on his sun lounger. "She should be worried I might take the opportunity to strangle her and blame it on the Condo Killer." They all laughed, except Deanne who floated away in a sulk to the other end of the pool.

"Oh, my giddy aunt, Condo Killer, is that what they're calling him now?" said Nancy Farr as she bobbed up and down in the pool on a bright pink pool noodle.

"Got a nice ring to it I think," said Linda Monostory, a fellow pool noodle floater, "Condo Killer, yeah I like that. I can see them making a movie of it. Wonder if I'll be invited to star in it?"

"It'll be a horror movie then?" said Bodo Kellerman. They all laughed.

"Bodo, you just be careful. My husband hears you say that, he'll likely feed you to the gator!" She wasn't smiling and propelled herself down to the far end of the pool to join Nancy.

"You've done it now Bodo," said Pete Boswell.

"Nah… Might cost me a large dry martini to get back in her good books though," he replied, and they laughed again.

The pool was more crowded than usual and some of the residents had to lean against the railings, or sit on the side of the pool dangling their legs in the warm water, which was more the temperature of a tepid bath rather than a swimming pool *Florida…*

"Hey, seriously though folks," said Jim Büettnerkraus who was sitting under a sun umbrella at one of the poolside tables, "My wife is scared to death. She's now insisting we get our locks changed, and, she says Frankie Armstrong was hauled off by the cops this morning, reckons he could be the killer."

"Nah," said Bodo, "Frankie Armstrong a killer, you're joking. He and the girl who was murdered, Lisa Ledinski, they were certainly seeing each other that's for sure. Virginia, who was there when they found the body, she told my wife Frankie had been taking this Lisa out, and he was with her the previous evening apparently. But Frankie a killer? No, I don't believe it. Obviously, the person who killed Lisa Ledinski has got to be the same guy who killed her sister, and we all know Frankie didn't kill Ava, so…"

"But he was arrested by the cops wasn't he - why would they do that if he wasn't implicated?" asked Jim Büettnerkraus. No one seemed to have a satisfactory answer to that.

Chapter 21

Day 7 - Monday

Detective Randazzo — Naples Police HQ

"So, Dale," Randazzo said, as they sat in his office, "Here's the initial autopsy results." Dale Vogel looked through the report, muttering as he did so, occasionally shaking his head.

"Compression of anatomical neck structures leading to asphyxia and neuronal death. Why can't they just say she was strangled?" he said. He finished reading put the report down on the desk. "What a waste," he continued, "I don't think I'll ever get used to this sort of thing. A healthy young woman, in the prime of life…"

"Yeah, it's tragic Dale. So, we now have something tangible to work with, the DNA. It's a male perp, hardly surprising. I've already called the chairman of Acadiana to tell him I'll be sending over some text for him to email out to all residents, all male residents that is, asking them to provide a DNA sample."

"You want them all to come here for that?"

"No, this is where you come in. I want you to go down there, talk to the association president, Rudy Sprouse, and arrange some place in Acadiana where we can set up a facility where the residents can attend to have their swabs done. We can send a couple of our people down there as soon as possible. And while you're there, take a DNA swab from Mr. Sprouse himself, and make sure he knows this DNA thing is ultra-confidential. He doesn't say a thing to anyone about us having the DNA, not to his wife, not to anyone. You make absolutely sure he understands the importance of keeping this strictly confidential. Lay it on thick, tell him he'll be in serious trouble if any word of this gets out, okay?"

"Understood boss, but supposing anyone objects, I mean they haven't been arrested, so?"

"If anyone objects, then we'll make it clear they're going to be considered the main suspect, and to expect all that comes with that prospect, including being arrested on suspicion."

"What about people who have gone back to their main home, or are away on a trip?"

"Yeah, well I thought about that. We tell them they have to go to their nearest local police facility to provide a DNA sample. Again, I want you to coordinate this with the association president. He should have an idea of all the resident's movements."

"Are we assuming the same guy killed both women, the gator lady and the sister?" asked Vogel.

"Not necessarily I guess we have to keep an open mind, but it seems a reasonable assumption at this stage, particularly if we believe the claims of Frankie Armstrong, that the latest vic found some incriminating evidence that could identify her sister's killer."

"Could be the killer isn't one of the residents at all? Could be anyone, someone who lives in another part of Naples, or further away for that matter, much further away."

"Yeah, I realize that Dale, but obviously, this exercise will either eliminate all the residents as suspects, or, identify the killer if he is a resident. And if he is a resident, my guess is he'll make a run for it."

"And if it turns out to not be one of the residents?"

"I wished you hadn't asked that question. Look, let's see how quickly we can set this up. Give the perp as little time as possible to react. We need to have everything in place, ready for when the condo president sends out that email. We've got to make absolutely sure he keeps quiet about it until he does, put the fear of God into him, and just hope that he's not the killer himself."

Chapter 22

Day 7 - Monday

Frankie

Frankie got his belongings back and left the Naples Jail Center. He declined the offer of a lift from Attorney Michael Riley. He wanted to walk for a while and think. He wanted to recall all the times he'd spent with Lisa in their brief relationship, wanted to cement those memories in his consciousness. It was all he had of her. He shook his head in disbelief as he walked along, *who knows what the future might have held for us?*

He knew one thing, it wasn't just infatuation, the thrill of someone new, he'd felt it deep in his being, *that connection just doesn't come along very often in life, sometimes never for some people, and now it's been snatched away.* As he walked along, his sadness morphed into anger, *If I ever find out who killed her….*

He felt his heart start to pound as his anger grew, then realized the futility of such undirected rage. *Save it until I can use it.* He came back to the present and realized he'd reached the bridge over the Gordon River. It had a view of the upper river on one side and the estuary on the other. It was another beautiful day. Crossing over the road, he stood leaning forward on the bridge rails looking down on Tin City, a collection of colorful riverside shops and arcades, a gateway to the busy estuary, thronging with watercraft, large, small, fast and slow.

A variety of speedboats, leisure cruisers and sailing yachts were moored along both the sides of the river. Tin City was buzzing with tourists. Everything looked tranquil and joyous, a far cry from the mood of his recent days. He was still finding it difficult to process the events of the last week, and the last twenty-four hours in particular. The detective's words haunted him, *if only I'd insisted on Lisa telling Randazzo about the backup disc right away?*

He turned away from the rail to continue his walk home when a middle-aged couple walked past him, pushing a buggy with a pretty white Maltese terrier in it. The dog sat in its carriage like the proverbial Queen of Sheba. Frankie had to laugh, there was no question who the boss was in that relationship. Then he remembered *Charlie!* Taking out his cell phone he called Joe. There was no answer and the call went to voicemail. He left a message.

"Hi Joe, I'm out of jail, so I'll get an Uber and come get Charlie. Thanks for looking after him. See you shortly."

When he arrived at Nelson's boatyard, Joe was standing in the yard talking to an elderly couple who were looking longingly at a forty-six-foot floating gin palace Joe had for sale. Joe told Frankie he wouldn't be long and to go in the office and help himself to a coffee while he finished with his potential buyers. Frankie poured himself a cup and watched out of the window as Joe shook the hands of the man and woman in turn. Frankie interpreted the body language of the couple as that of people who had just bought themselves a dream. The wide grin on Joe's face when he turned around, confirmed his impression. The couple drove out of the boatyard in a white drop head Bentley - *Naples*, thought Frankie

"Belinda's on her way here with Charlie, shouldn't be long," said Joe as he entered the office. He shook Frankie's hand vigorously. "Let me grab a coffee and you can tell me all about the shenanigans that got you into such a tight spot." Frankie filled him in on all that had happened since Ava's untimely death.

"Yeah, heard all about that of course. I was going to call you, but the yard's been so busy of late. I hardly get a chance for anything else. I read about your heroic dive into the bay."

"Hardly heroic, but you know what the press are like – why spoil a good story with the facts?"

"I guess you're right, but still, at least you tried. Then her sister, unbelievable," said Joe shaking his head. "Sounds like you'd gotten really fond of this Lisa girl, must've been gut wrenching to find her dead like that."

"It was bad Joe, still is. I just can't take it in, she was special if you know what I mean?"

"I do Frankie, same with my Belinda. If I lost her, I wouldn't know what to do."

Just then Frankie's cell buzzed with an incoming call. He answered, it was Detective Randazzo.

"Where are you Mr. Armstrong? I wanted to catch you before you got back to Acadiana. I gave them specific instructions not to let you go until I'd had a chance to speak with you, but, anyway …" Frankie told him where he was. "Okay, well you don't tell anyone about us having got DNA from the crime scene, its vital we keep that confidential for the time being, understood?"

"Yes Detective, understood. I assume you're going to take samples from all the residents?"

"We are, well all the male residents, and as you'll appreciate, I'd like to give them as little notice as possible."

"Can you force them to provide samples?"

"Ultimately yes, so no one is going to get out of providing a sample, unless they choose to make tracks, in which case… So, when you go back to your condo, you don't tell a soul, understand? If you want to help us catch the killer of your friend Lisa, you keep quiet, got that?"

"Yes Detective, got that. Mum's the word?"

"What?" came the reply.

"Sorry, yes Detective, I'll keep my mouth shut."

"Okay, good, just make sure you do."

"Who was that?" asked Joe as Frankie finished his call.

"The detective warning me not to tell anyone about the DNA they found at the murder scene. I'll tell you about it later. Look, here's Belinda with Charlie. There were hugs from Belinda and a big welcome from Charlie.

*

Frankie arrived back at his condo, having taken an uber rather than wait until Joe could give him a lift. There wasn't much evidence of the police search, other than a few items being put back in the wrong place. As he went to the kitchen to make some coffee, his cell phone buzzed. He looked but didn't recognize the number. He answered.

"Hi Frankie, Roger here, Roger Tuckerman. Someone said you'd been arrested, what's going on buddy? We're all worried about you. Myrtle said I should try to call you, find out if you're okay, or if we can help?"

"I'm okay thanks Roger, just the cops being overzealous, I guess."

"But why you Frankie, I mean you were the one who discovered her body. How could they think you had anything to do with her being killed?"

"Well, I was the last person to see her alive, at least as far as the cops know. I mean obviously the actual killer was the last person to see her alive. I'd taken Lisa out for dinner the night before and later we had coffee in her condo. She was perfectly all right when I left her, but as you know, the next morning I found her dead." There was silence at the other end of the line.

"You still there Roger?"

"Yeah, still here Frankie, just trying to take it all in, such a shock, such a waste."

"I know, I'm still finding it hard to process it and… Well, look Roger, I have to go, got to call my partner in the UK and it's getting very late over there."

'Yeah, sure Frankie. Anyway, let me know if we can do anything to help, won't you?"

"Will do Roger and thanks for calling."

"No problem Frankie. Oh, by the way, do you think the cops have any idea who the killer might be, and why Ava and Lisa were killed?"

"Don't think so Roger, not yet anyway, but…" *Shit, nearly let the cat out of the bag then*

"Sorry Frankie, you said but, and then I lost you."

"No, nothing. Listen Roger, I really have to go and thanks again for calling.

"Okay Frankie, bye for now."

Frankie poured himself a coffee. *Was I being pumped for information, or was that just genuine concern? Get a grip Frankie you're becoming paranoid, Roger's a friend, why wouldn't he be concerned?*

Frankie went to sit in the lanai and opened Skype. Derek answered on the second ring.

"Where the fuck have you been Frankie? No contact for two days."

"And hello to you too Derek."

'Sorry Frankie, just got a bit worried. I think I'm getting sentimental in my old age."

'No, it's okay Barnsie, as it happens, I have had a bit of a rough time of it the last few days."

"Sorry to hear that Frankie. Women trouble?"

'Sort of but I'm afraid it was serious stuff."

Frankie went on to tell Derek all about Lisa, how they hooked up, then finding her dead, and being arrested as a suspect. When he'd finished Derek remained silent for a few beats, then spoke.

"That's really tough Frankie, I can't imagine what you went through finding her murdered. Are you okay now though, not okay, but...you know? Obviously, they've let you out of jail."

"Yeah, but I'm still a suspect."

"Really?"

"Yes, but hopefully not for long. They got DNA from the crime scene, which is why they let me out. And now they're going to test everyone. Well, all the male residents here, so if it is one of them, which seems likely, then I'll be off the hook. And more to the point, they'll nail the vicious bastard who murdered Lisa, and Ava of course."

"Anything I can do Frankie? Do you need me to come over there? I will if you need support, you know that."

"No, you idiot, I can look after myself, but thanks for asking."

"Yeah, okay Frankie. So, what are you going to do now?"

"Not sure about tomorrow. But right now, I'm going to take my dog for a long walk and get some fresh air."

Chapter 23

Day 7 - Monday

The Perp

"Tell me exactly what he said again, word for word and don't leave anything out." He listened intently. "Fuck! there's only one reason they let him out so quickly, they've got some DNA from the condo."

"Not necessarily, there could have been other reasons."

"Oh yeah, what reasons? Look you dummy, take his release together with the word 'but' and it's the only thing that makes sense."

"How so, I mean…"

"Look, chances are he was going to say something, something like 'now they've got some DNA'…"

"You're letting your imagination run away with you. How can you possibly know what he was going to say?"

"You're right, I can't know, but my *imagination* as you call it, has my self-preservation antenna on full alert. And I'm not taking any chances. It's okay for you, it's my DNA they might have, not yours. I told you there might still be traces, but oh no, you were so fucking confident. We should've chopped her hand off like I said. "Jesus Christ, I'm fucked!"

"Listen, I don't think …"

"That's just the fucking problem with you, you don't think!" He cut the line and put his cell down on the kitchen counter.

"Shit shit shit," he said through gritted teeth and got up and walked round the kitchen raising his hands held in tight fists "Fuck!" he shouted at the ceiling. *"DNA… how could there have been any DNA left? So fucking incompetent".*

The perp realized he had to make some very quick moves. There was little doubt in his mind that now they now had a DNA sample, and they'd soon start asking all Acadiana residents to provide a sample. Even if he was wrong, he couldn't afford to take any chances. *If I wait until they ask for DNA samples from us all, and then I run, I might as well pin a sign on my back saying I'm guilty. But if I leave before they ask, there'd be sufficient reason for doubt, just a coincidence…?* He looked at the clock, *No time to waste.*

Picking up his cell he called his wife. When she answered, she wanted to know all the latest about the killings. He'd called her previously to keep her up to date with the dreadful events, naturally, but she'd also had calls from a couple of her gossipy friends from Acadiana, so was well up to speed. He quickly changed the subject and went through the motions of asking her how she was, how her uncle was and listened patiently to the answers, then he got into it.

"Now, you won't believe this Mable, but the reason I'm calling is that I've just had a call from the UK, about one of my distant relations."

"Just give me a minute," his wife said, "can't hear you properly, someone just turned the TV on." A few moments later she came back on the line, "sorry honey, you were saying?"

"Yes, I just got a call from England. Apparently, I have, well had, a wealthy relation I knew nothing about, and she died recently. They want me to go over to sort out some legal stuff. It's an urgent matter they said."

"I didn't know you still had any contact with your relations in England. Didn't you tell me all your relations died out years ago?"

"Well I did, but it seems not all of them were dead. And it could be that there's serious money involved. That was the suggestion by the guy who called me. He hinted it could be a lot of money. He told me they'll call me right back with details, so I don't want to block the line here."

"Jeez honey, how weird is that?" And how did they manage to locate you after all this time?"

"I don't know sweetness, one of the things I need to ask when they call back. But listen, I need to think about getting over there pretty soon. The guy said there's going to be some sort of legal process in the next day or two. I need to get over there without delay he said, otherwise I could miss out on a fortune. His exact words."

"Are you sure this is on the level? I mean you hear about all sorts of scams these days."

"No, he knew too much personal family history. But of course, I'll make sure when he calls back. You know me honey, no one pulls the wool over my eyes."

"That's true. Well how long are you thinking of going for, I mean this is all a bit sudden. We're due to go the Naples Phil next week. It's your favorite, Rachmaninov's second piano concerto."

"I know, but…look Mable, the sooner I get over there the sooner I can get this sorted out and get back. I'll pack a few things and get on my way."

"What right now? What's the hurry treasure? Is it really that urgent?"

"Well I can't see the point in waiting around and possibly missing out on this fortune he said is waiting for me. But if you don't want me to go, I know you've been looking forward to that concert, I mean…"

"No, no I didn't mean to be awkward. You must do as you think best. Like you say, it would be a shame to miss out on some family fortune or whatever. I completely understand honey. I'll get Betty to come with me, but it won't be the same."

"I'm sure you'll have a great time with Betty. Look I'll get on to the travel agent then pack a few things and get on my way."

"This is all, all so sudden honey. You just make sure you keep in touch with me and let me know where you are and how you are. And don't forget your passport,"

"Oh thanks, I won't," he replied, *both of them....*

*

The last place he wanted to go back to was the UK, but it was the only place he could think of. He had to get out of the US, away from the reach of the American authorities. He knew they would find it next to impossible to get a DNA sample from him once he was in the UK. Plus, they wouldn't know where he was, he'd make sure of that. And he had somewhere to stay. As he sat in the back of the taxi, on his way to Fort Myers airport, he wondered if they could lift a DNA sample from his condo, but he figured they'd need some sort of search warrant for that sort of thing. And he couldn't see how they would get that, given there was no proof he'd committed any crime.

Nevertheless, he'd made sure to bring along all his personal items such as toothbrush, razor and made sure he'd put any cups or food implements he'd used in the dishwasher, before he left, and switched it on. Just to be on the safe side, he'd brought along all the clothes he'd worn recently and that hadn't been washed. He made sure to wipe down any obvious surfaces he might have left traces on. From Fort Myers RSW Airport, he took the first flight to Atlanta he could get on. He planned to book the transatlantic flight once he got to Atlanta, after making one last phone call to Acadiana.

Chapter 24

Detective Randazzo

Rudy Sprouse's hands were shaking as he set his phone down on the table. Detective Randazzo had sworn him to secrecy, as had his deputy who came to see him the previous day. The detective had given him final details of his plan and he waited nervously for the detective's email to come through. He was instructed to copy and send it, verbatim, to all residents, even the ones who weren't present. Rudy thought about the media circus, reporters camped outside. He couldn't turn the TV on without seeing Acadiana in the headlines. Condo of Gruesome Twosome Slayings, was one of the phrases that had caught on, referring to the two killings at the once peaceful Acadiana condo complex.

Who would have believed it? he mused as he waited. He wanted to tell his wife about the DNA thing, but the detective had warned him not to. His PC pinged as an email came through. It was from the detective. He printed it off and went on the lanai to sit down and read it.

Dear Acadiana resident

<u>URGENT – Please acknowledge receipt by return email and then read.</u>

<u>Failure to acknowledge receipt will result in an immediate visit by the police.</u>

As you are all well aware, there have been two recent killings at Acadiana. As part of our ongoing enquiries we require all and any male resident, renter, or guest who has stayed at Acadiana in the last seven days, to attend the president's condo this afternoon between 12:00 midday and 1600 hours to provide a DNA sample. This is a quick and painless mouth swab procedure. After acknowledging receipt of this email, please call Rudy Sprouse ASAP to book your appointment.

This is a request at present, but please note that refusal to comply will result in your immediate arrest on suspicion of committing a serious crime, and/or obstructing the police in their pursuit of evidence of a serious crime.

Detective Sam Randazzo

Naples City Police Department

Tel; (239) 213-4822

Rudy read it again and shrugged, then went back to sit at his PC to copy and paste the email on to a broadcast list. The detective had instructed him to call any of the recipients who didn't respond within fifteen minutes of him sending the email, which he was to send out at 10:30 a.m. He told Rudy to re-emphasize that unless the request was adhered to, the detective wouldn't hesitate to locate the resident, wherever they were, and take them into custody. They would then have their DNA taken regardless, and that as a minimum, charges of obstructing the police in the course of their duty would be brought against any person not cooperating or complying with the request. Rudy pressed the Send button and waited for the responses.

He didn't have to wait long. First Matt Monostory, then Sean Stipp, then Bodo Kellerman, Dr Schaefer, Steve Farr, the replies came thick and fast. The detective had asked Rudy to make a list of all males in residence at the time of the two killings. He'd made it in Excel, then checked it for accuracy with his wife. She knew everything that went on in Acadiana. Well, almost everything. She certainly knew who was there at any given time. He rearranged the list to alphabetical and ticked off the names against receipts as they came in.

At 11:30, Rudy's cell buzzed, he answered. It was Detective Randazzo.

"So, Mr. Sprouse, how many replies do we have?"

"I was just about to email you a copy of the list showing all the replies so far. Hold on and I'll send it now. Here goes. That should be with you in a few seconds." There was silence at the other end then Randazzo spoke.

"Yep, got that now. Three no responses."

Yes, and yes, I have tried calling them. I managed to get hold of Nick Ammer who is driving back to Michigan. He says he'll reply when he gets a chance, but no problem and happy to have the test done whenever and wherever."

"And Bill Ferenczi?"

"Yeah, haven't been able to get him. I've asked my wife to see if she can find out where he is, or more to the point, where he and his wife are. They go everywhere together. Hanne, my wife, she thinks they may have gone on a cruise, so we'll find out and I'm sure I will be able to get him pretty soon. So that just leaves Hector Carmouche."

"And…?" asked the detective, "do I sense there's some problem here?"

"Not sure, but his wife Mable, she's away visiting a sick uncle. But my wife is in contact with her pretty regularly and she called her to find out where Hector is. She says he left for the UK yesterday. Something about an urgent legal matter to do with some distant relative who died recently."

"What? Did hear you right? The UK as in the United Kingdom, Great Britain?"

"Yep, that's the place. Apparently, he has roots there, maybe born there, I don't know. I didn't want to ask any further. I thought that was more your department."

"And that was yesterday," said the detective, "before anyone knew about the DNA tests we'd be asking for?"

"Apparently, yes. And before you ask, no I did not breathe a word about the DNA thing, not even to my wife, so."

"Hmm, well there was only one other person who knew," said the detective. "I'll get back to you Mr. Sprouse, and good work, thanks."

Frankie's cell chirped, he answered.

"Mr. Armstrong?"

"Yes Detective, what can I do for you?"

"Did you tell anyone, and I mean anyone, about the DNA tests, or about us finding DNA? Think carefully before answering Mr. Armstrong, think very carefully."

"I don't have to think carefully Detective. No, I didn't tell anyone." Frankie said. "Why do you ask?"

"You sure about your answer Mr. Armstrong?"

"Look Detective, I don't like the insinuation. What grounds do you have for doubting my word?"

"Not a great question coming from you Mr. Armstrong. But if you did tell anyone, I'll find out, and you my friend, will be in more trouble than you can imagine." Frankie thought back carefully about his conversation with Roger Tuckerman. *I didn't mention DNA at all, nothing I said could have been taken as having anything to do with DNA, could it?*

"Look Detective, can we stop with the threats. If you want me to help, please tell me why you doubt my word on this. Okay, I, well we, should have told you right away about Lisa finding that backup, but that was different." There was a long silence.

'Detective, are you still there?"

"Yes I am. Have you spoken to Mr. Hector Carmouche recently, in the last forty-eight hours?"

"No, I haven't. Why?"

"I guess you'll find out soon enough. Hector Carmouche left the country yesterday, urgently, late afternoon or early evening. Looks like he might be the only one who won't be available for a DNA test, very convenient right?"

"So, everyone else has agreed to have the DNA test? "

"Seems so yes," Frankie breathed a sigh of relief, *so Roger's not in the frame.*

"When you say Hector left the country, where did he go?"

"The UK apparently, some story about an urgent legal matter to do with a recently dead relative, something like that."

"But this was before anyone knew about the DNA thing? So maybe it was a genuine situation, just a coincidence?"

"Yeah, a coincidence, right."

"Have you any reason to believe otherwise?"

"Yes, my skeptical nature, my long experience of convenient coincidences and my ability to smell a rat."

"Do you really suspect Hector Carmouche is the killer?" I can't think of anyone more unlikely. And Hector was one of the first on the scene when Ava fell into the water. No, make that the first one, apart from me. He provided the flashlight if I remember correctly. How could he have been the one who pushed her in, then been at my side when I was trying to rescue her?"

"I can't answer that now, but however unlikely, it wouldn't be impossible. He could have just gone round in a circle."

"Maybe he could have Detective, but isn't it more likely that he's gone to the UK for a legitimate reason and is completely innocent? And with respect, aren't you getting ahead of yourself? I'm assuming you haven't yet checked the DNA of all the other residents. And even then, there's nothing to say the killer was a resident or visitor to Acadiana."

The detective didn't reply.

"Detective?"

"Yeah, okay, just something tells me it's just too pat. I'm going to go call his wife now. She's also away, but thankfully, still in the USA. I'll see what that brings. But you're absolutely positive you didn't say anything about DNA to anyone."

"Absolutely positive Detective."

Chapter 25

Day 8 — Tuesday Manchester UK
The Perp

The pilot announced they were on their initial descent and would be landing at 6:30 a.m. at Manchester Airport, nearly an hour ahead of schedule. Hector looked out of the window at the gray clouds scudding past. His heart sank. He thought about his condo in Naples and his walks along the beach, the warm weather, the spectacular sunsets. But he had no choice, it was time to disappear for a while and wait it out. He'd figure out some sort of plan that would enable him to get back to Florida.

Maybe I can find a new identity? And it doesn't have to be Naples, there are lots of other places that would suit my needs. Maybe I could even find a new wealthy wife? He smiled at the prospect, then was brought down to earth literally as the plane pancaked on to the tarmac. A few people let out an involuntary scream. The pilot spoke on the public address system and apologized, saying there were tricky crosswinds. *Or maybe he let that gorgeous looking stewardess land the plane?*

The taxi ride to his house just on the outskirts of Harrogate was tedious and expensive. It was some years since he'd been back home, and things didn't seem to have improved much. More traffic, more congestion, the roads and general infrastructure had clearly been originally designed for another era. The view of the moors as they drove over the Pennines were considered attractive to some people, but not to him, and the last few miles were along roads that were more suitable for the occasional horse and cart, than any kind of modern automobile.

He'd asked the taxi driver to drive into Harrogate first so he could stock up on essentials, then directed him to the agency where he'd left the keys when he moved out all those years ago. He'd kept in touch with them by phone initially then by email. He made sure not to miss any payments for their services, which were to visit the property each month and make sure there were no leaks or other maintenance matters needing attention.

The agents were fascinated to meet the absent owner and the young lady who handed the keys over, asked him too many questions. He deflected without appearing secretive. A low profile was the order of the day. The taxi made its out of the suburbs of Harrogate and they were soon heading towards the moors. Arriving at the farmhouse, the taxi driver got his luggage out of the trunk. He thanked the driver and paid him, then unlocked the front door. The place smelt musty and damp. Dropping his luggage on the hall floor he went around the house checking the lights and heating, then opened the kitchen window.

He'd called ahead from Atlanta to ask the agent to switch on the hot water, and the heating. Taking his groceries into the kitchen, he turned the bags out on to the kitchen table, then turning on the tap, he took a cup from the cupboard, washed it, opened the packet of tea bags, dropped one in the cup and filled the kettle with water.

While he waited for the water to boil, he looked out over the rear garden. The agent had arranged for a monthly visit by a gardening service, so it was reasonably well maintained. The weeping willow had grown considerably since he planted it all those years ago. He sighed, poured the boiling water into the cup and stirred. He opened the bottle of long life milk and poured some into the cup, sat down at the kitchen table, sipped his tea and thought about the events which led to his meeting up with Ava again after all that time, and how it had resulted in catapulting him back to the UK. Back to where it all began *Who could have predicted this would happen? A chance in a million, no, make that a chance in a trillion...* He took another sip of his tea.

*

When Cornelius Hayes was a young lad growing up on the outskirts of Harrogate, Yorkshire, he soon developed the urge to leave. He was eleven years old in 1969, a defining year in many ways. Lots of new things were happening, the world was changing big time. The swinging sixties were still swinging - the supersonic Concorde took its first test flight, John Lennon and Yoko Ono appeared naked on their new record album cover, The Rolling Stones founder, Brian Jones died, a car driven by Senator Edward Kennedy plunged off a bridge killing Mary Jo Kopechne, and Neil Armstrong became the first human being to walk on the Moon.

Con and his older cousin Hector lived in a row of terraced houses, with tiny front gardens and small enclosed paved back yards They lived just ten doors from each other. And they weren't just cousins, but best friends. Just two years separated them in age. Con and Hector both developed a love of all things American. They couldn't get enough of American movies in particular and loved the old ones the best.

Anything that featured cowboys, gangsters, rock and roll singers and big American cars were their favorites. They watched all the movies starring Humphrey Bogart, George Raft, Edward G Robinson, John Wayne, Elvis Presley and Marilyn Monroe, especially Marilyn Monroe, several times over. Such was their love of old classic America, Con's mother said he and Hector should have been born a few decades earlier.

"So how old do you think we have to be, to be able to go and live in America Hector?"

"Dunno, eighteen maybe? We've got to leave school then get a job, save up some money first."

"So, I'll have to wait another seven years?" asked Con.

"I guess," said Hector.

"But you'll be eighteen in just five years?"

"Yeah, but maybe we can go when I'm nineteen and you're seventeen?"

"Yeah, that would be great. I mean you wouldn't go without me would you Hector?"

"No, I wouldn't Con."

"So, it's a plan then, a promise? We'll leave school get jobs, save up then we'll both go to America together?"

"It's a promise Con, a solemn promise."

"What's the difference between an ordinary promise and a solemn promise Hector?"

"Well, one you might break, but a solemn promise is one you have to keep, no matter what."

"We should have a blood handshake. I saw it in a movie once, it seals the deal forever."

"Blood?" said Hector, "whose blood?"

"I'll go get my knife," said Con. And he did. They cut each other's palms, grimacing as they did so, then made a handshake. Blood dripped from their hands on to the tiled floor as they carried out the ceremony. Just then Con's mother appeared in the kitchen. After admonishing them for being stupid, she washed and cleaned their wounds, which were thankfully just superficial. Then she bandaged their hands up, trying not to smile as they explained what they'd been doing.

Con laughed out loud at the memory, *didn't quite work out that way did it Hector?* Hector and Con remained best friends

194

throughout their young lives, until Mary Kershaw moved in next door to Hector. She was a year younger than Hector, pretty and precocious. At first both boys rejected her efforts to befriend them, but as they grew older and Mary grew more attractive, Hector succumbed and began 'going out' with Mary. Going out at sixteen, included holding hands, going to the cinema, snogging on the back row and sometimes going dancing together to a school Hop or a coffee bar.

Con felt excluded and became increasingly miserable. He was in the middle of taking his GCE exams and although normally a bright intelligent boy, his grades suffered. When he got the chance to talk to Hector about their future plans and mentioned their previous aspirations to go to America together, Hector laughed and said it was just a thing kids did. He said Con shouldn't take it so seriously and told Con he should find himself a girlfriend as well and start growing up. He even said Mary had a friend who she could encourage to go out with Con, but Con rejected the idea. He hoped that Hector would get fed up with Mary, but that didn't happen for a long long time, too long.

Chapter 26

Day 8 - Tuesday Naples

Frankie

Frankie answered his phone.

"Frankie, I've been trying to get hold of you, didn't you get my emails, I thought maybe they'd thrown you back in jail, what's happening?"

"Sorry Barnsie, I got distracted, been unable to think straight since Lisa died."

"Look Frankie, maybe you should think about coming back home. I'm serious."

"Can't do that yet Barnsie, got to see if I can help find the killer. I'm just too involved, practically and emotionally. Like I said, I had serious hopes for some sort of long-term relationship with Lisa. Maybe I was dreaming I don't know but I can't just walk away now and act as if nothing happened. I have to do something."

"Jesus Frankie, you're something else. So, what exactly are you thinking of doing? Why not just leave things to the authorities? They have the resources and more important, you're going to get in trouble again if they think you're interfering. I know you, and you're an obstinate bastard. Mostly that's a good trait, but sometimes..."

"Yeah I know Barnsie, but like the man said, a man's godadoo what a man's godadoo."

"Be serious you arsehole. Look, is there anything I can do to help?"

"Maybe there is Barnsie. The detective handling the case thinks a guy called Hector Carmouche is a potential suspect. I'm not so sure. But in the absence of any other suspect, I suppose…"

"Who the hell is Hector Carmouche when he's at home?"

"Funny you should use that expression. His home was here, still is here, in Acadiana. He's one of the residents. He's an okay guy as far as I'm concerned, but like I say, the detective in charge, guy called Randazzo, he's got a bee in his bonnet about this Hector Carmouche."

"So how can I help find a guy who's living in Florida?"

"That's just it, he's gone back to the UK. Hector's wife says he got a call from solicitors, or someone in the UK, about some legal matter to do with inheritance or a recently dead relative, something like that and he left in a big hurry it seems, so who knows, maybe the detective is right?"

"Okay, so Hector Carmouche. Name like that, you sure he's a Brit?"

"I'm pretty sure he is. He told me his family were British. I know his name sounds French or something, but I looked it up, and there are some families with that surname in the UK, so it looks like their ancestors travelled around a bit."

"Any idea where in the UK this Hector's gone to?"

"No, I have absolutely no idea where you could look. I don't have a clue where his original family might have lived in the UK, but maybe you could get someone to do some research? The unusual name should make it easier."

"Okay, Frankie, I'll get the genius tech Gareth on it. If there's any data relating to this guy or his recently dead relatives, Gareth will find it. I'll let you know. Now go relax and recharge those batteries, go fishing or something, okay?"

"Okay Barnsie, I promise. Give my best to everyone back home." Frankie cut the connection and wondered if Detective Randazzo had had the results of the DNA swabs yet, and if he'd learned anything further from Mrs. Carmouche. The media horde was still camped outside but had been moved out of the parking lot and on to the street following a formal complaint from the condo president Rudi Sprouse.

Somehow, the media had got wind of the DNA testing and were trying every which way to find out if a suspect had been identified. The police silence on the matter was driving them nuts. Frankie was equally curious. He called the detective.

"Mr. Armstrong - see I now recognize your number. Don't ask, I know the question and the answer is no, we don't have a positive result. One more left to go. The guy who was driving back to Michigan, but I expect that to come in at the latest tomorrow."

"Did you interview Hector's wife?"

"I did, over the phone. I don't suppose what she told me is confidential, as you're free to call her yourself. In fact, I'd be pleased if you did call her, because I got precisely zip, nada, nothing. She said he left almost immediately after the call and she didn't really have time to ask her husband any more questions, and she hasn't heard from him since he left. Unusual don't you think, not even to contact his wife to tell her where he is?"

"I admit it does seem a bit odd Detective. I don't suppose you know which flight he took?"

"Yes and no to that one. We managed to locate the taxi driver who took him to Fort Myers airport, where he got on a flight to Atlanta. But, we haven't been able to find him travelling on any flight departing Atlanta for anywhere else yet, but we will. Still convinced he's innocent?"

"I'm not really convinced he's the killer, if that's what you're asking. The killer could be any one of Ava's clients. Someone who lives in another nearby condo complex, or maybe somewhere else in Naples altogether."

"That's true Mr. Armstrong, and if we had the backup that your girlfriend found, we might have had a better chance of knowing which of Ava's clients the killer might be."

"Fair enough detective, but I can only apologize so many times for that. If it's any help, I've asked my office back in the UK to see if they can find any information on Hector Carmouche, try to locate any relatives of his, living or recently dead. Do you happen to know when Hector moved from the UK to come to the US?"

"I do as it happens, yes. It seems he moved here some 35 years ago, when he was 30 years old. Lived in Chicago, where he worked as a structural engineer. Apparently, he was head hunted by an American company early on. He moved here with his wife, no children as far as we can tell. They got divorced shortly after moving to the US. Some years later, he moved down to Florida and lived in Tampa for some time, before buying a condo in Naples, in Acadiana in 2010."

"So, he's lived in Acadiana for nine years? Do you know when he married Mable?"

"Five years ago, I believe."

Frankie had wandered over to the lanai as he was talking to the detective. He looked out now over at the pool. It was busy. His ears should have been burning.

"So, where does it go from here Detective?"

"We keep on digging. There's more forensics to come, so maybe that will reveal something more, and by the way, you're not completely off the hook Mr. Armstrong."

"You can't be serious Detective. Do you really still consider me a suspect? You think I'm the killer?"

"I keep an open mind Mr. Armstrong. In this business you don't make too many presumptions, or should it be assumptions. Whatever. But to answer your question honestly, if I really thought you were the killer, I'd have found a way to keep you in jail. So, the fact that you're out, tells you where my mind is on this. However unlikely it might be that you're the guilty party, I'm not ruling you out altogether, got that?"

"And how do I convince you I'm not the one who killed Lisa?"

"Oh, that's really simple, you help me find the guy who is. You just get those guys in that office of yours in the UK to get their collective asses into gear and locate Hector Carmouche. My gut never lies to me. Goodbye Mr. Armstrong."

"Goodbye Detective," replied Frankie, but he'd gone.

Chapter 27

Cornelius Hayes

Cornelius had been a good student in his early years. He was naturally bright, as his school report attested, but a bit of a daydreamer. All that changed, his tutors noticed, just about the same time he and Hector no longer seemed to be such close friends. At first, his form class teacher was worried by Con's sullenness. A normally happy go lucky child became unusually quiet and uncommunicative. No longer was Con's hand one of the first to shoot up in response to a question addressed to the class.

His form teacher, Miss Mason, was so concerned she considered going to see his mother, but after talking to the headmistress, she accepted that his mood change was probably down to puberty. And it seemed that the headmistress was right, because about a month after her talk with the headmistress, Con, buttoned down and worked so hard, he was consistently in the top three or four in the class. Nevertheless, she still noted that he no longer played with his cousin at break time. Although in different years, Hector being older, Con and Hector would always be seen playing football together in the school playground or chatting and laughing with their mutual friends.

All that seemed to have changed and the two seemingly inseparable friends hardly seemed to mix now. She shrugged in resignation. She'd also taught Hector two years previously and noted how similar both boys were in attitude, intellect, and looks for that matter. She had huge experience at (informally) assessing the potential of the children she taught, and she was rarely wrong. Both boys had huge potential in her opinion. She just hoped she'd been able to help release that potential but would also like to think they would get back together in the future as friends.

It wasn't to be. Hector left school and became an apprentice with Melthrop's Engineering where he showed real promise. Melthrops sent him to a technical college where he graduated with a BSC degree in engineering. Cornelius chose a different path. Always fascinated by flying, he took the exam for entry into the Royal Air Force and managed to get on a special program for trainee pilots. He was soon transferred to RAF Brize Norton in Oxfordshire, the largest RAF Station in the UK. Not only did he enjoy the pilot training program, but took full advantage of the lively social life around Oxford. On their weekends off, he and his pals would often travel to London, where they would party all weekend, finances allowing.

RAF personnel, and in particular, pilots, seemed to possess a fatal attraction for the opposite sex. Con made full use of this peculiar alchemy to enjoy life to the full. More often than not, Con and his pals would wear their uniforms when they went out socializing in London. This always ensured entry into establishments that would otherwise be out of bounds for a lad from Yorkshire. It was in one such club, The Golden Archway, that he met a very attractive Pan-Am Air Stewardess called Ava.

It was lust at first sight (again) and she invited him to an impromptu party at the hotel she and her fellow crew members were staying at. It was a very brief, booze fueled one-night stand. Con would not have remembered her name, nor anything much about their night of passion, had it not been for an incredible coincidence of time and place so many years later.

The RAF became his life. He had many chances to marry, but always fled when things got too serious. The idea of marriage terrified him. Commitment was something he couldn't face up to. Sometimes he wondered if he would have had a happier life with a wife and children, but eventually concluded he'd been right to resist when he saw the marriages of some of his friends fall apart.

Eventually he retired from the RAF on a good pension and bought a remote farmhouse on the outskirts of Harrogate. It was in a dreadful state of repair, almost falling down, but that suited him. He needed a project. He'd always been handy at repairing stuff and could turn his hand to most things. He was obliged to bring in the occasional contractor for some of the work, but the vast bulk of it he did himself. The farmhouse was also remote, which was one of the attractions of the place.

Despite his successful career in the RAF, he could never shake the feeling of being cheated, that he'd missed out somehow. Whenever he felt this, he quickly admonished himself and buried the thought. He wasn't unsociable and didn't mind company, but only on his terms. When he left the RAF, he didn't bother to keep in touch with his friends from the service. Most of them had families and he'd never really developed any close relationships anyway. He had a few local acquaintances, mainly people who had been involved in some aspect of his house restoration project. But he kept them all at a distance.

He was a typical thrifty Yorkshireman, careful with money, but he'd indulged himself and bought a baby grand piano. Cornelius's mother was a frustrated musician herself and had insisted that Con take piano lessons as a child. He resented it at the time, but now he played for hours at a time. If he felt the need for female company, he'd travel to Leeds where he could find and pay for such company when he needed it. It suited him that way.

Chapter 28

More prattling round the pool
Day 8 - Tuesday

Pam Büettnerkraus was doing lazy lengths in the pool, effortlessly navigating around Jane Hamilton who was lying on her bright green pool mattress in the shallow end of the pool.

"I'm doing my best to get in your way Pam, but you're such a good swimmer. I could never swim like that, maybe I'm the wrong shape?"

"Remarks like that are tempting providence," muttered Sam Bogdasarian who was sitting on the edge of the pool dangling his legs in the water.

"Hey, I heard that. You're not in such good shape yourself Sam," she replied to the slight. She looked round for her husband who was busy chatting to Steve Farr. "Hey husband of mine, are you going to let him get away with that? Go punch him on the nose."

"Yes dear, later I promise."

"Jeez, such chivalry," said Jane. "You know I think I might just trade Jim in for a newer model, a toy boy. I've got the money," she said in a loud voice to all assembled.

"Will I do Jane?" I'm not that young, but I sure could do with the money," said Bodo

"Dream on Bodo boy," replied Jane, "I heard the only thing you're good at in bed, is snoring." They all laughed as Bodo feigned hurt. Nancy Farr, who was sunbathing on one of the sunbeds, spoke.

"I guess they didn't identify anyone through the DNA testing?"

"No one arrested yet that's for sure, but I think they have at least one more to come through. Two of the guys left before we were all told about the test, no make that three including the Ferenczi's. They left to go on a cruise. Nick and Mary Ammer left to drive back up to Michigan early in the morning, the day we all got the email. He called me to ask what was going on. Note, I left out the expletive. Rudy had called him, told him he had to go get a DNA test done as soon as he got back to Michigan. Said he should go to his local police station and tell them to contact the detective in charge of the investigation here, that Randazzo guy."

"Yeah, I heard that too," said Bonnie Ferenczi "but what about Hector? Word is he rushed back to the UK, something about an inheritance, a fortune I heard."

"Yeah, lucky Hector. Nothing like a rich relation's will reading to get people motivated to travel," said Roger Tuckerman, who was sitting at a poolside table reading a newspaper.

"On the other hand, could be that Hector is the killer, making up a story to cover his getaway 'cos he didn't want to give a DNA sample?" replied Bonnie.

"Could be, but he left before anyone knew about the DNA testing, so how would that work?" asked Bodo.

"Yeah, you're right Bodo," said Bonnie, "but someone killed those two gals, and it's more than likely it's one of us residents what done it." No one replied to that.

Chapter 29

Day 9 - Wednesday Naples

Frankie

Frankie came in from his morning jog, showered, fed Charlie his breakfast, then set his own breakfast out on the counter in the kitchen.

"Hot one today Charlie," Frankie said. Charlie looked up briefly from his food but didn't reply. Frankie was about to start his breakfast when his UK mobile rang or played the Third Man theme to be more accurate. It was Barnsie.

"Got anything interesting for me Barnsie?" asked Frankie.

"Yes, at least I think you'll find it interesting. The genius that is my nephew, Gareth. By the way, have I ever told you that genius runs in my family?"

"Many times partner, many times."

"Okay, so, where was I? Oh yes, Gareth, he's managed to find a guy called Cornelius Hayes, who lives just outside Harrogate, Yorkshire. He's the cousin of a guy called Hector Carmouche. Don't ask me how he did it. Gareth started to explain, but it was giving me a headache, so I asked him to stop. He couldn't find any other living relatives, or recently deceased relatives, so this is all we got."

"He can't find anything recent on this Hector Carmouche guy though, just some records going back years. Gareth found a marriage certificate for him dated, let me see…, yes, he married a Mary nee Kershaw in 1980, at, hang on a minute, I can't pronounce this… Saint Aelred of Rievaulx Catholic Church in Harrogate."

"Well done that Gareth, buy him a beer for me." Frankie said and began to consider his next move.

"So, Frankie, you want me to send anyone to see this Cornelius character, see if he can shed any light on this where Hector Carmouche guy might be? I could send Mike Bingham, the ex-cop guy we've used before when we've been chasing cheating spouses and so on."

"No, I'm thinking it might be better if I came back and took care of this myself."

"Really? You're going to come back for this?"

"Yes, I think so. The detective on the case still considers me a suspect, at least he says he does, but I think he's still mad at me for withholding some info I had, info that might have helped him find the killer?"

"Why would you have done that Frankie?"

"It's complicated, a backup disc Lisa found, but it'd take too long to explain now. I'll tell you everything in detail when I get back."

"Okay Frankie, you sound rattled."

"Yeah, I know. Maybe I'm losing it?"

"Where are you going to stay, I mean when you get back here. Are you and Penny still speaking?" Thinking back to his last phone conversation with his wife, he hesitated, then replied.

"Good question. I'll call her. After all it's still half my house, and that's where all my stuff is, so yes, I plan to stay there, but if things are too unpleasant, then I'll move out to a hotel."

"You can always stay with us Frankie, you know that, right?"

"I know, but I'd just feel awkward. Anyway, I'm not planning to stay away from here that long. Just see if I can get a handle on what's happening with this Hector guy, then I plan to come back. I'll go make some calls and book a flight back home."

"Okay Frankie, let me know what time your flight arrives, and I'll come collect you from the airport."

"Not necessary, the flight will get in very early morning and it's just as easy to get a taxi, easier these days than you trying to find me at the airport. I'll get myself to the office later in the day."

"Okay bud, well have a safe journey."

"Thanks Derek."

*

"That Detective Randazzo?"

"Sure is Mr. Armstrong, what can I do for you now?"

"Just checking really, but I assume there are no restrictions on me travelling, I mean back to the UK?" There was silence at the other end. "Detective?"

"Yeah I'm here. I guess there aren't any formal restrictions at present, no, but I could always find a reason to impose some. Care to explain your reason for going back now?"

"Following your orders really. I intend to find Hector Carmouche and try to establish if he's innocent or guilty of something."

"I see, you're going to do my job for me are you?"

"I don't know about that, but I don't see how you can find him. I guess you could call the authorities in the UK but seems to me you don't have any valid reason to ask for him to be apprehended. Best you can say is that he may be able to help you with your enquiries. That's not going to shoot to the top of their priorities is it? The UK police are already overwhelmed with domestic crime. They hardly have the time or resources to go chasing after the likes of Hector Carmouche, a guy who may be completely innocent of any crime, and on whom you currently have no evidence of wrongdoing."

"Wow, that's quite a speech Mr. Armstrong."

"Sorry, I can go on a bit sometimes."

"You sure do, but I have to concede you do make perfect sense on this occasion - I'm sorry to say. But tell me this, do you have any idea where Hector Carmouche is, do you have information you're once again not disclosing to me?"

"No, I don't know where Hector Carmouche is. One of my guys has done some research and found out where a cousin of Hector's lives, so once I get back to my office, I might well be able to find out more. One thing's for sure, neither you, nor I are likely to find Hector Carmouche from here in Naples Florida."

"I hate to admit it, but you're right again. So go Mr. Armstrong. But if I find you've misled me in any way, I'll come and find you myself, wherever you are. That's a promise, no make that a threat, understand?"

"I think I get your drift."

"Good and goodbye."

Chapter 30

Hector Carmouche

Back then

Hector was surprised when Mary, his wife of six years, said she wanted a divorce. This unexpected event came just two years after they'd laid down their roots in the USA. Somehow, they'd managed to have a row about what color they should paint the main bedroom of their new house. It was a nothing row, and Hector fully expected they would kiss and make up, but Mary had other ideas. She kept on and on at him, way beyond anything reasonable he thought. She refused to make up and shunned his attempts at reconciliation.

On that Friday evening, they'd both had drinks on the way home from their respective places of work. She had a job as a pay clerk in a building firm. When he'd tried to start a civilized conversation, asking about her day, she taunted him about an attractive man she'd met at the office. She hinted at sexual lunchtime trysts. He roared at her, calling her a bitch and a slut. She screamed back that he was fucking useless as a husband. Hector snapped and lashed out. He hit her so hard she was propelled across the room hitting the wall and sliding down to the floor.

Despite the red mist of temper, Hector couldn't help noticing a smile of satisfaction on Mary's face as she sat there, wiping the blood from her mouth with the back of her hand. Hector realized he'd been had. She started screaming at the top of her voice that she was being murdered. He seriously considered killing her there and then and was only saved from turning his thoughts into action by the shouting of their neighbors, who were now furiously banging on their front door.

The police had been called and arrived a few minutes later, sirens blaring, blue and red lights flashing. Hector sat on the couch and waited. He was arrested and charged with assault and battery. They took him to the police station where he was obliged to give fingerprint and DNA samples, then spent two nights in jail before being allowed out on bail. His lawyer talked to his wife's lawyer and she agreed not to press charges, providing she got an uncontested divorce and everything they jointly owned, including the house.

Agreement to her terms was the only way he could avoid a potential criminal record and the prospect of being kicked out of the USA. *Game set and match to Mary.*

Looking back, he realized he'd been well and truly played, even from the day they met maybe? She'd taken everything, everything he'd worked for. She'd left him with nothing, just the clothes he was wearing. There were no children thankfully, she'd always said it wasn't the right time. He now realized on reflection, there was never going to be a right time. So, it was a case of getting the divorce over and moving on.

He was still a relatively young man, healthy, not bad looking and, there were plenty more fish in the sea – he liked fishing. But he foreswore marriage ever again. Since coming to America, he'd also developed a love of American Football and now, his adopted American football team the Chicago Bears, had just won the Super bowl. *Life wasn't really all that bad.*

Over the next few years, Hector rebuilt his life and prospered. He wasn't one for looking back and put down his disastrous marriage to Mary as one of life's lessons, a lesson he only needed to learn once.

Chapter 31

Day 9/10 - Wednesday/Thursday

Frankie

Frankie called his wife Penny to tell her he was coming home and would be staying a while.

"How long is a while?" she asked without enthusiasm.

"Not sure, a week maybe longer."

"Okay, the bed in the spare room is made up. May I ask why you're coming back?"

"Business, a few matters I have to take care of. I imagine I'll be out a lot, so I won't be under your feet. I might need to stay away for the odd night as well."

"It's none of my business Frankie. You do as you please, you're a free agent."

"Look Penny, let's not make it any harder than necessary. I'll see you tomorrow. Maybe we can talk. I know that's a bit sooner than we planned but something's come up and I have to deal with it, so we're going to be seeing each other sooner than intended."

"I'm not sure what there is to talk about, but I suppose we have to at some stage. I'll see you when you get back."

Frankie took a taxi to Fort Myers airport, from where he flew to Philadelphia to catch the overnight transatlantic leg of the journey. Once the American Airlines flight to Manchester had settled into the cruise, he had a glass of wine and took a sleeping pill and managed to sleep most of the way back to the UK.

*

He was still asleep when the airliner bumped on to the runway. It was late February, early morning and still dark. For once it didn't seem to be raining, but he knew that could change within minutes in this part of the world. *Welcome home.*

Penny wasn't home when the taxi dropped him off. He was grateful for the time alone to re-adjust. He showered, found some croissants in the fridge, made some coffee and had breakfast, then hung up what clothes he'd brought and sought out something more suitable for the rigors of northern England in winter. Charlie had given him a big lick when he'd said goodbye. Joe's wife was thrilled to have the chance to look after Charlie again, so Frankie knew he was in good hands. He missed Charlie already, *how do dogs manage to steal your heart?*

He was greeted at the office, a couple of hugs, some handshakes.

"Welcome back stranger," said his friend and business partner Derek Barns *Barnsie* who gave him a big bear hug. "Come into the office, sit down and I'll bring you up to date with where we're at with trying to locate your mysterious Mr.

Carmouche." They sat. "You'll be pleased to learn that we, when I say we, I mean our own pet gumshoe Mike who has great connections everywhere. In this case, the airline industry. Mike managed to find a passenger record of one Hector Carmouche arriving back into Manchester Airport two days ago.

Flew in from Atlanta on Delta 4579. The bad news is, he's disappeared. Mike can't find any trace of him after that, so your only chance at the moment is to see if his cousin has any idea where he might be. Here's his cousin's address," and he handed Frankie a piece of paper.

"Bilton, Harrogate?"

"Aye lad, darkest Yorkshire. Make sure you take your passport, they don't like strangers up there."

"I'll make sure and be careful Barnsie," he said, punching his partner on the arm. "Can I borrow a car? I put mine into storage when I left as I thought I'd be away for six months."

"Yes sure, take mine. Listen why not let Mike Bingham tag along, I mean you don't know what you might be getting yourself into."

"You worry too much Derek, I'm a big boy now. I can take care of myself."

The day turned out fine, cold, sunny and bright. He drove along the M62 motorway over the moors and into Yorkshire. There were a few remnants of snow on the top of the hills, but the moors lower down were mostly bathed in sunlight. The rugged landscape appeared as a patchwork of colors, covering stunning sweeps of open moorland. A huge panorama with shades of green, brown, tan, red and russet, all shading from dark to light as shadows of clouds scudded across the pale blue winter sky.

Frankie was so busy taking in the view, he nearly missed his turn off and was blasted by the horn of a huge lorry, as he had to swerve ungracefully in front of it and across into the nearside lane to take the slip road. He waved an apology to the lorry driver and got a finger in return. *Knights of the road…*

It was just past midday as Frankie was approaching Bilton so he decided to look for a pub for a bite to eat. He drove round a bit, confident he would find a pub and eventually found himself on a small lane with a very traditional looking establishment called The Fox & Hounds. He parked the car, went inside, walked up to the bar and ordered half a bitter from a stern looking woman he took to be the landlady.

"Half a bitter it is," she said, as if mocking him for not ordering a pint."

"Thanks," he said putting a five-pound note on the bar, "do you have a sandwich menu or anything?" She turned back as she opened the till to place his money in it.

"No, I don't, this is a pub, we sell beer," she said, came back with his change, put it on the counter then walked away and disappeared from view. Frankie picked up his drink, then looked down the bar at the only other person in the pub. He was sitting on a stool and dressed in a tweed jacket. He sported a fine set of mutton chop whiskers and was smiling broadly. He raised his glass to Frankie then said.

"She's a one off is our Gladys, got all the charm of a rattlesnake," and with that he guffawed, slapped the bar and slurped his pint.

"Is she always like that?" asked Frankie

"I've known Gladys since she was a girl, and to be fair, I think she's mellowed quite a lot of late." He laughed again. "Don't take it personal, just the way she is, heart of gold really. Help anyone out in a fix."

"Good to know," said Frankie, "but I'm not sure I believe you. Cheers." Frankie raised his glass of beer to the man.

"Cheers," said the man, "So what brings you to this neck of the woods, you're not a local and we don't get that many strangers in this time of the day, especially midweek?"

"Just some business stuff." Frankie was aware that the slightest hint of anything untoward could spread like wildfire in these tightknit country communities. Gladys came back into the bar. Frankie's glass was now empty. Gladys glared at him.

"You want another beer?" Her look said he'd better buy another beer or leave. He chose the latter.

"No, I'd better be on my way, thanks for the hospitality," he said as he walked towards the exit. He heard the man laughing again as he walked out of the door.

The GPS on his phone took him first down a dead end, then along a nearly impassable farm track, before he finally found the lane that led to Moor View. It was high up on a small hill and had views of the surrounding farmland. He pulled up on a patch of dirt track in front of the house. *No other car here, bad sign.* It was a large solid looking traditional farmhouse, built in local yellowy gray stone, hewn out of some nearby quarry no doubt. He knocked on the imposing big wooden door using the big brass knocker, there was no bell push. No answer. He tried again, same result. He took a walk around the side, then through a side gate round to the back of the house.

It was difficult to tell if it was occupied or not. The house was in good order, well maintained, no peeling paint. He walked around the front again and sat back in his car trying to decide what to do. Meanwhile inside the house, Cornelius Hayes was also trying to decide what to do. Frankie got out of the car again and went back to the front door. He used the big brass knocker again, nothing. He tried slamming the flat of his hand several times on the front panel of the door. Then he looked through the letterbox, put his mouth to the letterbox and shouted.

"Mr. Hayes, are you in there?"

There was no way anyone inside could not have heard Frankie knocking on the door, so either the house was empty, or someone didn't want to come to the door. Frankie stood back and was about to grab the brass knocker gain, when he heard a bolt sliding and the door opened. Frankie took a breath.

"Hector?" he asked. The man in front of him looked like Hector, albeit he had a small goatee beard and wore glasses.

"Sorry, I'm not Hector. I assume you're talking about Hector Carmouche, I'm his cousin Cornelius. People always used to get us mixed up. We always did look alike. So, who are you and why did you think you'd find Hector here? As far as I'm aware, he still lives in sunny Florida." Frankie was still struggling with the likeness.

"I was led to believe that Hector had rushed back to the UK, something about a relative dying and leaving him, I don't know, some big fortune or something. I asked my office to do some research and they could only find you, his cousin, so I came to ask if you might know where he was."

"Well I'm sorry to disappoint you Mr.?"

"Oh, sorry, Frankie, Frankie Armstrong."

"Well Mr. Armstrong, I haven't seen Hector for a long long time, probably ten years or more."

Frankie couldn't get over the man's likeness to Hector and something in the man's demeanor just didn't compute. He decided to push.

"Look, would it be possible to come in and I could explain a bit more. Maybe you could provide some clue as to who this relative might be and where Hector might have gone?" The man hesitated, then seemed to come to a decision.

"Okay, but I'm going out soon, a dental appointment so I can't be late."

"I understand," said Frankie stepping over the threshold. The man showed Frankie through a spacious hallway and into a large sitting room with, old fashioned comfortable looking furniture. The inside of the house was all exposed stone, with a stone floor, littered here and there with rugs. An idea occurred to Frankie *worth a try*.

"Sorry," he said, "but it was quite a long journey to get here. Any chance I can use your bathroom?" The man looked uncomfortable, then replied,

"I'll show you, follow me," and led the way up a wide staircase to the landing. He pointed to a bathroom on the right. "In there," he said motioning to a door. Frankie opened the door and went into the small bathroom, realizing the man wasn't going to let a stranger loose in his house. He looked around quickly, found what he wanted, then flushed the loo, turned the taps on for a while, then opened the door.

The man stood there holding a double-barreled shotgun, pointed directly at Frankie's midriff.

"Did you find what you were looking for? You must think I'm really stupid Frankie, what did you take, the toothbrush, ah no, my razor?"

"The toothbrush and just the razor blade," said Frankie."

"Put them back Frankie, just drop them in the sink. And please don't try anything. I won't hesitate to pull the trigger if I have to. We're miles from anywhere here, so…" Frankie did as he was told. "Now walk down the stairs in front of me and turn right into the kitchen," Frankie obeyed. "Okay, open that top drawer the one on the extreme right, that's the one."

"Now take out the roll of tape and walk in front of me into the dining room." They walked out of the kitchen, into the hall. "Open the door on your left." It opened into a dining room with an oblong oak table and eight chairs. "Over there," the man pointed to the far side of the dining table with his gun.

Once Frankie was at a satisfactory distance, the man told him to stand still, then holding the gun with one hand, he pulled one of the dining chairs out, turning it so it faced outwards away from the table. The chairs were the traditional farmhouse ladder-back type with raffia woven seats. The man instructed Frankie to take his jacket off and put it over the back of the chair, then roll his shirt sleeves up.

"Okay Frankie, sit down on the chair and place your left arm along the arm of the chair."

"I know this is a well-worn cliché," said Frankie, "but you'll never get away with this Hector. My office knows I was coming here."

The man laughed.

"Not Hector Frankie. You're going to have learn to call me Cornelius, Cornelius Hayes esquire. But hey, ditch the formalities, you can call me Con for short. At least for the brief time we're going to spend together."

"But you are the same person I know, or knew as Hector?"

"I am indeed Frankie boy, one and the same. Now please, just do as you're told." Said the man waving his gun to emphasize his authority. Frankie complied and laid his arm along the arm of the chair. The man continued. "Now, using your right hand, tape your left wrist to the arm of the chair. Make it nice and tight, no cheating or I shoot. Frankie had to use the fingernails of his left hand to pry of the tape from the roll, then he carried out the man's instructions and wrapped the tape around his left wrist securing it to the arm of the chair.

"Now bite the tape through, leave a nice long piece of tape off the roll and place the roll on your lap."

Frankie did as he was told, "Okay, now put your right arm along the other arm of the chair. That's it. Now just keep still." The man came forward and rested the barrels of the shotgun in Frankie's lap.

"The safety's off so one wrong move and I pull the trigger. I hate to think what a mess it will make of you Frankie, so keep quite still. No heroics okay?" Frankie shrugged. The man tucked the butt of the gun under his arm, with his right-hand finger on the trigger. With this left hand he took hold of the roll and pulled a long piece off with his teeth, then looking Frankie straight in the eyes, the man stuck some tape on the top of Frankie's right wrist, letting the weight of the roll drop it to where he could get hold of it and wrap it under the arm of the chair and back over the top of Frankie's wrist.

He did this four times with the gun still resting on Frankie's lap, before he was happy with his efforts. He backed away, disappeared for a few seconds then came back with some scissors. Standing behind Frankie, he cut the tape, then knelt down at the side of the chair, away from any danger of a kick from Frankie, and taped Frankie's lower legs to the chair legs. Coming back around to face Frankie, he looked at the bonds and nodded. Then he went around the back of the chair again, checked Frankie's jacket pockets and took out Frankie's car keys and mobile phone and put them on the other side of the dining table.

"Okay, that should do it for now. That was quite hard work, I think I deserve a cup of tea. Would you like one as well Frankie?" Frankie glared. "I'll take that as a no then," and the man disappeared again, reappearing some minutes later, mug of tea in hand. He sat down on one of the other chairs, then got up and maneuvered Frankie's chair so that Frankie was now facing the inwards. The man went back to his chair on the opposite side of the table and sipped his tea.

Chapter 32

Day 10 - Thursday Naples
Detective Randazzo

"Hey Dale, where's the fire?" said Detective Randazzo to his colleague when he rushed into Randazzo's office without knocking, a piece of paper in his hand. "You look as if you're being chased by a bear," which came out as *bayor*.

"Sorry boss, but I thought you'd like to know, we've got a hit on that Hector guy's DNA."

"You do? Come on in and sit down. I'll see you later Denise, I need to deal with this."

"Yes sir," said the Criminal Researcher, "just let me know when you're free." She closed the door on her way out.

"Yeah, Chicago PD has a record of one Hector Carmouche arrested in 1986 for beating his wife. They took his fingerprints and DNA."

"They were taking DNA way back then?"

"Yeah, they were ahead of some other forces on that one. Anyhow, I anticipated that you'd want to find out if it was a match as soon as possible. So, as you were out most of the day, I took the initiative and sent it to forensics for a match and guess what?"

"Come on Dale, have we nailed the guy or not?"

"That's just it boss, it's not a match."

"What! Not a match, are they sure?"

"They are one hundred percent positive. They said there were some similarities, but nothing unusual, said it could be a match any one of millions of Caucasian males."

Randazzo stroked his chin.

"I must be slipping. I was sure, absolutely sure…" he said shaking his head.

"So, what now boss?"

"We keep sifting through the evidence, interviewing people and generally keep digging until we get some sort of lead. At the moment we look like a bunch of fools. Two murders within days of each other, in an otherwise peaceful neighborhood. I just don't get it."

"Didn't you say that the British guy, Armstrong, didn't you say he's gone back to the UK to look for Carmouche?"

"I did yeah. Better see if you can get some contact details for him. I 'm sure we have his email somewhere. We need to tell him. I'll look for it. Ask that Rudy Sprouse guy, the president of the community, he'll have his email if we can't find it."

"On it boss."

Chapter 33

Day 10 - Thursday (UK) Continued

Frankie

Frankie watched the man sip his tea. *I walked straight into this one. Barnsie will crucify me... if I ever get the chance to tell him about it.* The man spoke.

"I underestimated you Frankie. I didn't think anyone would come looking for me here, least of all you. But then I didn't have much time to make proper plans. I should have thought my plan through better. Still, as they say, we are where we are."

"And where are we exactly Con? Okay, you've got me trussed up like a chicken, and maybe you now plan to kill me as well, but where's that going to get you? Detective Randazzo knows I've come over here to look for you, plus my business partner knows I've come to see you, specifically at this address, so when I don't get in touch, they're going to raise the alarm and come here looking for me."

"I realize that Frankie, but at least I now have time to think. It's a tight spot I'm in I'll grant you, but I've been in tight spots before and I'm still here, to fight another day. I'll figure something out. You ever see that Cary Grant movie, erm..., got it, North by North West?"

"What?" said Frankie.

"Well, the bad guys kidnap Cary Grant and need to make the cops think he's killed himself, so they pour liquor down his throat, put him behind the wheel of a car on top of a steep hill, fix the brakes, then let the hand brake off and Cary Grant goes careering down this steep hill. Trouble is, he manages to come to a stop without getting hurt, but that's the movies not real life."

"You're quite mad Con, you realize that don't you?"

"Just kidding you Frankie, I'm sure I can figure out something better for you, I just need a while to think it through."

Frankie doubted Con would get away with killing him, *but that won't be much comfort to me if I'm dead*. He decided he needed to keep Con talking. *Maybe I can eventually persuade him the game's up and there's no point in killing me.*

"So Con, how did you get away with switching identities, and where's the real Hector? I assume he's not still alive?"

Cornelius Hayes laughed a dry laugh.

"I suppose there's no harm in telling you now. You sure as hell won't be passing on the information. Can you see out there, in the garden?" Frankie turned and looked through the window, "See that weeping willow, that's where Hector is."

"You killed him?"

"I killed him, but it wasn't really my fault. I liked Hector. No, I loved Hector and he let me down, we were best friends.

But he broke his promise, and it wouldn't be an exaggeration to say he broke my heart. He ruined my life, so I took his life, literally."

"How could he have ruined your life?"

The man got up and walked around the room, then came back and sat in his chair.

"Okay, well I've never told anyone else, so I guess it would be good to tell someone. You're a safe bet, as one way or another, you're never going to be in a position to tell anyone else." Hector stopped talking and gulped down the rest of his tea. He began. "It all goes back to when we were kids." And he told Frankie about how as children, he and Hector had developed a love of everything American. Cornelius Hayes described how Mary Kershaw's family had moved next door to Hector in his late teens, and how this led to the disintegration of the friendship between the cousins. Con said he'd hoped that Hector's infatuation with Mary would wane and that their own friendship would be resumed, but realized eventually, that wasn't to be.

He told Frankie about joining the RAF and how it became his life, then about retiring on a full pension in 2009, after thirty-four years of service. He told him how he'd bought this house they were sitting in, as a wreck. He explained he needed a project to replace the inevitable void he knew he'd feel after leaving the RAF. Frankie realized Con was finding the telling of his story cathartic…*maybe, just maybe, I can develop some sort of relationship with him that might make it harder for him to kill me? Nothing to lose by trying.*

"Did you and Hector communicate at all during that time, I mean after he'd met this girl, Mary did you say her name was?"

"No, we didn't. I thought about Hector and I knew from mutual acquaintances back in Yorkshire that he'd moved to the United States with Mary, but no more than that. At least not until much later."

"You never married?"

Con allowed himself a self-deprecating laugh.

"Yeah, I married the RAF. Oh, I had lots of girlfriends, affairs, flings whatever you like to call them, but nothing serious. It sounds pathetic, but I think maybe that experience of Hector breaking his promise when we were kids did something to me, made me suspicious and wary of commitment. Maybe I'm exaggerating, I don't know, but there was one other relationship that did have an impact on my life, my later life that is, and quite a big impact at that."

"I'll come back to that later maybe?" he said thoughtfully. Frankie made a mental note to remind him, the man continued.

"So anyway, back to my leaving the RAF and taking this project on," the man said looking round at the house, "I won't bore you with all that though, I'll fast forward about nine months after I'd bought this place. One evening, out of the blue, that phone rang." He nodded at a phone on a side table. "Unusual to have a land line these days isn't it? Anyway, I answered the phone and recognized Hector's voice instantly. He said, 'is that Con?' I couldn't speak for a brief moment. I asked him how he was, and he did likewise. I tried to be civil, but inside I was angry with him, angry at how long it had taken him to contact me again."

"How had he found out where you were, and how to contact you?" asked Frankie.

"The internet, he said. Paid for some service that claimed they could find anyone. I don't think it would have been that difficult, I don't know, vote register, everyone's on all sorts of databases these days, I really don't know, does it matter?"

"I guess not," said Frankie *but it helps me string out this conversation until I can think of something…*

"We chatted for well over an hour, maybe an hour and a half I don't know, mostly about old times. He asked me if I'd ever got hitched, and I told him no. I asked about Mary, if they'd had kids. He said there were no kids and that Mary was history. He reckoned that Mary was originally motivated by envy. She'd been jealous of our friendship. A bit late to discover that I thought. Breaking our friendship up was apparently what she wanted to begin with, but then she saw him as a way of getting out of the UK and into America.

Hector said she used him, then when they'd moved to the States and she judged the moment was right, she goaded him into a huge argument. He told me he completely lost it and hit her. He was arrested and would have been convicted, but she said she'd drop the charges if he gave her everything. He reckoned it was worth it to get rid of her. He said he couldn't risk getting a criminal record. If he did, it would mean he'd be kicked out of America.

But I just couldn't feel sorry for him, he should have kept his word. He said he'd tell me more about it when he came over. 'What, come over here?' I asked, and he said yes, he'd like to come over and see me, and 'would that be okay?' Told me he was moving from Tampa to a place called Naples on the Gulf of Mexico, said it was a really nice place. Lots of great beaches, lots of fishing and very secure, hardly any crime. But then he went on to say that the realtor or the lawyers had messed up and he had about three weeks when he'd be homeless, that is from the time he had to vacate his apartment in Tampa, to when he could take up residence in the condo he'd bought in Naples. Told me it was a place called Acadiana."

Con stopped talking to take a drink of his tea, "Oops, empty," he said. "So, where were we, oh yes. So, Hector came to visit. We got on just like we had when we were kids. We were just so alike, in personality and looks. Then within a few days, Hector got the flu. Having spent all that time away, he just wasn't inoculated against our bugs, and the damp weather here didn't help. He couldn't believe it was so gray and cloudy all the time and rained so much. He became very ill with the flu, took to his bed, well my bed actually. He asked about getting a doctor, but I persuaded him it would pass eventually and said I'd look after him. See the plan was already forming in my mind and the fewer people who knew Hector was here, the better, as far as I was concerned."

"His realtor emailed him to say he needed some more documents completing, but Hector was in no state to deal with it, so he asked me to sort them out for him. I had no idea what to do, but Hector talked me through it all. He had all his personal stuff on his laptop, so it wasn't too difficult. Hector said it would be better if I were to pretend to be him, rather than try to explain that I was acting on his behalf, as they may not think that acceptable. Otherwise they would need a load of power of attorney forms completing and he wasn't sure how that would work out timewise, plus other legal complications of me being a Brit and so on. He gave me all his passwords or told me where to find them. He trusted me completely."

"Anyway, it all got sorted and Hector was looking forward to going back to Naples and to his new home. Said he was starting again, shaking off his old life and starting anew. A fresh chapter in his life he said. I don't know if something had happened in Tampa, he never said, and I never asked. Maybe a relationship that went sour, maybe an affair with a married woman that got found out, I don't know. But he didn't really talk much about Tampa. Anyway, it came to the last three days of his stay and he was feeling better, said we should go out and celebrate. He ordered a taxi and we went into Harrogate."

"We went to a sumptuous restaurant, The Rostbury I think it was called, something like that. Not sure it exists now. We had lots to drink, far too much. We got a taxi home and carried on drinking. Hector had some bourbon he'd brought over with him and we got stuck into that, although I made sure Hector drank most of it. Then I brought up the broken promise, the promise we'd made to each other in blood, and how disappointed I was when he broke that promise."

"Hector reacted. I knew he would, I banked on it. He'd always had a bit of a temper, maybe that's another thing we had in common. We fought, a really vicious fight. Years of angst coming out of me, all that bitterness about being betrayed. Funny how things that happen to you as a kid stay with you all your life, become amplified as you get older even maybe? The fight moved out of this room and into the hall. You'll have noticed the stone floor. Hector was much more the worse for drink, so I had the advantage."

"I wasn't sure how I was going to do it. In truth, I don't think I knew until that moment, just how serious I was about killing him. Eventually I managed to land a big old punch and he fell backwards, hit his head on the floor. I heard a noise, something between a thud and a crack. Hector was out for the count. I got hold of that marble statue over there, the one on the hall table, with the idea of finishing him off, but he was already dead, stone cold dead."

"I checked, and the back of his skull was smashed, a pool of blood spread across the floor. I was exhausted, drunk and fell asleep on the floor beside him. Eventually the dawn light woke me up." Con stopped talking and looked down at the floor.

"You weren't sorry you'd killed your cousin, your childhood best friend?" Frankie asked.

"Not really. Seemed to me fate had stepped in to put things right. Hector robbed me of the life I could have had in America. If he'd stuck to our promise, none of this would have happened. So now I reckoned it was my turn."

"You decided to become Hector?" said Frankie, "steal his identity?"

"Yes, I did. I decided I could be Hector from then on. The situation was ideal, much better than I could have hoped for or planned. He was moving to a new place, where as far as I knew, no one knew him, least not that well. We looked very similar. I had access to all his private stuff, his bank details, pretty well everything. Like I said, he'd given me his password details when I helped him with the problems with the realtor. In fact, I was Hector, as far as the realtor was concerned."

"I searched his luggage, he'd only brought hand luggage, so I had his passport and his flight ticket back to a place called Fort Myers, just a taxi ride from Naples. I had the address of his new condo, everything I needed to become Hector. Why I even had access to his online banking, which Hector gave me details of when I was doing the realtor stuff for him."

"So, you buried him in your garden?"

"Yup, and planted a weeping willow, planted the tree as a marker."

"So how did you explain your prolonged absence to people round here, your neighbors etc.?" Asked Frankie. *Keep it going Frankie the longer the better, the office bound to get concerned about me not checking in. Barnsie knows I wouldn't stay out of communication for long, not how we work together. If he calls my mobile and doesn't get an answer, he's going to really get worried.* Con began speaking again.

"I made up a story about going to Australia, then maybe travelling the world. I didn't have any close friends round here. I engaged a property agent to look after the house, check on it now and then, make sure it hadn't been broken into, make sure the heating was on if there was a really cold spell, all that sort of stuff. I left my bank account in place and my pension got paid into it to take care of any expenses here. All contact with anyone over here from then on was by email, so no one suspected anything. A few acquaintances had known that I'd had my cousin from America staying with me for a while, but no more than that."

"So, your plan to become Hector worked, you even got married as Hector?"

"Yes, I did, hilarious I thought. And things were going great until... well, this is where I need to tell you about something that happened many years ago. As I mentioned, when I was in the RAF, I had a rare old time, especially in the early years, partying most weekends, girls galore. London wasn't too far away and we made the most of that. On one such occasion I met a girl called Ava, an American air hostess." Con stopped talking and looked meaningfully at Frankie.

"Ava? Not Ava Ledinski?"

Con laughed

"As it turned out it was her, but neither of us were aware of the coincidence to begin with. When I first went to live in Acadiana, neither of us recognized each other. We'd both aged quite a lot since our brief fling all those years ago. Even when I was introduced to her as Ava, it still didn't ring a bell. I'd never known her last name anyway and Ava's a common enough name. I couldn't remember her, any more than I could remember any of the girls I'd slept with all that time ago. We were all pretty drunk most of the time."

"So, you killed Ava because she recognized you?"

"Yes and no. It wasn't as simple as that."

"Oh, I think it was. You killed Ava because she knew you weren't who you said you were. It doesn't get much simpler than that."

Con's face turned red and contorted. He stood and shouted at Frankie, spittle flecked Frankie's face.

"You know nothing! It was her fault, if she hadn't been such a stupid greedy bitch."

Frankie was alarmed at how out of control Con had suddenly become. He waited for the man to calm down and sit down, then asked

"Greedy how?"

"Ava was no saint. She gave piano lessons and other services as well to certain clients, then she blackmailed them, blackmailed me!"

"Yes, I know she was probably blackmailing men she had sex with, but not about you as such. So, you killed her because she was blackmailing you?"

"Yes, but not just about the sex. She was doing that alright, but she was also threatening to tell Mable who I was, that I wasn't really Hector Carmouche. It wasn't just the damage she would do to my marriage, which would have been bad enough, but if my true identity was revealed to anyone, that would lead to the authorities getting involved, and my whole plan would unravel. The ultimate probability would be that the authorities would find out that I'd killed the real Hector Carmouche. I couldn't take that risk."

"How did she know? I mean couldn't you convince her you were really Hector Carmouche, the look alike cousin of the guy she knew in London?"

"Maybe I could have, but for one little problem. Like I said, neither of us recognized each other when we first met, although she did say I reminded her of someone. But then we had sex. I really did go for piano lessons to begin with. I learnt to play when I was a kid. I've even got a piano here you might have noticed. Anyway, we had sex and that's when she realized who I was. See, I have a very distinctive birth mark on my stomach, just near my penis, looks like a pyramid, uncannily like a pyramid. As soon as she saw it, the penny dropped, for her that is."

"She said we'd met before and had sex before. I was confused. But then she told me she used to be a Pan Am Stewardess based in London and I remembered her too, sort of. She searched her memory for my name and then the bitch said. 'I remember, Hayes, Cornelius Hayes, RAF. Why are you calling yourself Hector Carmouche?"

"I was fucked, in more ways than one, and she knew it. She thought I was worried about having stolen Hector's identity, she didn't realize I'd also killed him to get it. She knew I was married to Mable, made demands and I paid up for a while, but then she got greedy. On the night she was killed, I'd arranged to meet her by the dock. She said we had to meet urgently. Turned out she just wanted to up the money I was paying."

"I was hoping to do a deal on a big one-off payment, but blackmailers always get hooked, not just the money but the power. I knew eventually I'd have to kill her but hadn't worked out how to. Then we were arguing on the dock and I saw that gator swim up in the water behind her. I couldn't believe my luck. You know the rest."

They were both silent for a few moments, then Frankie spoke,

"Feel better now Con?"

"How do you mean, oh, offloading on to you? Yes, I think I do. I suppose I've always really wanted to tell someone the whole story, but obviously I couldn't before. But now…yeah, it feels good I mean especially as you ain't going to be able to tell anyone else." He laughed.

"You haven't a hope of getting away with this," said Frankie, "even if you get rid of me, someone is going to find you and…" just then Frankie's phone pinged with an incoming email. Con picked it up.

"Handy, no password, tut tut tut Frankie, should be more careful."

"Unlike you Con, I don't have much to hide." Con read Frankie's email, then read it again. He looked perplexed to begin with, then he smiled a big smile and started laughing. His laughing became more hysterical. He stood up and tears ran down his face, then he finally brought his laughter under control. During this time, Frankie had taken the opportunity to test the bindings on his left arm. As he'd been wrapping the tape around it with his right hand, he'd kept his left arm raised from the chair arm to provide for some movement. Hector wiped his eyes with a tissue.

"Something obviously very funny in that email, care to share the joke?"

"Well… it looks like Hector's ridden to the rescue again, this time from the grave." He read the email out to Frankie.

Mr. Armstrong. I don't know how far you've got in trying to find Hector Carmouche, but you can call off the dogs. He's not a suspect anymore. We've got a sample of his DNA from when he lived in Chicago and it isn't a match. I re-state, Hector Carmouche's DNA is not a match for the DNA we found at the crime scene. Call me if you would like more information.

Detective Randazzo

Naples Police Department

"Must have been the time Hector was arrested for beating his wife up. But you know what this means don't you Frankie? You're the only person who now knows the truth. The cops still think the original Hector and I are the same person. Hilarious don't you think? All I have to do is figure out how to get rid of you without me being implicated. No mean feat I grant you, but if I can figure something out, I'm home free. I can go back to Naples and resume my life over there as Hector."

Franke's heart dropped, but he felt he had to keep the man talking.

"So, you admit to killing Ava and I assume you also killed Lisa?"

"Yeah, it does seem logical to assume that doesn't it? But you'd be wrong," he said leering.

"Wrong in what way?"

Con seemed as if he was about to answer, then looked at his watch.

"My my look at the time. I need to make some plans. First I need to get your car out of sight. Don't have many visitors, but no point in taking chances eh?" And with that, Con picked Frankie's keys up off the table, checked the bonds holding Frankie arms to the chair then left the room. Frankie heard the front door slam shut.

He quickly got to work on trying to free his arms, the left one allowed him to try and twist the tape, but it was strong stuff. He then concentrated on his ankles.

Con had taped them to the legs of the chair around Frankie's chinos, so there was some wriggle room. He twisted and turned and managed to stretch the tape that was binding his right ankle to the chair leg. He leaned over nearly toppling himself to the floor but managed to retain his balance sufficiently to stretch his leg out, forcing the tape down and off the chair leg. With his now free right leg, he used the heel of his shoe to tease down the tape holding the other ankle to the chair, whilst simultaneously pulling up with the other leg. It worked and now both legs were free. He realized his next move would be critical.

He was running out of time and needed something quick and effective. He stood up and bent forward with the chair now on his back and sidestepped to the nearest wall, then twisted with all his might and smashed the bottom part of the chair against the wall. The bottom spindles gave way and the chair started to disintegrate. He made the same move again and again until he was left with just the chair arms still taped to his own arms, albeit with a few large wooden splinters hanging off.

He moved to the hall and positioned himself by the side of the door so when it opened it would hide his presence. He needed a surprise attack to have any chance of succeeding. Eventually the door opened and then closed exposing Con's back to him. It was now or never. Frankie swung his arm with all his strength and hit Con on the side of the head. The wooden arm of the chair taped to his own arm made a formidable weapon and he felled Con with the first strike.

Con was now on the floor rolling around and moaning. Before he could recover, Frankie jumped on top of Con and hit him again on the same side of the head, then on the other side with his other wooden arm. Con stopped moving. Satisfied Con was now out for the count, for a while at least, Frankie went to find a knife or some scissors. Once he'd freed himself from the tape and the chair arms, he found the roll of tape and went to work on trussing up the now unconscious Cornelius Hayes.

Chapter 34

Plod to the rescue

The police arrived within fifteen minutes of Frankie's 999 call. Frankie found the shotgun, which Con had hidden in a hall cabinet when he went to move Frankie's car. He left it where it was but pointed it out to the two constables who were the first ones to arrive. They called for an ambulance, un-taped the injured Con and put him in handcuffs. They asked Frankie if there was anyone else in the house, then asked him for details of what had happened.

As Frankie began to tell them, one of the constables stopped his colleague and suggested it would be better to wait for CID. A couple of detectives rolled up a short time later and took over. The ambulance arrived and two policemen accompanied Cornelius to hospital. Frankie told the detectives what had happened and the events in America leading up to him coming to look for Hector.

"Do you feel you need medical attention Mr. Armstrong, perhaps see a doctor?"

"No, I don't need a doctor, but I would like to call my business partner, tell him I'm okay," said Frankie.

While Frankie called Barnsie, the senior detective got on his phone to request a scene of crime crew come to the house, making particular reference to the probability of a body having been buried in the garden some ten years previously.

Derek hit the roof when Frankie told him what had happened.

"You're not safe to be let out on your own, you fucking crazy man. I told you to take Mike. Are you hurt?"

"A bit bruised, that would be both my body and my ego, but I'll recover. You'd be impressed with the way I escaped. The guy was going to kill me, no doubt about that."

"And you say there's a body buried in the garden? Jesus Frankie, you're a one-man disaster area."

Frankie was taken down to the police station where he made a formal statement detailing Con's attack on him, the story he told and his stated attempt to kill him. Frankie was thanked, then given tea and biscuits while he waited for Barnsie to turn up to take him home. The police insisted on keeping his car as part of the crime scene paraphernalia.

*

A body was found where Cornelius Hayes had told Frankie he'd buried it, but even before that, Cornelius Hayes confessed to the police to killing his cousin Hector Carmouche. His story to the authorities ran along similar lines to the one he told Frankie, though entirely slanted towards it being an accident as a result of a fight which Hector started. Hector's death was an accident he claimed, self-defense. In the end the Crown Prosecution Service decided against charging him with murder and charged him with the lesser crime of aggravated manslaughter.

Cornelius was also charged with assaulting Frankie and taking him prisoner. Frankie was angry that they had declined to charge Hayes with kidnap and attempted murder, but the CPS said there wasn't sufficient evidence to convict him on such a charge. Hayes was arraigned in custody for a trial date two months hence.

Frankie's statement had included details about how Hayes stole his cousin's identity and lived as Hector Carmouche in Florida for over ten years. Even getting married to a US citizen using that false identity. He told how Hayes had confessed to the killing of Ava Ledinski, but this last price of information was considered hearsay and in any event, outside the jurisdiction of the British authorities.

Nevertheless, the American legal authorities were eventually allowed to come to the UK and interview Cornelius Hayes. They duly obtained permission to obtain a sample of his DNA, which proved he was at the crime scene where Lisa was killed. Subsequently, they applied for a warrant to extradite Cornelius Hayes to the USA to face a charge of homicide in relation to the death of Lisa Ledinski. A separate warrant was applied for in relation to the death of Ava Ledinski. Both warrants were granted, but the action of those warrants would be subject to the outcome of the trial in the UK, and only actionable on completion of any jail term in the UK, imposed by a British Court.

Frankie was the main, indeed, the only witness for the prosecution. So, his testimony was vital to secure the conviction of Cornelius Hayes in a court of law. The CPS was more than a bit twitchy when Frankie told them he was going back to Florida to complete his extended vacation. They agreed to this, only on condition of him agreeing to return to the UK for the Court case. He was more than happy to give them the assurances they sought, especially as they said he would be reimbursed for any expenses relating to his return.

Frankie had returned to work at his company's offices in Manchester, where he was feted as a hero, and asked over and over to tell his story of his fight and his escape from the clutches of Cornelius Hayes. Articles were written about him in the Manchester Evening News and in all the national newspapers, but he declined TV interviews and generally shunned publicity. He was grateful when things died down. Frankie didn't have to wait long for the next political scandal about Brexit to push his story out of the news.

During this time, Frankie was living back at the house he owned with his wife Penny. He'd been hoping they might use the opportunity to discuss some sort of reconciliation. Not a resumption of their marriage as such, but maybe something better than the present antagonistic situation. He still loved Penny on some level, and he was sure she still had feelings for him. But if anything, Penny seemed even more remote than ever. He'd tried to start a conversation about the possibility of a more platonic future relationship. *We got along well enough in the past, so who knows?* thought Frankie. He knew he could never love Penny the way he used to, not after Lisa, *but maybe we could just rub along together and get by? Lots of married people do.* But she didn't want to know.

His patience finally ran out and told her he was going back to Naples on the next available flight. She told him it was of no consequence to her. He wrote her a letter which he left on the kitchen table the morning he left for the flight back to Naples. In it he told her he'd instructed a lawyer to begin divorce proceedings. He finished saying he hoped they could achieve an amicable settlement and wished her the best for the future.

Chapter 35

Coming Home

Arriving back in Naples, Frankie arranged to collect Charlie and moved back into his rented condo. He was greeted warmly by the other residents, who all wanted details of the traumatic events surrounding his finding of the man they'd all come to know as Hector Carmouche. Frankie fended them off, promising he would tell all in the fullness of time, but refused to say any more than that. He then made the call he knew he had to make.

"Well well, our very own hero Mr. Frankie Armstrong, you're back."

"I'm back Detective and I guess you need me to come and see you?"

"Nope, I'll come to see you. I need to get out of the office, I go stir crazy if I have to spend more than a day in this place. Be with you about one o'clock if that's okay?"

Detective Randazzo arrived on the dot. Frankie made them both coffees.

"Okay, so I know the official version of events, and you know that we've applied for extradition to get the cocksucker back here so we can charge him with the murder of Ava Ledinski, and the murder of her sister, your girl Lisa."

"Yes, I did know Detective and I'm looking forward to him eventually facing justice over here for what he did."

"Me too Mr. Armstrong, me too. And I have to say, he might have gotten away with it, but for you."

"Maybe," said Frankie, "but maybe not? He would have had to have got away with killing me, and that wouldn't have been easy. But then again, he did have the luck of the devil, so who knows?"

"You're right, and no point in speculating. Look, what I really wanted was your unofficial version of events. I mean, your formal statement covers pretty well everything I guess, but I'm interested in the informal story, the nuances of the situation. You know what I mean?"

"Yes, I think I do," said Frankie and told the detective the entire story from when he first arrived at the house, his capture, Con's story through to his escape and the arrival of the police. The detective listened in silence as Frankie retold the events. When Frankie had finished, he made them both fresh coffees.

"That's some story Mr. Armstrong. I'm impressed and that doesn't happen very often."

Frankie nodded his appreciation. The detective took a sip of his coffee then continued.

"What gets me Mr. Armstrong, is how come the authorities over there only charged him with assault and attempted manslaughter? Over here he'd have been charged with murder one for killing his cousin for sure, and attempted murder in your case. He'd have been in the slammer now, probably on death row."

"British justice Detective. The CPS are a law unto themselves," Frankie laughed at his description *irony?* "My guess is they don't like to take chances, so maybe they went for what they think a jury would convict on, given the available evidence. My evidence was uncorroborated, my version of events, verses his, so…? But from the story he told me, there's no doubt in my mind, that he did have premeditated intent to kill his cousin, albeit a latent intent. All those years of resentment built up to a crescendo of hatred and violence."

"He was consumed with rage and envy and he acted on that with the sole intent of killing his cousin and stealing his identity."

"So, how long d'you think he'll serve over there, I mean before we can get our hands on him back here?"

"Depends. Theoretically, he could get off without even being given a custodial sentence at all in the UK. Or, maybe as little as a couple of years, less time served on remand."

"Sounds like he'll get an easy ride over there then. But it doesn't matter 'cos when I get him back here, he's gonna pay, believe me!"

"I'm looking forward to that Detective. I'm not normally a vengeful man, but this is all too personal for me. He not only stole Hector's life, but he probably stole my future with

Lisa." Frankie stopped talking unable to carry on. The detective looked away and gave him a minute.

"Going back to your account of his confession to you," said Randazzo, "the one thing that really bugged me was that he didn't actually admit to killing Lisa Ledinski, have I got that right?"

"You have, and I found that curious as well. I mean the man was definitely going to kill me, so what had he got to lose by admitting killing her?"

"Do you think it's possible he didn't kill Lisa?"

"I think he did, he must have. The DNA proves it. But in truth, I really don't know Detective, I really don't."

"Well, that's okay. When I get him here, I'll beat a confession out of him myself. I believe he killed that beautiful girl and her sister, no matter what he says." They both stayed silent for a couple of beats, then the detective spoke again.

"I noted your formal statement didn't say anything about the email I sent you about the DNA. I mean who could've believed that twist?"

"No, I didn't. I thought it might confuse things. Trying to explain that the historical DNA sample you'd got your hands on was from the real Hector Carmouche and not Hector Carmouche the imposter. In any event, I didn't see what it would add to the case against him in the UK Courts."

"Yeah, I can see that. And by the way, I'm real sorry about that, my timing wasn't great was it?"

"You can say that again. He rightly presumed you had his DNA from the murder scene, hence the reason he ran. But when he saw your email about the DNA sample eliminating him as a suspect, he couldn't believe his luck. He realized he could get away with resuming his life as Hector Carmouche.

Randazzo shook his head.

"Man, that really floored me when I found out. When I told the rest of the guys, their collective jaws hit the ground. If he'd managed to kill you without being found out, chances are he'd be back here now, home free in more ways than one."

"But would he have got away with killing me? Not likely, but then again, the man had the luck of the devil," said Frankie.

"He did, but his luck ran out thank God. Hey, on a different subject Mr. Armstrong, what are your plans now? I see you've got your little doggie back and you've come back alone, so…?"

"Yes, I think I mentioned previously that I had a few problems at home?"

"You did, but none of my business."

"Well, it doesn't really matter now. My wife and I are getting divorced, so who knows, I might try to get work over here, apply for a green card maybe. You don't happen to have a job for me do you Detective?"

"I'm not sure I could handle you as a work colleague Mr. Armstrong. With all due respect, you seem to be a magnet for trouble, and I have plenty enough of that already." The detective laughed. "So, you're planning to stick around for a while?"

"Yes, I am, at least until they haul me back to the UK to testify. Can't think of a better place than Naples to be right now."

Chapter 36

Springtime in Naples

Frankie

Springtime is the best time in Naples. As the winter season comes to an end in late March, the Snowbirds all return home to the north and the population of places in southern Florida plummets. The beaches are uncrowded, the roads are all but empty and you can guarantee you'll get a table at any of the many restaurants. Yet the weather if anything, is at its best.

Frankie had spent the last few weeks relaxing in the sun, swimming and chatting by the pool. No matter how many times he told the story, the residents loved to hear it again and again. Always with new questions about his dramatic confrontation with the Hector Carmouche imposter.

The local press and the national media also couldn't get enough of the story. The media loved sensational news and they obviously thought it didn't get much more sensational than this. A man killing his own cousin, burying his body in the garden, stealing his identity then living for ten years in Florida as his own cousin, even marrying in his cousin's name. And then to top it off, committing suicide! There was talk of a movie.

The headline writers had a field day, *Dead Ringer* was a particular favorite. Frankie's own favorite was *Killed Copied and Conned.* Frankie reluctantly appeared on a couple of news channels and gave some newspaper interviews, before calling a halt to it all. It took a while, but eventually the story became last week's news and Frankie's life went back to something like normal. His divorce was going through, and even though his solicitor told him he was being too generous in his settlement agreement with Penny, he didn't really care and wanted it to be over so he could just get on with the rest of his life.

Then in mid-April the CPS contacted him by email to say a final date for the trial had been agreed and he should prepare to make himself available, and make sure he would be back in the UK least four days prior to the trial for pre-trial briefings etc. Frankie contacted Detective Randazzo, who had also been made aware of the trial data date. He told Frankie to keep him up to speed on developments as the trial proceeded.

Chapter 37

The Letter

A few days after he'd been informed of the trial date, Frankie took Charlie out for his morning walk and as he passed the condo's mailboxes, he noticed he had mail. As usual, it was mostly junk, apart from two genuine looking letters. One, he recognized as the monthly bill from his landlord, and another bulkier letter. He looked at the white envelope. It was addressed in neat longhand to Francis Armstrong Acadiana, 242 Bayline Drive Apt 206, FL 34103 USA and marked Private & Confidential.

The letter had a distinctive postmark, *Wakefield Prison*. He took the envelope upstairs and placed it on the dining table, then fed Charlie, had his shower and prepared his own breakfast. He ate his breakfast reading the UK news on his iPad, then tiring of the ongoing Brexit debacle, he turned on the TV to watch the American news. He switched channels from CNN to MNSBC, then to Fox. He shook his head. *Same events, wildly different interpretations.*

The news hadn't changed all that much, the truth he reasoned, was somewhere in the middle. Trump was still detested by the Democrats but supported by the Republicans. He glanced at the unopened letter on the table, then got up and made a second cup of coffee, brought a clean knife back with him to the table and slit the envelope open. He began to read.

***

Dear Frankie (may I still call you Frankie?)

Being in prison has given me plenty of time to think. I told my lawyer I wanted to write to you to explain a few things. He cautioned me against it, said putting anything in writing might prejudice my trial in the UK, but I don't think that's going to matter in the long run. I'm not sure if they read outgoing letters in remand prisons, but I'm not taking the chance and I've offered a £100 to one of the guards here to smuggle it out of prison and send it from a post office. If you're reading this, then he's kept to the bargain. My lawyer says I might well get a non-custodial sentence, we'll see, but regardless of the outcome of the trial over here, there is still the question of my subsequent extradition to the US, which my lawyer says is inevitable, so I want to tell you a few things. Again, I won't explain any more about the incident involving Ava and the unfortunate circumstances of her demise, only to say that it was an accident, an argument that got out of hand. I sincerely regret that she ended up killed by that alligator.

But I did want to write to you about her sister Lisa. I did not kill Lisa Ledinski. However, I asked my lawyer, and he confirmed what I already suspected, which is that if I was present when she was killed, I'd be considered just as guilty as the person who actually did the killing.

Frankie put the letter down and went to make another cup of coffee. *Ha, it's finally dawned on the guy that he's in deep. Maybe he's probably just discovered Florida still has the death penalty?* Frankie had studied the criteria for the death penalty and concluded that Cornelius fitted that criteria on a number of counts. *Now he's saying he didn't do it, but realizes that he'll be found guilty of murder, so why this letter pleading innocence?*

Frankie was conflicted about capital punishment. On the one hand, he felt it was entirely unacceptable on so many levels to take the life of another person in cold blood, no matter what they'd done. On the other hand, he thought, *why shouldn't someone pay with their own life, if they've taken an innocent life themselves?* In the case of Cornelius Hays, one way or another, he'd killed at least two innocent people that Frankie knew of, and if you included Lisa, that made three. *Who knows who else this monster has killed in the past? The way I feel about him killing Lisa, I could happily execute him myself.*

Frankie took his coffee and the letter on to the lanai, placed it on his desk, then sat down and watched the bay for a while *He's probably crapping himself at the thought of being found guilty of homicide over here, then facing the death penalty. All those years on death row, not a great thing to look forward to that's for sure Maybe that's some form of justice in itself?* He picked up the letter again. Charlie had followed him on to the lanai and lay down with his head on Frankie's bare feet. Frankie bent down and stroked Charlie's head, then continued reading the letter.

***

I am not guilty of killing Lisa Ledinski. You must believe that. You probably think I'm panicking at the thought of being found guilty of murder in Florida, and you'd be right. I'm very much aware of the potential, if not inevitable consequences, but that would still be a gross miscarriage of justice. I am innocent, at least in relation to the killing of Lisa Ledinski. So, I'm writing to you in the hope that you will bring the guilty party to justice. I know you were very fond of Lisa Ledinski and I'm really sorry she's dead.

Frankie put the letter down on the table briefly and took a sip of his coffee. *The guy who killed his own cousin and was going to kill me, now wants me to believe he didn't kill Lisa, why? In any event, nice to think fear is going to haunt him every day of his life from now on.* Frankie continued reading.

I'll begin at the beginning, the letter continued, *A few days after Ava met her unfortunate death, we were all having a few early evening drinks around the pool, when Roger Tuckerman sidled up to me. He nodded for us to move away from the main crowd to a table at the far end of the pool. He was a bit the worse for drink and asked me what I thought of Ava's death, or 'that bitch Ava' as he put it. I made no comment. He asked if I'd been messing about with her. I said I had no idea what he meant, but he said he knew I'd had piano lessons and wagged a finger at me. He was pretty far gone. He then told me he'd seen me.*

Seen me what? I asked. He told me he'd seen it was me who was arguing with Ava that night on the dock. Said he hadn't told anyone because he was glad the bitch was dead. Told me she'd been blackmailing him, and then he started to cry. I told him he'd had too much to drink and suggested he go back to his condo and get some rest. He just got up and wandered off back to the crowd at the other end of the pool and started drinking more beer. I left.

The next day, I bumped into him in the parking lot and he pulled me to one side. He reminded me of our conversation the previous evening and again promised he wouldn't tell anyone it was me that killed Ava. I told him it was an accident. He said she was obviously blackmailing me, and I couldn't deny it. Said he couldn't think we were the only ones either. He said she'd told him she had a video of him being caned and having sex with her and she'd threatened to show it to his wife if he didn't pay her a monthly fee. He was worried the police might find copies of the video if one really existed. Said he hadn't slept properly in days. I could tell he was drinking too much, the worry was obviously driving him insane. Everyone knew by that time that the cops suspected someone had broken into Ava's condo the same night she'd been killed, and stuff had been taken. Roger put two and two together, and concluded it was me who'd gone in and taken her laptop and stuff. I admitted it was me and told him to stop worrying, the videos would never see the light of day. That same evening I was going for my walk on the beach and Roger ran after me and asked if he could walk with me. He talked and talked about the videos and made me promise I wouldn't now start blackmailing him myself. I told him again he should stop worrying, we were both victims. Then I opened my stupid big fat mouth and told him I was concerned about there being a backup, I said that nobody wouldn't back up such valuable material. After that, he just wouldn't let it go. So, I told him I had a plan to sort it, but he kept on worrying. I decided it was safer to have him in on the job, rather than him be a loose cannon. I felt I had to involve him so that he had as much to lose as I did if anyone ever found out about it all. Oh, I forgot to say, I assume you'd guessed I'd bugged Ava's condo? Obviously, that's how I knew about your girlfriend Lisa finding the backup, right? I heard you and her discussing her finding the backup. Then of course you watched one of the videos, and as luck would have it, it was one of Roger with Ava. I heard you talking about a cane and laughing, so I drew my own conclusions about what you'd seen. I called Roger, who now kept his phone on all the time, keeping it under his pillow on vibrate at night so it wouldn't wake Myrtle. I told him that I now knew where the backup was and was going to break in and get it. I hinted that you might have seen him on one of the vids. He wanted in on the break in. I got it all arranged, bought some cheap horror masks, and we wore plastic gloves. It was never my intention to kill Lisa, didn't want the heat of another killing. I reckoned the cops would pull out all the stops if there was another death. So anyway, we broke in as soon as you'd left, well I picked the locks. Lisa was asleep. We grabbed her and taped her mouth shut to stop her screaming, then, when we were binding her hands, she broke free. She fought like a wild cat, she reached up and pulled Roger's mask off. He let go of her momentarily, and then she tried to pull my mask off, but I arched my head back and she scratched me on the neck with those very sharp nails of hers. Roger was going berserk saying she'd seen his face. I'd managed to hold her down until she ran out of steam, then suddenly, Roger lunged, got his hands round her throat and started to strangle her. I couldn't stop him. I tried to, told him to stop, I really did, but he killed her. We tidied up and left, taking the backup, the cash and of course the bugs. Afterwards I got very anxious, wondering if we'd left anything behind that might incriminate us. I was particularly worried about the cops possibly finding my DNA at the scene, and as you know only too well, I was right to worry.

Frankie stopped reading and put the letter down. *Roger, my good friend Roger, I can't believe this!* Frankie felt incandescent with anger, his breath came in short gasps, tears of rage streamed down his cheeks. He got up and walked the length of the apartment, then back again to the lanai and looked out but saw nothing. The raw emotion of loss struck him again like a knife in his heart. He and Lisa had only known each other a short time, but they'd connected. He knew she felt it as well. There was no doubt in his mind that he'd found his soulmate, and then she was snatched away, for what? *She'd done nothing wrong, nothing!*

Frankie wanted to go and kill Roger there and then, strangle him as he'd strangled Lisa. Frankie stopped, took some deep breath and concentrated on calming down. *Maybe this is what the letter is supposed to do, maybe it isn't true, maybe I'm being manipulated again?* He had to think, not react. He couldn't keep still, he had to get out into the fresh air.

"Come on Charlie, let's go for a walk," Charlie's ears picked up at the word walk. He was at the door waiting by the time Frankie had found his leash. Half an hour later Frankie returned to the condo much calmer. He gave Charlie some fresh water, then went back to the lanai and resumed reading the letter.

During our little chat back at my house in Yorkshire, you said I must have known the cops were going to ask everyone at Acadiana to take a DNA test. Well I didn't know, not as such, but I guessed. I was always concerned about that scratch. We'd cleaned her fingernails with the nail brush we found in her bathroom, scraped them clean. By the time we'd finished, Roger said there was no chance of them lifting any DNA from her nails, but I wasn't so sure. I was right, we obviously didn't get rid of all the traces. Anyway, when Roger told me about your conversation with him, I made him repeat it word for word. There was something about that conversation, Roger said he thought you'd said but, when he asked you if the cops knew anything, then didn't finish the sentence. That put got my antenna on full alert. I knew you'd been arrested on suspicion of her murder and then freed. I knew they would have taken your DNA as a matter of course, and that any DNA they found under her nails wouldn't match, hence they let you out of jail. I couldn't be absolutely sure, but I couldn't take the chance. If they had my DNA, I obviously couldn't submit to a test, and if I waited for them to ask for one and then I ran, it would be a clear indication of my guilt. So, when Roger called me to tell me about your conversation, I called Mable, and made up a story about receiving a call from the UK about a dead relation and a possible big inheritance. It was the best I could do at short notice and not a bad plan in the circumstances. And, I might have got away with it, but for you. But, no point in going over that is there?

The big thing here is, I'm innocent. I didn't kill Lisa Ledinski, Roger Tuckerman did. He'll obviously deny it, but I can give you proof. It happened just as I've described. You now want that proof I suppose? Go to my bedroom in my condo and look in the wardrobe. On the top shelf, right at the back (you'll need to use the steps which are in the kitchen closet) you'll find a false panel, the cops will know how to remove it. Behind the panel you'll find a key stuck to a small magnet attached to the wall. Take that key to Hideaway Storage on Pine Ridge Road. In storage box 3099, you'll find Ava's laptop and the backup disc, but no cash I'm afraid. I took that with me. I got rid of her iPad and the secret camera thing she used in the bedroom, smashed them up and chucked them in Venetian Bay. The backup disc will have at least five sets of fingerprints on it. I'm assuming Ava's, her sister Lisa's, yours, mine and most importantly, Roger Tuckerman's. We wore gloves of course during the break-in, but I made sure Roger (unwittingly) handled the backup disc afterwards as insurance. Despite everything, I really liked you Frankie, you're one of the good guys.

Frankie looked up from the letter then down at Charlie.

"He really likes me Charlie. This from the guy who was going to kill me a few weeks ago, and no doubt bury me under the weeping willow tree, along with his cousin Hector. The guy who was his best friend as a kid, *Jesus Christ, what kind of twisted mind…*" He shook his head in disbelief and went back to finish reading the letter.

You won't hear from me again Frankie, ever. I know that detective guy over there, Randazzo, is relishing me being extradited back to the USA so he can have his big day in Court, but he's going to be disappointed. Give my best wishes to all at Acadiana, we had some good times.

I've written a separate letter to Mable, though I doubt she'll ever forgive me.

Have a good life Frankie

Yours

Cornelius Hayes - aka Hector Carmouche

Frankie went back and re-read the last paragraph again, then went to find the envelope and looked at the date of posting *five days ago, shit!* Frankie went and sat in front of his PC and Googled Wakefield Prison UK. Google provided details - The largest high security jail in the UK, it also provided the phone number and name of the Governor. Frankie found his UK mobile phone and dialed the number. After a few frustrating minutes navigating the electronic answering process he finally got to speak to a human being.

"Wakefield Prison, how can I help you?"

"Yes, can I speak to the Governor's office please, it's urgent?" said Frankie

"May I know the nature of your call please?"

"I'm in the USA and I've just got a letter from someone in your jail and I think, well it could be he's contemplating suicide."

"I see sir, I assume your concern is about one of our inmates?"

"Yes, it is but..."

"Have you seen the news today sir? I only say that because we did have an unfortunate death in the prison yesterday. Would your enquiry relate to a Mr. Cornelius Hayes by any chance?"

Chapter 38

Detective Randazzo

Checking his watch, he called the Naples Police Department and asked to speak with Detective Sam Randazzo. They connected him to the detective's office. His assistant answered.

"Dale Vogel speaking."

"Frankie Armstrong here, is Detective Randazzo available please?"

"Oh, hi Mr. Armstrong, he's a bit busy at the moment. Can you call back?"

"I think he'll want to hear what I have to say."

"Uh oh, that sounds ominous. And we were having a nice peaceful day today for a change. Hang on." Frankie heard Vogel shout, "Sam, the British guy, Armstrong, needs to speak with you. Yeah, I told him, but he says you'll want to hear what he has to say, sounds like trouble."

Frankie heard the reply.

"It's always trouble with that guy. It follows him round, put him through to extension 24. Hello, Randazzo here. This had better be good Armstrong, I'm in the middle of an important meeting."

"I've had a letter from Cornelius Hayes, and you need to read it."

Randazzo said nothing for a few seconds, then asked,

"Does he confess to the killing of Lisa Ledinski?"

"Well, no, he doesn't…, but look, you really need to see what he has to say."

"Does he admit to being there when she was killed?"

"He does. But like I say, you really need to read it. He says he didn't actually do the killing."

"Can you get here now Mr. Armstrong? Sounds like we might get two murderers for the price of one."

"On my way."

Frankie was ushered into Randazzo's office as soon as he arrived at the Naples police headquarters. The detective was sat at his desk signing some papers.

"Come in Mr. Armstrong, take a seat." Frankie sat on the opposite side of the desk to the detective. Frankie made to hand the envelope to Randazzo, but the detective held his hand up and went to the door.

"Dale, Christina, get in here now will you?"

Dale Vogel and a glamorous blond woman entered the office. Dale pulled two more chairs up and they all sat. Randazzo held out his hand for the envelope, but Frankie hesitated.

"Before I hand this over, can I have a few minutes with you in private Detective?" Randazzo looked perplexed.

"Okay..." he said, looked at the other two and they left the office. "And close the door behind you. I'll call you when we're done," he said. They left and Randazzo opened his hands inviting Frankie to speak.

"I have something to say, before you read the letter. Might as well get it out of the way."

"This sounds ominous, carry on."

"Well, maybe, I don't know, maybe I should have said something at the time..."

"Something, like what something?" asked the detective getting exasperated.

"Well, when I told you about Lisa showing me the backup disk, the night we returned from Pepe's Pizzeria, when I went and got my laptop and we watched one of the videos."

"I remember you telling me that yes. And you said you didn't recognize the guy who was being caned. Are you now saying something else?"

"Not exactly, it's true I didn't recognize him, couldn't see his face clearly at all."

"But?"

"But I thought it he had a similar physique to one of the residents, Roger Tuckerman, the guy who was being caned I mean, that's all."

"You lied to me…why? What the fuck were you thinking?" the detective's voice had risen several decibels by now and he slammed his fist on the desk, "you'd better have a good explanation for this Mr. Armstrong."

"I didn't lie," replied Frankie raising his voice to the same level. "Hand on heart. I honestly couldn't have said it was Roger Tuckerman on that video, I didn't see his face, just saying that he had a similar physique. You know, similar sort of body shape, the way he held himself, I don't know. Sometimes you don't quite know, but kind of sublimely something… something niggles. Maybe I should have said something? But Roger was a friend, a good friend I thought I knew him, and I knew he couldn't possibly have any involvement in any of the killings, break ins, whatever. I thought him incapable of harming anyone, let alone killing someone."

"And, it was obvious, Frankie continued, "there were likely to be any number of other men who'd had videos taken of them having sex with Ava, and presumably being blackmailed. So, it could have been anybody. Then when you found the DNA and Roger passed the test so to speak, that settled any scintilla of doubt I may have had…" Frankie ran out of steam.

"But now?" said Randazzo.

"Well now…, now you need to read that letter Detective. I just wanted to explain…"

"One last question before I read it. Did you tell this Tuckerman guy, or Hector Carmouche for that matter, did you say anything about the DNA test we were arranging?' And don't lie to me Mr. Armstrong."

"No, I didn't, not a word. Hector, well Cornelius, you know who I mean, he worked it out, me being released so quickly mainly. He thought there was a possibility he may have left some DNA under Lisa's nails. Anticipated you'd be asking for DNA from all the residents. That's why he ran when he did. It's all in the letter. He realized he had to run before you'd told everyone you wanted DNA samples, otherwise you'd know he was guilty..." There was a long silence while Randazzo digested what he'd just been told.

"Any more or is that it?"

"I'm afraid there is one more thing yes. I thought you might have been told already, but I guess telling you wouldn't be a priority."

"Priority, what are you taking about Armstrong, spit it out for Christ's sake."

"Hector, I mean Cornelius Hayes, he killed himself in prison yesterday."

Randazzo got up and paced round the office shaking his head.

"So, the fucker's cheated us. We don't get to nail him for the killing of these two women. Jesus Christ almighty! I was looking forward to grilling that asswipe, grilling him till he sweated blood, I wanted to scare the livin' shit out of him, I wanted him to suffer" He looked at Frankie, "Wait up, that's not the whole story is it?"

"Not quite, please read the letter Detective." The detective came back to his desk, sat down and held out his hand for the letter. Frankie passed it over to him. Randazzo took the letter out of the envelope and began to read. He stopped reading, went over and opened door and called for the others to come back in.

"Please sit. This," he held the envelope up, "this is a letter sent to Mr. Armstrong here, from Cornelius Hayes, previously known to us as Hector Carmouche. I'll read it now and pass it on to you each page by page, then we'll discuss the contents once we've all read it, okay?" The other two nodded. "There is one thing to add. It seems that since sending this letter, Mr. Hayes has taken his own life in prison. It happened yesterday okay?"

The other two looked shocked but nodded. Randazzo began reading, shaking his head now and then. He passed pages to the others as he finished reading them. When they'd all finished reading the letter he said.

"Okay, Dale, call the condo president…," he looked at Frankie.

"Rudy Sprouse," Frankie said.

"Yeah, Rudy Sprouse, tell him you need access to Carmouche's condo. Take Joe with you, get the key, take some evidence bags and go and retrieve the stuff from the storage locker and bring it back here pronto. I'll alert the forensic guys and the techies. We need to see what's on the laptop and the backup."

"On it boss," said Vogel and left.

"Christina, go make two copies of that letter then bring them all back to me. And arrange for a squad car and two officers to come with me to Acadiana to arrest Roger Tuckerman."

"Yes sir," she said and left the room.

Randazzo rubbed his forehead.

"I really don't know what to say to you Mr. Armstrong. I'm trying to assess the implications of what you've told me, how much damage you might have caused to the investigation by not telling me the guy in the vid might have been Tuckerman."

Frankie started to protest but Randazzo held his hand up.

"Yeah I know, you didn't recognize him at the time." The detective walked to the window and looked out for a few minutes, then turned and looked at Frankie

"You still think it was right not to have said anything to me about maybe, possibly, thinking it might have been Tuckerman?"

"Yes, I do. I mean hindsight is a very exact science Detective. We all make errors of judgement, it's easy looking back. And you know I'd have done anything, anything for things to have not turned out as they did, but I can't turn the clock back can I?"

"I guess not. Anyway, we can talk later if needs be. My priority now is to get this joker under lock and key. We'll talk again very soon I'm sure Mr. Armstrong."

"Am I free to go Detective?"

"Yes, you are, but don't leave Naples without checking in with me first, okay?"

"Okay, but will you let me know what happens with Roger Tuckerman and the evidence in the storage locker?"

"Yeah, I suppose. Considering your involvement in all this, I think that's fair enough. Let's just hope this Tuckerman guy hasn't skipped. I'll let you know."

Chapter 39

Finale

Frankie felt deflated after talking to the detective and decided to drive down to Naples pier and watch the people fishing, chew the fat with some of the guys there and try to forget all about the letter and its implications. He fell into conversation with an old timer called Nick, a guy whom he'd spoken to many times previously. Nick was a squat strong looking individual, always had a big Cuban cigar hanging out of his mouth. Nick lived in a place called Falling Waters, which Frankie knew, having stayed there briefly one time when he first visited the area.

Frankie loved the smell of Nick's cigar smoke. They stood leaning on the railings of the pier, looking out over the gulf and watching pelicans diving into the clear turquoise water in their never-ending quest for food. He and Nick talked about fishing, and about the red tide which had spoilt the fishing for the last couple of years, but now seemed to be in decline. Nick was just telling Frankie about a five foot shark he'd caught off the pier the previous week, when Frankie's cell chirruped.

"Sorry Nick, I need to take this," he said.

"Mr. Armstrong?" Frankie noted the urgency in the voice.

"Yes."

"Could you get back to Acadiana, pronto, we have a situation."

"A situation, sorry who is this?"

"Sergeant Baker sir, I'm the senior police officer here at the moment. Detective Vogel is on his way. He asked me to call you. I accompanied Detective Randazzo to interview this Roger Tuckerman guy. When we got there he was out, so we waited. When the guy arrived, Sam, I mean Detective Randazzo, he told him we needed him to come down to headquarters to have his fingerprints taken. The guy cut up rough, got all belligerent. Detective Randazzo told him if he refused, we'd have to arrest him there and then, do it the hard way. Then the guy pulled a gun and shot him, dragged him inside."

"Shot Randazzo? How bad is he?"

"Not sure, but bad enough. Shot in the thigh I think, could be a flesh wound, could be worse. We need to get Sam out of there. But this Roger guy says he'll only speak to you, says you're his friend. It's a really bad situation. Medics are standing by, but the guy's off his head. We can't risk shooting our way in. I think he's crazy enough to kill Detective Randazzo."

Frankie was already running along the pier. He could hear the sound of the emergency vehicle's sirens through the sergeant's phone.

"Just leaving Naples Pier now sergeant, he said breathlessly, "where's Myrtle, Roger's wife?"

"She's here with me in the parking lot. She was out at Publix when we called. She's frantic, but the guy won't talk to her, only to you, hurry Mr. Armstrong."

Frankie arrived at Acadiana, identified himself to the officer at the gate, and was taken swiftly through the throng who were corralled at the north end of the parking lot. People shouted at him as he made his way through. Some of the residents shouted his name and encouragement, others obviously from the media shouting questions. Frankie was taken into the south stairwell. There were several police personnel waiting, all wearing bullet proof vests.

"Sergeant, this is Mr. Armstrong." The sergeant broke off from what he was doing and shook Frankie's hand.

"Call me Jack, be easier. What do I call you?"

"Frankie will be just fine Jack."

"We just disabled the elevators. You know Tuckerman lives on the top floor, right?"

"Yes, 301, been there a number of times."

"Good, so you know the layout?"

"I suppose I do, yes."

"That helps," said the sergeant. "I don't know if the guy's been drinking or just gone crazy, but he's talking nonsense. Wants us to provide a plane for him to fly out of Naples Airport. Says he's not messing around. Maybe he's seen too many hostage movies I don't know, but the guy is serious. I think he might just flip."

"Well I'm more than happy to help Jack, tell me what you want me to do."

"Well, he says he wants you to help him negotiate his escape, or whatever he thinks he's doing."

"Me?"

"Yeah, you Frankie Armstrong. Look we need to talk the guy down before he takes complete leave of his senses and kills Sam in there. He's threatened to do that a few times now. I don't know how bad Sam's injury is, but I can't just wait until he bleeds out, or the guy carries out his threat. Worst case, we storm the place, guns blazing, but that's a huge risk for Sam. I don't give a shit about shooting the guy, and if it comes to it that's what we'll do. You have any ideas, d'you think you can talk some sense into this crazy guy?"

"Don't know, but I'll try. Can I go up on my own?"

"No, but you go up and we'll wait at the top of the stairwell where we can see you, but Tuckerman can't see us, okay? Now look, it could be that the guy will start shooting anyway, so I have to tell you, you're risking getting shot here, maybe killed. No other way to say it, so you don't have to go."

"I know Jack, but… let's just do it."

"You got moxie Frankie. Okay, here put this on," he said handing Frankie a vest, "and let's mic you up." The sergeant fitted Frankie with a mic and earpiece. "All set?" Frankie nodded, then moved up the stairs quickly. The sergeant and two other police officers climbed up the stairs behind him. They reached the top floor, opened the door on to the passageway that ran along the outside of the condos to each front door, and stopped.

"You know how to shoot a gun Frankie?" asked the sergeant.

"I was in the military, so yes. I haven't handled one for a while, but anyway, I don't think it would be a good idea."

"Okay, well it's your show now. So how d'you want to play it?"

"I think I'll stand to the side of the door and see if I can talk to him, try to get a measure of his state of mind, okay?"

"Sounds good. Go, and good luck Frankie."

"Thanks," said Frankie, and showed Jack his crossed fingers. He approached the side of the condo door.

"Roger," he shouted in a loud voice, "Roger it's me Frankie, Frankie Armstrong. Talk to me Roger."

"Hi Frankie" said a surprisingly calm voice from the other side of the door. "Thanks for coming, I knew you would."

"How can I help Roger? You seem to have got yourself into a heap of trouble. How about you let the detective go? I understand he's hurt."

"Hey Frankie, you've known me for long enough now, do I seem stupid to you?"

"No Roger, never thought you were stupid. But don't make things worse for yourself. You have to let the cop go, he needs medical attention. If you kill him or he dies, they'll just storm the place, you know that." There was silence, then Roger spoke.

"I'll let him go if you take his place Frankie, how about that?"

Frankie looked round at Jack who was leaning out of the stairwell, out of Roger's line of sight. He grimaced, which Frankie took to mean, *up to you buddy.*

"Okay," said Frankie, "best way to do this is you let me in and then we let the detective go, right?"

"You got a gun Frankie? Cos if you have, I'll shoot you without hesitation, friend or not, right?"

"No gun Roger. No tricks, just open the door."

The condo door opened outwards to the right, into the passage, blocking any view from the top of the stairwell. Frankie looked back at Jack, who gave a thumbs up. Roger slowly opened the door and pointed a large handgun at Frankie's chest.

"Take off the mic and vest, throw them right up the passageway, well away from this door," said Roger. Frankie did as instructed, "now, turn around." Frankie was wearing a blue T shirt, cream shorts and casual shoes. There was nowhere to conceal a gun.

"Pockets?" said Roger.

"My wallet and cell."

Okay, we might need the cell, but take it out of your pocket and let me see you switch it off." Frankie did as he was told. "Okay, come in." Frankie walked through the door and it swung shut by itself. Detective Randazzo was tied to a chair with a piece of blue rope. His left trouser leg was soaked in blood and he seemed barely conscious. A tourniquet made out of a couple of tea towels knotted together was tied around the detective's upper thigh.

"You've got to let me get this man out of here now Roger. What say I get hold of him and drag him out into the passage? You can keep that gun pointed at me while I do it. You could easily shoot me if I tried to escape or anything. What d'you say?"

Roger seemed to mull things over.

"I will shoot you Frankie, you know that don't you?"

"I think I got the message loud and clear, yes. Can I undo that rope?" Roger took a deep breath then exhaled. Frankie smelt the booze.

"I guess so, but I ain't kidding Frankie," Roger raised the gun and pointed at him as he went over to untie the bonds holding the detective. As soon as Frankie released Randazzo, the detective slumped forwards and groaned. Frankie held him under his arms then laid him down gently on the floor. He then turned the detective over on to his back, grasped him under the arms again and dragged him backwards toward the door.

"Just turn the knob Roger, so I can back out into the passage. I'll lay him down out there and come straight back in. You'll have your gun on me the whole time, okay?"

Roger moved to the side of the door, reached over and turned the knob at arm's length, Frankie pushed the door open with his backside and dragged the inert body of Detective Randazzo out into the passage and laid him out flat, then came back in, the door swung shut behind him. Roger motioned him into the lounge with his gun.

"Sit down Frankie, make yourself at home," Frankie could hear movement outside as the police officers quickly moved in to rescue the detective. He hoped it wasn't too late. Frankie sat down on the sofa.

"Coffee Frankie, or maybe something stronger?" Roger held up a bottle of Jack Daniels. Join me in a shot of Sinatra Select I think it's called, over $150 a bottle. Great sipping bourbon Frankie, like to try some?"

"Why not?" said Frankie.

Roger picked up a glass from the drinks tray on the coffee table and handed it to Frankie, keeping the gun trained on him all the time.

"Please help yourself if you don't mind Frankie, pour a good slug." Frankie poured himself a generous four fingers worth, then took a good swig.

"Hmm, that hits the spot. So, where do we go from here Roger?"

"I really don't know Frankie. Any suggestions?"

"Yes, give yourself up?"

Roger laughed.

"No point Frankie boy. I ain't stupid. If they're asking for my fingerprints, then they want to match them to something incriminating. I wondered how long it would take Hector to give me up. That would be Hector who isn't Hector of course. When did he tell you?"

"He wrote me a letter. Told me the whole story, at least his version of it. Said you killed Lisa, said you strangled her."

"Well that's no great surprise. Suppose I said that it was Hector who killed her, would you believe me?"

"No Roger, I don't know if I would. After all, I fell for your bullshit phone call about how worried you were about me, when all you were doing was trying to pump me for information. You're a good liar Roger. For all I know you could well be capable of murder."

"Well, as it happens Frankie, this time I'm telling the truth. I didn't murder your Lisa, but either way. I know the law. Doesn't matter who actually killed her. Hector, or whoever he is, he and I, we both go down for it. And in

Florida, that's likely to be a one-way street. So, Frankie, I have absolutely nothing to lose do I? Might as well go for broke."

"You don't know then?"

"Don't know what Frankie?"

"Hector, well the guy we knew as Hector, he killed himself in prison yesterday."

"He what…!? Well well well, so no live witness. Shit, I might have gotten away with it, not now though I guess." Roger Tuckerman hunched his shoulders and wound his head around.

"Feeling stressed Roger?" said Frankie.

"Yeah, some I guess."

"Look Roger, you know how this is going to end. Why prolong the agony? Give yourself up man."

Roger laughed.

"Been in tight spots before Frankie, and the golden rule is you never give up." Roger took another swig of bourbon, then said. "So, Frankie, time to go. Tell those fuckers I want a plane, minimum three seats, a prop, nothing fancy. Tell 'em to have it ready at Naples airport in the next half hour, fully fueled, minimum range one thousand miles. Tell them to clear the condo parking lot. I want a car, one driver. Everyone else disappears. I see anyone too close, other than the driver, I start shooting okay? Come on Frankie, don't look so serious, cheer up, we're going on vacation." Roger laughed again.

"Even if they agree to all that Roger, where are you going to go? There's no way you can escape now, just give yourself up."

"I told you Frankie, I got nothing to lose. I go, it won't be at the end of a needle or being gassed to death, no sir. Then there's the public humiliation of stories about getting my ass caned, to say nothing of Myrtle finding out. So, get on that fucking horn now and tell them." Roger's smile had evaporated, he was all business now. Frankie switched his cell back on and made the call.

"Detective Vogel says they're unlikely to get a pilot to volunteer to take a gunman up in a plane."

"Yeah, I guessed that duh! Tell them I don't need a pilot. But tell them not to try any tricks, like only putting a couple of gallons of fuel in it. If they mess with the plane, you'll be with me Frankie. If I go down, you go down."

"Okay," Frankie said into his cell, then turning to Roger he said, "they heard all that, so they say they'll do as you ask. But it might take them a while."

"Tell 'em that fucking plane better be ready to go by the time we get to the airport. So that gives them about fifteen, twenty minutes max." Frankie relayed his instructions.

"We'll do our best, tell him," came the reply.

The stairwell was cleared, as was the entire condo parking lot, but for a single squad car with a driver standing by the driver's door. Roger kept Frankie close as he descended the stairs. Once outside he told the driver to stand away from the car. Keeping the gun a few inches from Frankie's back he instructed him to pat down the driver, check his ankles, then told the driver to stand some distance away while Frankie opened all the car doors and trunk lid.

Roger walked around the car inspecting the insides. Frankie wondered if they would have a sharpshooter take Roger out in the parking lot. Would they take the risk? No shot rang out and the three of them got into the car, Roger and Frankie in the back. They drove toward Naples airport with two police squad cars some distance in front and behind. Roger yelled at the driver.

"Tell your boss to lose the escort cars, now! If I see any police presence or anything I don't like, I'll kill Frankie here and then you, then myself." The driver used his radio to pass on the message and the cars disappeared. *Maybe they'll take him out at the airport?* thought Frankie. They arrived at Naples Airport. As airports go, it was small. There was no elaborate security, or barriers. It wasn't a commercial airport as such, mostly used for private planes, flying lessons, local sightseeing tours, but also used by private jets bringing the wealthy for some R & R at their luxury beachside homes in Naples and other locations along the Paradise Coast.

They drove straight on to the airport apron. Just one small light aircraft sat alone on the tarmac.

"That looks like our ride Frankie," said Roger. The driver took them to the aircraft where they got out.

"Go, skedaddle," said Roger to the driver. "Now stick very close to me Frankie, I'm sure some sniper has a bead on me, and you're probably the only thing that's coming between me and the guy pulling the trigger." They approached the aircraft. "A Cessna 172 Skyhawk, "ideal," said Roger. "Get in Frankie."

Frankie hesitated, he wasn't fond of heights or flying. He wasn't afraid of much, but flying, that just didn't seem natural to him in any way. He accepted he had to fly sometimes otherwise what kind of a life would you have, but preferably on big sturdy planes with two pilots. This small plane didn't exactly instill him with confidence. It had just one propeller at the front and wings across the top held on by one strut on either side of the fuselage.

Flimsy was the word that popped into Frankie's mind as he looked at the small aircraft - that and the thought that he was a hostage, and about to fly with a pilot who was a homicidal maniac who said he had nothing to lose. *Well at least this should make Barnsie laugh when I tell him, if I get the chance to tell him that is.*

"Look Roger, you don't need me now do you? You've got your plane and, well, I'll just be an encumbrance. And as Rudyard Kipling said, 'he travels fastest who travels alone.'"

"Yeah, well fuck Rudyard Kipling, get in Frankie or get shot. Your choice." Frankie clambered into the passenger seat.

"Guess we won't need to file a flight plan with the control tower," said Roger, smiling as scanned the airfield. Seemingly satisfied, he started the engines and checked the instruments and dials, tapping the fuel gauge a couple of times.

"Full tank," must think we're going to Cuba or South America." he laughed "Okay let's get this baby airborne."

Roger started checking a few things.

"When did you learn to fly?"

"Nam, helicopters mainly but I can fly anything with wings fixed or otherwise. And if I say so myself, I'm a great pilot. So don't fret Frankie, you're in safe hands."

Irony on steroids, thought Frankie.

"Let's see, we'll just switch off this transponder. I'm sure they've put some sort of tracking device on this baby, plus they'll be monitoring us using all kinds of technology shit. No worries though."

Roger cranked up the engine, released the brakes and they taxied out to the end of the runway then made a ninety-degree turn. Roger looked around, made some final checks looked at the dials on the dashboard, then revved up the engine till the propellers all but disappeared in a blur of speed. He took the brakes off and they hurtled down the runway, taking off into the clear blue Florida sky. Frankie felt his stomach drop.

The plane rose steeply, then banked right and they were soon flying over the Gulf of Mexico. Frankie could see Naples Pier out of the left window, the turquoise sea and the almost white sandy beaches on the right as they leveled off turned right and flew low and parallel to the coastline.

"Where are we going exactly?" asked Frankie.

"Not sure yet Frankie, but I'll know it when I see it."

"It, as in?"

"As in an airfield. There are hundreds, many hundreds of little airfields in Florida. I'm looking for one that fits my criteria, and we need to find it before sunset." The plane banked to the right a bit more and they began to fly inland. They climbed a little and Frankie could see for miles.

"And what would your criteria be Roger?"

"Well, something that's not too big and not too small. One with a good few cars parked on the perimeter. A bit further north yet though."

"Then what?"

"We land and steal a car Frankie."

"And then?"

"We go on the run. Not the greatest plan in the world, but the best I can do at short notice. My guess is, they'll know where we land within minutes. But I'm counting on them not being able to muster the ground troops for a while, so that should give us a bit of a head start."

"Then what?"

"Look Frankie, I'm making this up as I go along, so one step at a time okay?"

"You'll be all over the news Roger, won't take long for them to find us."

"Depends. If I get the chance, the moustache will be gone and I'll shave off all my hair. That should stump them for a while, we'll see. Everyone needs a little luck Frankie."

"And what about me Roger? What do you propose to do about me?"

"Let's call that part work in progress, depends on events. Hopefully I won't have to shoot you Frankie, but if push comes to shove, well..."

"Why not just let me go Roger? Drop me off in some remote spot where I won't be able to raise the alarm for a while. I mean, what's the point of shooting me. Don't you remember, I'm your friend, and I'm the guy who's helping you escape now. Doesn't that count for anything?"

"Yeah, I guess it does, but in the circumstances... If I get away, then who knows, Frankie? If I get to live, then maybe you get to live? We'll see. Uh oh, this looks promising." The plane suddenly banked steeply towards a tiny airstrip by the side of a big lake and surrounded by trees. There were a few cars parked along one side of the airstrip.

"Here we go Frankie boy." Roger took the plane low over the airfield, then up and round to approach from the opposite direction. Roger dropped the plane heavily on to the grass runway. It bounced clumsily then Roger slowed it down to taxi speed. He had the gun on his lap where he could easily grab it. It was pointing at Frankie, but Roger had both his hands busy steering the plane. He read Frankie's mind.

"Don't even think about it Frankie. I have the reflexes of a cat, a very fast cat."

A man rushed out of a wooden hut with a windsock on top of it and ran towards the aircraft. He looked old but obviously quite fit. He was shouting up at Roger, crisscrossing his hands in a way that Frankie took to mean they shouldn't have landed there.

"Play along with me here Frankie. Your life depends on it."

The man shouted, trying to be heard above the propeller noise, then Roger reduced the engine revs and they could hear him.

"This is a private airfield sir, you can't land here," he shouted, "Please take off again, there's a commercial airfield just fifty miles due north of here, you can't miss it."

"I understand, but my friend here's just had a heart attack," Roger shouted back, "I think he's dying, we need to get him to a hospital urgently," Roger brought the small aircraft to a halt, and cut the engine, then opened his door and pocketed the gun. "If you want to live Frankie, make as though you're dying, slump forward a bit. Make one wrong move and the man gets it, then you're next. Roger went around to the other door. "Please help me get my friend out will you?" Frankie did his best to look ill whilst clambering out of the small door and sliding backwards down to the ground.

"I gotcha son," said the man as he took Frankie's weight.

"D'you have a car we can use sir?" Roger asked the man.

"Better'n that son I'll drive you. I know the way to the hospital, be quicker if I take you. C'mon, hurry up, your friend looks to be in a bad way." Frankie couldn't help stealing a look at Roger, who winked. *Gallows humor*

As they drove away at speed, Frankie noticed another plane landing on the airfield.

"Well I'll be damned, another plane that shouldn't be landing. What in the name of Henry Ford is going on here? Still gotta get your friend to hospital first, the airfield'll have to wait." The man put his foot down and turned right on to a bigger road. "Keep breathing son, be there in ten minutes tops," he said. The man picked up speed. Roger and Frankie were both sitting in the rear. Frankie realized Roger had also noticed the arrival of the other plane. He kept looking out of the rear window.

"Okay old timer, stop the car."

"What?"

"I said, stop the car." Roger waggled his gun by the side of the man's head so he could see it.

"What in tarnation is this, a stickup?"

"You could call it that Jack, yeah, so just pull over and get out of the car."

The man kept driving. A loud siren could be heard in the distance behind them, gradually getting louder.

"I'm going to count to three, then either pull over, or I shoot you in the head."

The man put his foot down and the car lurched forward.

"Shoot me buddy and we all get to see our maker," said the man.

Roger clicked the safety off, then started to count.

"One..., two...," the man didn't slow down. Frankie lurched sideways and tried to grab the gun. The sound of the shot was magnified in the enclosed space. The tires squealed, the car lurched as the sound of the siren got even louder behind them. The car suddenly came to an impossible bend. A second shot rang out as Frankie managed to wrestle the gun out of Roger's grip. The car left the road, then a third shot rent the air and Frankie felt a searing pain in his head, combined with a weird feeling of weightlessness as the car left the road and sailed into the air. Frankie had a brief feeling of euphoria, then felt a tremendous impact, combined with an explosion of sound and force that shattered the brief silence. Then everything went black.

Chapter 40

The awakening

"It's your round Frankie, come on, no argument, get the beers in, you tight fisted son of a bitch… Look I think his eyelids moved, fluttered a bit, didn't they?" he said to the nurse.

"I think he might be trying to speak, put your ear to lips, but careful you don't nudge one of those tubes out," she said to Derek.

He bent over and listened, then stood up and smiled.

"What did he say?"

"I think he said a couple of rude words, well one rude word followed by an adverb. Off is an adverb isn't it?"

The nurse laughed.

"If you say so, never was much good at English grammar."

The light gradually filtered through as Frankie slowly opened his eyes, he closed them again quickly.

"Too bright," he said, then it went dark again. He slowly opened his eyes again and had no idea if it was minutes later or days later, maybe weeks, *who knows, who cares..?* Then he was awake. He looked to his right.

"Barnsie, what the fu…" He realized he was lying in a bed *what are you doing in my bedroom?*

"Frankie wake up. Wake up Frankie."

"Okay, okay…," he said and tried to sit up. It hurt, everywhere.

"Hang on, said the woman's voice, "let me help. Now let's sit you up and get you more comfortable," she said, "oh, and welcome back." The nurse helped him up to a sitting position, plumping pillows and placing them behind his back.

"Where've I been?" he asked, his mouth felt funny, "and what the f.., I mean what are you doing here Barnsie?" He looked at the nurse. "Sorry, I'm in hospital?" Then the memories started to come back.

"Am I alright Barnsie? I feel sore all over?"

"Yeah, you're okay, but you've been in bed for just over three weeks partner, so I guess you'll be bed sore as much as anything. You've had a rough time Frankie."

"Three weeks!? My head hurts as well," Frankie went to put his hand up to his head.

"Careful there Frankie, they had to operate, remove a bullet. You're lucky, boy are you lucky. They thought you'd be okay, but they couldn't be certain, not until you woke up. I think the doctor's coming to see you now. He'll explain a lot better than I can."

The doctor duly arrived, white coat and a clip board in his hands.

"Look Frankie, while the doc talks to you, I'll go and call some people, let them know you've woken up, Randazzo said to call him as well when you came out of it. And Penny's been going frantic, plus the guys at the office are waiting to hear. Back in ten."

Some hours later when they'd taken out the feeding tubes, generally tidied him up and he'd had a little snooze, he felt quite a lot better. The doctor had described his injuries and the procedures he'd gone through. He then conducted some tests, walking (very wobbly) eyesight, memory, strength and some other tests he didn't quite understand. Apparently satisfied, the doctor left with warnings about taking it easy and not rushing things.

"Take time to recover young man." He said. *Young man, almost worth getting shot to be described as a young man.*

When Derek returned, he asked if they were going to let Frankie out.

"The doc said I could leave as soon as I could function properly, walking, going to the bathroom, all that sort of stuff. Hopefully in a couple of days' time."

"And about your injuries, no permanent damage?"

The doctor said I'd been very lucky, due mainly to the trajectory of the bullet. It hadn't done any serious or long-term damage as far as they could tell. His actual words were, and I asked him again so I could write it down." Frankie looked at the piece of paper in his hand " 'you were lucky that bullet missed your brain's high-value real estate, such as the brain stem and the thalamus,' See Barnsie, as you might have guessed, my brain is full of *high value real estate*."

"Yeah right, I know what it is full of, and the word begins with B," they both laughed,

"Ouch that hurt," said Frankie, "no more jokes for a while please Barnsie."

"So, what's the routine when you get out Frankie?"

"He said I'll need time to recover fully. Warned me to take it easy and not try to rush my recovery. Said he'd let me go, providing I have someone to look after me for a couple of days, at least until I can look after myself. But the sooner I get back to a normal routine, the better."

"Normal Frankie? That'll be a first, you've never been normal in any meaning of the word."

"Yeah, yeah, very funny Derek."

***

A week after Frankie had left hospital, Barnsie left to go back to the UK. He'd flown over to Naples as soon as he'd heard about Frankie's situation but now, after such a long unplanned break, he needed to get back to run their business. The events surrounding Frankie's shooting and the car crash, made headline news in Florida, the wider USA and even featured on some of the world's news media for a time.

When Frankie's neighbors, and the condo president Rudy Sprouse, heard what had happened, they quickly got access to Frankie's condo and took care of Charlie while Frankie was indisposed. Frankie's reunion with Charlie was an emotional affair for both of them. By the time Derek had left to go back to the UK, Frankie was back into a routine. His morning jog replaced with a brisk walk for the time being, but each day he felt more like his old self.

Detective Randazzo had phoned as soon as he heard that Frankie was back in the land of the living. He expressed his relief at Frankie's recovery and thanked Frankie for having helped to rescue him. He'd suggested they wait until Frankie felt fully recovered before they met to discuss their recent and mutual traumatic events in detail.

"Call me as soon as you feel okay to meet. I'm on restricted duty until my leg fully heals, but I'll rearrange my schedule to suit. No rush, but I guess the sooner the better."

Frankie called Randazzo the day after Barnsie had left for the UK and was now in an uber on his way to Naples Police HQ. As soon as he entered police headquarters and they realized who he was. People came out to see him, and either shook his hand or slapped him on the back, or both. One young policewoman gave him a prolonged hug. He eventually made it into Randazzo's office. The detective got up and hobbled over to Frankie as he entered and shook his hand warmly.

"Great to see you buddy, nice haircut." Frankie's hair was still recovering from being completely shaved off on one side.

"Thanks, it's the new look, all the rage now." They both laughed. "and how are you getting along Detective? That leg wound looked pretty bad at the time?"

"Yeah, I lost a lot of blood, so it was touch and go for a while. If you'd waited another ten or fifteen minutes, they said it might have been too late. They say I'll probably always have a bit of a limp now, but no long-term serious damage. You?"

"Well the bullet entered my brainpan, but thankfully missed the vital bits, missed my brains, or 'high-value real estate' as the Doc described it. Said I could have easily been paralyzed or worse, but they were able to get the thing out and I should be as good as new in time. I still have some blurring of my vision, but they say that should also improve. So, a lucky escape Detective."

"For both of us. Hey but now we're fellow victims, I think we can drop the formalities, don't you Frankie?"

"Suits me Sam," they both smiled.

"How do you want to do this Frankie?"

"Well, as I've been out of commission for longer than you, I think I get to ask you questions and see where we go from there, okay?"

"Fair enough Frankie, shoot…sorry, wrong expression in the circumstances."

"You could say that… So, I assume you retrieved the laptop and the backup, from the storage place, and saw the videos on all Ava's blackmail victims?"

"We did, but we also got details of her client's names, addresses etc. She kept them all on spreadsheets. She was one very organized blackmailer. We already had some data that we'd got from the PC she used in the music shop where she worked. But that didn't make much sense without the other stuff on her personal laptop. We're now able to separate her legit clients from the, shall we say, less legit clients? Having said that, we have found some cross overs. That is, some people who apparently started out genuinely wanting piano lessons, but ended up having sex lessons instead, or maybe as well as?"

"I was obliged to watch some of the vids myself. Man, she was a busy girl. And I have to tell you, she had some very interesting clients. Some quite powerful people, and some not so powerful. Among them were a couple of *pillar of the community* types. Many lives could be ruined if what's on those vids got out. We've had to restrict access to the videos to just two people who can be trusted completely, I hope? I saw the video of Roger Tuckerman of course, the full version. Why do people want to have themselves treated like that?"

"I don't know Sam, way beyond my understanding. Okay, so what about Roger Tuckerman, where is he, still on the run? I mean, I've obviously read the newspaper reports.

But I'd like to know the official police version of events, from the time I left with Roger on that trip to Naples Airport."

"Okay, well as you might have guessed, the guys had planted a tracking device on the plane we got for Tuckerman and you, plus they had another plane in the air a couple of minutes after you'd taken off. Our plane flew at higher altitude so you wouldn't have been aware of it. As you descended toward that airfield in Lakeboro, the guys were on the horn to the local sheriff and he organized a squad car to pick up our man at the same airport, minutes after you'd hijacked the man and his car."

"I just have to tell you that it wasn't a hijack at first. Roger made up a story that I'd had a heart attack and the guy offered to drive us to the hospital."

"Yeah, I heard, the old guy told us. He is one smart cookie that Roger, or was maybe? So, anyway, our man was on your tail when your car left the road on that sharp bend. The driver was an old guy called Ron Bogdasarian. He got thrown out and broke nearly every bone in his body, but he'll live, thank God. Take him a while to recover, but the long-term prognosis is good. Tough old cookie. You, as you know, got shot in the head, but miraculously no other injuries apart from bruises and scrapes."

"You were double lucky, in that a trauma hospital was less than twenty miles away, so they got you stabilized pretty quickly. I think you spent a couple of weeks there then they transferred you to Naples NCH, which is where you woke up. They told me their main concern was the coma. They couldn't say if or when you might come out of it."

"And the million-dollar question Detective, what happened to Roger Tuckerman?"

"Okay, well just typical ain't it? The villain of the piece, he got away without any serious injuries it seems. He was certainly fit enough to run. He didn't hang around and by the time our guys got there he was running up the road, albeit, dragging one leg a bit our guy thought. But he was still fast enough. The police driver stayed behind trying to get you and the car driver picked up and hospitalized, while our guy went after Tuckerman. He was gaining on him and Tuckerman knew it."

"Then, when our man was about fifty yards away from him - our man not being in the first flush of youth and somewhat overweight, a guy called Marco Gullace, Tuckerman climbed a high wire mesh fence at the side of the road. Marco was in no fit state to follow him over the fence, said the guy was like a monkey the way he went over. Anyway, Marco went to look for a gate. It was going dark by then apparently, but he managed to find a gate further along the road. It had a big notice on it which said, Danger no unauthorized entry – Gator Farm."

"I don't believe it," said Frankie, "you're kidding me…?"

"I'm not. Can you recall what shoes Roger was wearing that day?"

Frankie searched his memory.

"Yes, I think I can. Light gray trainers, sorry. I think you call them sneakers. White socks too, why?"

"That fits."

"Fits what?"

"The official line is that Roger Tuckerman is still on the run, a wanted man. But the truth may be somewhat different. No one was prepared to follow him into the gator farm, especially at night. Entirely understandable. So, they contacted the guy who owned the farm and at sunup the following day, and with the help of some of his guys, they searched the farm. There was no trace of Roger Tuckerman, but they did find some gray colored sneakers, partially chewed up. Forensics weren't able to make any connection to Tuckerman, but…"

"You're seriously suggesting Roger was eaten by a gator?"

"Wouldn't be the first time such a thing happened, as you well know. The gator farm guy said that gators wouldn't go out of their way to attack a human being, but if they thought they were being threatened, attacked, or their young were in danger, they wouldn't hesitate. Apparently, there were lots of big momma gators with baby gators in that swamp. Which isn't surprising, as the place was specifically created for breeding."

Frankie sat back in his chair to take in what he'd just heard.

"That would be…"

"Yeah, I know, poetic justice."

"And some," said Frankie.

Chapter 41

Another letter

Frankie left the police HQ, having agreed to meet Sam Randazzo for a beer in a few days' time. On the way back he mulled over what he'd been told.

"Wow," he said out loud, the Uber driver responded.

"Sorry did you say something sir?"

"No, well yes, but I was just thinking out loud."

"Yeah, I do that all the time," she said.

Frankie walked through the condo entrance and collected his mail as he passed the mailboxes. Once in his condo, he made a coffee, checked Charlie's water, took his mail to the lanai, sat down and started to sift through the various leaflets and envelopes. He came to a cream-colored envelope with the address written in a hand he instantly recognized. He took a gulp of his coffee, put the cup down, ripped the envelope open, took out the three sheets of cream paper and began to read.

Dearest Frankie

I guess you'll be surprised to receive this letter from me, particularly in the light of our previous conversations which resulted in our divorce proceedings. I accept that your reaction to this letter might well be 'oh not again' and you'd be justified in that, but hear me out and maybe, just maybe, you might think again.

When you left for Naples the last time, I decided to seek help and went to consult a psychologist. It took a while but maybe we got to the root of my problem, which seems likely to be my decision not to have children. I've tried to justify that to myself, told myself that children aren't necessary to have a well fulfilled life and I still believe that. I just think that it was a mistake for me. It may suit some women and that's okay, but deep down I think I really wanted a family. My own upbringing wasn't that great as you know, so that probably contributed. Anyway, I'm not going to beg, or ask you to feel sorry for me, you wouldn't want me to, but I am asking you to think if you'd be prepared to give it another go. You know what they say — three times a charm!

I've kept up with your recent adventures, via Barnsie and the press. You're quite the hero. You probably have women trying to knock your door down and I don't blame them. But I don't care about all that hero stuff. I know the man I married. I just want you to think about my proposal.

Love always

Penny

He read it again. Sighed, put it down and went to make another coffee. He took his coffee back on to the lanai and sat and sipped. *And if she changes her mind again, what then? On the other hand, I do still have deep feelings for Penny. But I have to admit, they're wearing thin.*

The doorbell chimed. Frankie got up and went to answer the door. He opened it and there stood a beautiful blond woman he recognized, *but where from?*

"Hi Frankie, remember me, Daisy Metcalf?"

It took Frankie a couple of beats, then it clicked.

"The reporter," he said.

"Glad you remembered Frankie. Hello Charlie," she said bending down to pet the dog. She stood up. "Aren't you going to invite me in?"

"Well I would Daisy, but I don't really have anything to say to the press at the moment, I mean..."

"I'm not here on business Frankie. Remember when we met, I said we'd have to leave the story about how you hooked up with Charlie here. Said we'd do that on another day right?"

"Yes, I remember, but I thought that was just... well I don't know what I thought..."

"Are we going to have this conversation on your doorstep Frankie?" she said with a big smile.

"Oh, no sorry, please come in." He showed her to the sofa, and she sat. He sat on the chair opposite. "Sorry, my manners? Would you like a coffee?"

"No, "fraid I haven't got time, chasing a story and deadlines to meet."

"I thought you said you wanted to talk about how I ended up with Charlie?"

"Can I ask you a personal question Frankie?"

"Sorry?"

"Can I ask you a personal question?"

"I suppose so, it depends on the question."

"I know about you and the young lady who was killed," Daisy said, "Lisa Ledinski, I know you were said to be romantically involved."

"Are you back to being a reporter now?" asked Frankie wondering if he'd just been suckered into an interview. "All that's been covered again and again by the media, but thinking about it, you didn't try to interview me about it."

"No, I've been on a special assignment for a while, drugs and corruption here in south west Florida. So?"

"This is off the record?"

"Completely off the record." she said.

"Well, yes Lisa and I were romantically involved, as you put it, but obviously... Is that the question?"

"No, sorry, clumsy me. The question is, are you romantically involved with anyone at the moment, or spoken for as my mom would have put it?"

Frankie looked down at the letter he was still holding in his hand.

"Fan mail?" Daisy asked.

"What? No, it's just a letter." He looked down at the pages he was holding. *Am I romantically involved at the moment?*

"The answer is no, I'm not in any close relationship, at the moment. Why?"

"Good, well unless you have a prior engagement, I'll pick you up tonight at 6:30 and take you to dinner, then we can talk about you and Charlie, okay? Any preferences for which restaurant?"

"Well, I like Cibao but, you know, it's up to you?" Frankie was still trying to figure out what was happening.

"I know that place, Neapolitan Plaza, right? Good choice, great cocktails. And sorry to be so forward, but I liked you from the minute we met. Mostly it's me fighting off guys trying to hit on me, but you, I don't know, I just kept thinking…I just liked what I saw, so… Life's too short don't you agree Frankie?"

"I do Daisy and I'm flattered."

"Don't be, you might not like me when you get to know me." She smiled again. "See you later Frankie." She stood up, then bent down to pet Charlie again, "bye little feller," she said, then walked to the door and let herself out, turning round to give Frankie a little wave as she disappeared through the door.

Frankie looked at Charlie.

"Did that just happen, or did I dream it?"

Charlie didn't reply.

Inspiration

My wife and I have had the great privilege of owning a condo in Naples Florida for more than a dozen years now. This book was inspired by an email I received in 2018, from one of our Naples condo neighbors when we were back in the UK. It read as follows: -

"You left just in time. There was a sighting of a 10 ft gator just 4 ft from one of the boat docks. I have a picture I can send if I can figure out how to send it. Be well, Linda"

***

Naples Florida is one of the most perfect places to live. Situated on the Gulf of Mexico, it offers stunning beaches, great fishing, a huge variety of wildlife, wonderful weather, especially in the winter and Springtime. Great restaurants and best of all, the people, who are wonderful. Everyone smiles in Naples.

Thank you

Thank you for reading this book. I hope you enjoyed it as much as I enjoyed writing it.

If you did enjoy 'CONDO' then please leave a review on Amazon if you have the time.

Happy reading

Kerry Costello

https://www.kerrycostellobooks.com/

Charlie - the only non-fictional character

Printed in Great Britain
by Amazon

40571736R00185